Point, Click, Love

BALLANTINE BOOKS TRADE PAPERBACKS NEW YORK

Point, Click, Love

a novel

Molly Shapiro

A Ballantine Books Trade Paperback Original

Copyright © 2011 by Molly Shapiro

Published in the United States by Ballantine Books, an imprint of The Random House Publishing Group, a division of Random House, Inc., New York.

BALLANTINE is a registered trademark and the Ballantine colophon is a trademark of Random House, Inc.

LIBRARY OF CONGRESS CATALOGING-IN-PUBLICATION DATA
Shapiro, Molly.
Point, click, love : a novel / Molly Shapiro.
p.   cm.
"A Ballantine Books trade paperback original"—T.p. verso.
ISBN 978-0-345-52763-9 (pbk.)—ISBN 978-0-345-52764-6 (ebook)
1. Female friendship—Fiction.   2. Online dating—Fiction.   I. Title.
PS3569.H34147P65 2012
813'.54—dc23   2011035974

Printed in the United States of America

www.ballantinebooks.com

9 8 7 6 5 4 3 2 1

Book design by Laurie Jewell

For Harry and Fanny,

the loves of my life

Point, Click, Love

Chapter One

It had been two whole years since Katie divorced Rob, two years since she declared she was through with men. "I'll never be with a man again," she had said, her family and friends nodding and smiling politely.

Back then, Katie knew they didn't believe her. She knew they thought she'd find a new husband within a year or two and get right back on track. After all, she was only thirty-two when she divorced. In fact, they thought she'd find someone even better than Rob. He'd be a big-time executive for a pharmaceutical company, make lots of money, and install Katie and her two children in a big McMansion overlooking a golf course. She'd drive around in a shiny black SUV and would never have to work again.

That was their fantasy, not Katie's. Katie no longer bought into all that crap. Pharmaceutical executives were dull, McMansions fell apart after a few years, and SUVs were bad for the environment. Hadn't they heard about global warming?

Katie was proud that after two years as a divorcée she had proven them all wrong. She really was through with men, or at least through with marrying them, living with them, cooking and cleaning for them, having their babies, and putting up with their endless deficiencies.

She hadn't always been so sure. When she first separated from Rob, she'd look around at all of her friends and neighbors who were still together and think, Everyone's so happy! Everywhere she turned there were young lovers walking hand in hand, smiling couples pushing strollers, and families kicking soccer balls on lush green lawns.

It didn't take her long to see past the illusion. Most of those young lovers were destined to break up. If they didn't break up, they'd end up getting married, having babies, being sleep deprived, arguing over whose turn it was to do the bath, and going to bed mad. And if they made it through all of that, they'd be too busy driving their kids to play dates and soccer tournaments, arguing about finances, and worrying about getting laid off to give each other a second glance.

No, Katie wanted no part of it. But what she didn't account for was that, sooner or later, she would need to have sex.

She considered a number of options. The first that came to mind was asking Rob if he would oblige. After all, sex was always good with Rob, and he was also still single. She had no feelings for him anymore and was sure he didn't harbor any for her either. Maybe they could factor in a few quickies along with child support and alimony. Katie instantly realized that would never work.

Then she thought about getting a female lover. But after watching one of those TV shows about lesbians, she concluded that they had the same issues as heterosexual couples but with a lot more props. Then she wondered about the props. Could she get by with a really good vibrator? But as much as Katie had become a genuine do-it-yourselfer, sex was one area where she definitely needed some help.

And so she decided to take care of her need for sex in the same way she took care of paying her bills, finding cheap airfare, and buying her kids' school uniforms—she went online.

Katie had seen ads on TV for online dating, so she picked the site that seemed the least likely to yield "true love." She typed in her basic requirements—male, twenty-five to forty-five, within a twenty-mile radius—then hit "enter." Suddenly her screen was full of fuzzy little photos of men of all colors, shapes, and sizes.

She felt like a kid in a candy store, only this was a store where all the candy seemed just a slight bit off. The Milky Ways didn't have any caramel, the peanuts in the Snickers were kind of stale, and inside the smooth colorful shells of the M&Ms lurked something dark and sinister.

At first, Katie was put off by all that facial hair, all those balding heads, all those big guts and bulging biceps. She kept thinking that these were "real" men. Not that Rob wasn't real; it was just that she'd never stopped seeing him as the seventeen-year-old boy she met in high school. They had started dating during their junior year, stayed together all through college, and married at twenty-two. After fifteen years together, Rob never seemed to change much. He maintained a full head of hair, was always clean shaven, and his body remained slim and lean. He was cute in a boyish, nonthreatening way—the kind of guy twelve-year-old girls would fall for.

As she scrolled through all those eager faces, she crinkled her nose, squinted her eyes, tilted her head. Maybe if she looked from exactly the right angle they would seem more appealing.

Katie knew she would have to let go of all her preconceived notions. Maybe it would be nice to be with a big, hairy, balding, muscular man. Maybe that was just what she needed.

The first couple of weeks on Match.com were a little bumpy, but once Katie got the hang of it, she was hooked. She would find a man she was interested in and send him a short, clever email, something about the movies he liked or the books he read or the places he'd been. When she consistently got no reply, she figured out that these men wanted to be the pursuers, so she sat back and waited. Sure enough, being the quiet, demure female worked online too, and there was no shortage of men to choose from.

She noticed that the young, cute ones were boring. "Hey, how's it going?" they'd write. "Nice day, huh?" "Can't wait for Friday night!" The older ones were more interesting. Katie had specified she wanted men under age forty-five, but that didn't keep the fifty-year-olds and even a few sixty-year-olds from trying to woo her.

One fifty-seven-year-old didn't have a photo up but described himself as a dead ringer for Clint Eastwood. Katie wondered why a Clint Eastwood look-alike wouldn't want his picture up. He told her he was a real estate developer who traveled regularly to Hawaii, Central America, and the Virgin Islands. He specialized in hotels but spent half his time helping low-income families build homes out of corrugated metal and cinder blocks. He was a gourmet cook, spoke eight languages (only three fluently), and owned homes in San Francisco, Miami, and New York City. He realized he was out of her age bracket but found that the women his age were too matronly. He reassured Katie that he always satisfied his girlfriends. He wrote that one former girlfriend in particular, age twenty-two, frequently contacted him, practically begging him to come back to her. She told him once that when she masturbated, she always thought of him.

At that point, Katie decided to move on.

It was at these times when Katie wasn't sure if she should laugh or cry. If she hadn't divorced Rob, she never would have gotten a glimpse of this strange, fascinating world, she told herself. But then she wondered if she wouldn't have been better off never having gotten a glimpse of this strange, fascinating world.

When Katie and Rob broke up, she knew it was right from the very first moment. She never missed Rob, never longed for him. What she grieved over was the loss of her marriage, that concept that she had completely bought into, that thing that would give her life meaning. Ever since she was a little girl, Katie had struggled with the meaning of life. What is it all for? she'd ask herself. She always concluded that it was love—family and love. While she was married, she had a nagging feeling that the love she felt for Rob wasn't exactly the stuff the meaning of life is made of. Whenever she saw a movie where the lovers fell passionately into each other's arms, she wondered if she had anything close to that with Rob. Even all those Bachelors and Bachelorettes on TV seemed more in love after knowing each other for a few weeks.

She then figured it all came down to lust, not love. That was what had everybody so confused. All those people on TV and in the movies and in books weren't madly in love, they were incredibly horny. There was no such thing as "love at first sight," it was just "I want to screw you at first sight." Katie wished they would show what happens after the love is finally consummated, after that first romantic kiss in the pouring rain, after the passionate night in bed, after the "I dos." All that love and passion did not—could not—last forever. Why couldn't people just admit it?

So if Katie's love for Rob did not equal the meaning of life, what was life all about? Getting bland emails from overgrown boys who couldn't put a sentence together, or explicit come-ons from rich old fogeys who mingled good works toward men with nasty deeds toward women?

Being single again made Katie feel like she had been plunged back into a world that she was finished with long ago. She felt like she was in high school again, and she was never one of those people who longed for the good old days. But she knew she had to find a way to make the best of it.

That's how she got through the pain of divorce and the heart-breaking loss of her marriage—making the best of it. "It is what it is," she kept telling herself, even through the tear-soaked viewings of her favorite romantic comedies like *Sleepless in Seattle* and *Something's Gotta Give.* Even through the pitying looks from the other moms at school, having to go back to work, slogging through the chores by herself, and attending dinners with friends where she was always the odd man out—Katie closed her eyes and repeated to herself, "It is what it is."

Everyone agreed that she was handling it all amazingly. One friend even wrote a letter about her to Oprah, and for a brief moment Katie was sure she'd be invited onto the show to discuss her incredible coping mechanism. She would write a book about it called *It Is What It Is,* and it would be a bestseller. She'd write about all her insights on love and marriage—"It's not love, it's lust!" "Marriage doesn't work!"—and it would change the way the country—no, the world!—looked at things.

But before she could do all that, Katie had to first convince herself, which would be tough, since no matter what had happened, deep down she still believed in love. Maybe Match.com could cure her of that.

During the two years in which Katie swore off men, it seemed that they had sworn off her too. It was as if they knew that she was not interested and would not respond to their advances. And, sure enough, there weren't any advances to turn down. But once Katie went online and decided to give men another shot, she found that men in the real world were all of a sudden noticing her. Dads picking their kids up at school, the checkout boy at the grocery store, the man behind the desk at the DMV.

One time Katie went out for lunch with her kids and noticed a guy sitting in the next booth with two other men. He was cute and looked at her a couple of times, but she didn't think anything of it. After the men left, the waiter brought over the man's card instead of the check.

"He paid for your lunch," the waiter told Katie as he handed her the card.

Katie was stunned, and her kids must have sensed it.

"What's that, Mommy?" asked her five-year-old daughter, Maggie.

"Just a card," Katie said, hoping the whole thing would fly over their heads.

"Did you know that guy?" asked seven-year-old Frank.

No such luck, thought Katie. "Um, yes, I think we went to high school together."

"Then why didn't you say hi to him?" asked Frank.

"I wasn't sure it was him."

"Why didn't he say hi? Why did he pay for our lunch?"

Initially flattered, Katie was starting to get annoyed. Why'd he have to do that in front of my poor kids? she thought to herself. Didn't they have enough to deal with, being from a broken home and all? "Maybe he was shy," she said to Frank. "Like you. You're shy."

Katie was proud that, for the two years after her divorce, everything she did was in the best interest of her kids. In fact, her follow-up book to *It Is What It Is* would be called *Is It Good for the Kids?* Katie had figured out that by putting her kids first, divorce could actually be relatively easy and painless. There could be no fighting with the ex, because that would be bad for the kids. After a while, she was even able to develop a genuine affection for Rob, simply because she knew that's what the kids wanted. Every now and then they'd ask, "Mommy, can we all have dinner together like we used to?" and she would say, "Sure, let's ask Daddy." Rob would always agree because he also seemed to intuitively know the secret to a no-hassle divorce. And by developing a good relationship with Rob, she managed to avoid the continuing anger and bitterness and grief that most other divorcées had to endure.

By focusing so single-mindedly on the kids, Katie was able to block out any thoughts about what was going on, or not going on, in her life.

But it was the sex, or lack thereof, that finally caught up with Katie. A base human need, like food or water, was what shattered her idyllic post-divorce world.

Almost all the Match.com emails that Katie received began with a compliment about her appearance: "Nice smile," "Great eyes," "You look much younger than 34!" So she was happy when one suitor named Nate wrote, "Nicely written profile. I read so many of these things and yours is hands down the best. Original, funny. Are you a writer?"

Katie was flattered. The fact was, she'd rarely written anything longer than a grocery list since college but had always wanted to be a poet. She'd written poems to Frank and Maggie on their birthdays every year from the day they were born, figuring that one day they would sit and read them all, one by one, in order. She knew her Match.com profile was no work of art, but she had labored over it for days and was glad that someone out there seemed to notice.

"Thanks," she wrote back to Nate. "Not a writer (I work in a bank). Always wanted to be a food critic though. Love to write, love food, and am very, very critical." Katie liked to throw things in her emails to scare men away, just to see if they'd come back for more.

"I love critical," Nate replied. "In fact, I broke up with my first wife because she wasn't critical enough."

Great response, thought Katie. But the best part was that he didn't feel the need to stick a smiley-faced emoticon at the end.

"That's strange," noted Katie. "My ex said the exact opposite about me. Maybe we should have swapped spouses."

"Definitely," wrote Nate. Short and sweet. "So how long have you been doing this online thing?"

"Only a month or so. I guess it's fun, except when it's depressing and soulless." Katie was feeling cocky. Could she really write the words "depressing and soulless" without making this poor guy go running for the hills?

"Yeah, I know what you mean," agreed Nate. "But I don't seem to have any luck anywhere else. I'm not much for the bar scene. Where do you go to meet people?"

"You know, the usual places," Katie answered, feigning knowledge about such things. "Airplanes, firehouses (I always liked firemen), the grocery store."

"All women seem to go for firefighters," mused Nate. "What is it? The mustaches? I've never met anyone at a grocery store. Which ones have all the action?"

"I like the Safeway on 75th and Spruce. Go around 6:00 and you'll catch all the ladies in their pencil skirts and pumps after work."

"OK. I'll definitely give that one a try," wrote Nate. "Next time you go there, look for me in the produce section. I'll be the guy fondling the melons."

And at that, Katie's heart sank, her hopes plummeting. Fondling melons? She tried reading it over and over again, looking for some way to make it sound not quite so perverted. But there was no way around it. It was perverted. Why did he have to go and use the word "fondling"? "Touching," "holding," even "caressing" she could handle. And what's up with the "melons"? "Cantaloupe"? "Honeydew"? If Nate was looking for a girl with melons, he might as well look elsewhere. And didn't he realize that their fledgling correspondence really couldn't support references to melon fondling? Katie was at a loss. She decided to close her laptop and call it a night.

Katie got one more email from Nate, asking, "Are you there?" But she decided to ignore it. Before going on Match.com, she never would have imagined ignoring someone's email, but she learned that in the dog-eat-dog world of Internet dating, you had to be firm. Still, she worried she wouldn't find another like Nate. Until Ed came along.

Ed was kind of a gusher. While most men chose one or two things to compliment, Ed complimented *everything*—her black hair, her blue eyes, her toned arms, her tiny waist, her taste in books, her favorite restaurants, even the fact that she had two young children, something Ed, at age forty-six, never had and seemed to regret. Some might have called his behavior over the top, but Katie couldn't help but fall for it. Rob rarely complimented her on anything, so she felt like she had a lot to make up for, and Ed was willing to do the job.

When Ed first emailed Katie, she was a little annoyed that he'd ignored her age specifications. Putting her potential beau's age limit at forty-five was already a stretch, so she wasn't sure how she felt about dating a forty-six-year-old. Still, she was taken in by Ed's boyish face, bright-blue eyes, and graying blond hair. And his profile was so perfect she thought for sure he had invented the whole thing.

He was raised in Los Angeles but had lived in the Midwest for the last twenty years, working as an executive for a technology company. He made at least $150,000 a year—Match.com stopped counting at $150,000, as if to say, "Why would you need to make any more than that?" Katie always found it strange that some people were willing to disclose their salaries, but she was happy to know. Ed went to Princeton for college, business school at Wharton, and in between spent a year in Paris working for an investment firm.

Then she stopped herself. Why do I care where he went to college? Katie wondered. I thought I was doing this for the sex. She realized that, when in bed with a man, it would probably be better to be there with a twenty-eight-year-old with an associate's degree from a junior college than a forty-six-year-old with an Ivy League education. At that point she had to admit that maybe she *was* looking for something more than just sex. Good conversation? Nice dinners in fancy restaurants? Maybe the symphony? He could always use Viagra if need be.

Frankly, Katie couldn't imagine why Ed was interested in her. It wasn't as if she didn't have confidence, but she knew her limitations and she didn't have a résumé that could compare to Ed's. So what was it about her? Was her smile really so inviting? Her arms so alluring? Her restaurant picks so interesting?

After only a couple of emails, Ed asked for Katie's number, and within seconds of sending it to him, Katie heard her phone ring.

It was one of those rings that pierces your body and runs up your spine. One of those rings that signals a call that might just change your life.

"Hello?" Katie answered, a slight tremor in her voice. This was the first time she was actually talking to one of her suitors.

"Hi there, Katie. It's Ed."

Katie liked how confident Ed sounded. He already seemed in complete control of the situation.

"That was quick," said Katie.

"I don't believe in wasting any time. When I see something I want, I go after it."

"So you already know you want me?"

"I know I'm intrigued enough to find out more about you."

"Intrigued, huh?" Katie had never thought of herself as intriguing, but she liked the sound of it.

"I'm all about finding great things in unexpected places," Ed said.

"Oh, yeah?"

"Sure. I'm in biz dev."

Biz dev? thought Katie. "I'm sorry, I don't speak that language."

"Business development. My bad. You hang around these technology types long enough, you start abbreviating everything."

My bad? Is this guy *trying* to sound like he's twenty years old? wondered Katie. "What do you do?"

"I look for small companies doing great things and buy them out."

"I see. Let them do all the hard work and then reap the benefits."

"Exactly!"

"So I guess you work with a lot of young people." The minute she said it, Katie realized she had said the wrong thing.

"Well, yes. But I don't consider myself an old fart yet."

"Oh, of course, I know. I'm sorry. I just meant—"

"I know, I know. Don't worry about it. It's true. Most of the people I work with are much younger than me. I tend to gravitate to younger people."

"Am I young enough for you?" asked Katie.

"I don't know. We'll have to see if you can keep up."

"I have to say, most of the guys on Match seem to be looking for younger women." Katie was always appalled when she came across men who unabashedly stated that they'd date only women at least five years younger than themselves.

"That's true. Most guys think younger is better. But in the past year I dated a woman in her twenties and a woman in her fifties. Age doesn't matter to me. It's who you are."

Katie couldn't help but be charmed by Ed. She liked how self-assured, but not arrogant, he sounded. Well, maybe a little arrogant. But maybe he actually had something to be arrogant about.

"So you want to give this a try, Katie? Would you like to meet for dinner?"

Katie had expected to be invited for coffee, maybe a drink. She liked that Ed went right for the dinner. "Sure. Why not?"

Katie was excited. She wanted to tell someone about her first Match.com date, but it was too late to call anyone, particularly her best friend, Maxine, who usually went to bed around ten o'clock. Maxine's husband, Jake, was a doctor and liked to get to bed early. Maxine and Jake had gone to a couples' workshop in San Francisco a few years ago and the counselor told them that couples have the best relationships when they go to bed at the same time. Maxine swore it had made her marriage better, but Katie couldn't imagine how much better it could have gotten, since it already seemed perfect to her. Maxine always had the perfect marriage, and as much as Katie tried to find a chink in Maxine and Jake's armor, she never could. It was real. But rather than envying her friend, Katie was heartened by Maxine's good fortune. Maybe, someday, it could happen to her.

Chapter Two

Maxine's life used to be an open book. She used to share her thoughts and feelings with the people around her—her family, her friends. Now her life was full of secrets. She thought things and did things that she didn't want anyone to know about. Like the fact that she spent hours at her computer going to celebrity gossip websites.

Maxine was sure people would be shocked if they knew. She had spent her childhood reading books rather than watching *Gilligan's Island* and *The Brady Bunch*, like her friends did. She didn't even own a television until she had her first child in her late twenties. She was an artist—a painter—and a philanthropist. She was married to one of the most renowned gastroenterologists in the country. She had traveled the world and spoke fluent French, some Italian, and a bit of Chinese. Her kids were little geniuses who attended the fanciest prep school in town and were fawned over by their teachers. But the fact of the matter was, with all this, she spent a good part of her day reading about the celebrities and stars—both big and small—who populated online resources, from People.com to TMZ.

She read about their triumphs and their tragedies, followed their career ups and downs, and looked at photos of their well-dressed children. She watched them lounge on the beach topless in the South of France and walk the streets of Santa Monica with Starbucks lattes in hand. But what she loved most was reading about their romances and breakups, marriages and divorces. For some reason, reading about Katie and Tom, Demi and Ashton and Bruce, and Lance and Sheryl and Kate and Ashley and that poor ex-wife who had stood by him through all those Tours de France and never uttered a bad word about him even after being dumped, made Maxine feel like she was on the verge of some kind of discovery about life, love, and marriage.

Maxine was particularly intrigued by the Brad/Jen/Angelina combo. Even before she became celebrity-obsessed, she was struck by Brad and Jen—the golden couple. Everything about them glowed: their shiny blond hair and sparkling white teeth and richly tanned skin. Maxine had the idea that her friends thought of Jake and her as the Brad and Jen of the Midwest. No, they weren't quite as tan, their teeth weren't so white, and their hair wasn't as shiny. But they were pretty people, smart, successful, wealthy. So everyone thought they had the perfect life.

Then Brad left Jen for Angelina.

Maxine was devastated.

She knew it wasn't about Brad and Jen—it was about Jake and her and the idea that there was no such thing as a perfect couple. If it could happen to Brad and Jen, why couldn't it happen to her?

At first she hated Angelina—those ridiculously plump lips and her haughty demeanor on the red carpet. And what about all those tattoos, the vial of blood around her neck, and kissing her brother full on the mouth at the Oscars? But after a while, she started thinking that Angelina did have more substance than Jen. She genuinely cared about the world around her and used her celebrity to make a difference for the poor and destitute. Sure, Maxine wondered about all those adopted kids, whether the couple was biting off more than they could chew. But their hearts seemed to be in the right place. Soon, Maxine accepted Brad and Angelina as a couple and decided it was better this way.

So she had to wonder: Was there somebody else out there who was even better for Jake than she was? Or perhaps there was somebody out there for her who was better than Jake. Maxine was never a grass-is-always-greener kind of woman, but lately she couldn't help thinking that maybe things could be better.

And that was her biggest secret of all. Her marriage wasn't as great as everyone thought it was.

Maxine met Jake when she was traveling around Europe after graduating from Wesleyan. None of Maxine's friends were interested in going with her, since they all had secured high-powered jobs or artsy internships, so she decided to go it alone. She would head from north to south, beginning in Amsterdam and ending in Sicily.

Amsterdam was the perfect place to start, full of beautiful young people who were eager to make new friends and show off their town. Her first day there, she met a bunch of college students at a coffee bar who invited her to a party that night. The moment she walked into the cramped apartment, she was blown away by all the men, one more handsome than the next, and she resolved to meet a boy and sleep with him that night.

It had been a while for Maxine. Although she had spent her first two years of college skipping from one boy to the next, her second two years were completely sexless. Maybe she was burned out, maybe she was too busy with her double major in painting and religious studies, or maybe she was just looking for something different.

She zeroed in on a tall boy with deep blue eyes and jet-black hair; his name was Maximilian. They immediately hit it off, calling each other Max and discovering their mutual love of art. Maximilian tried to teach Maxine how to properly pronounce van Gogh. Maxine told Maximilian she wanted him to take her to his place, and he readily agreed.

Maxine stayed in Amsterdam an extra week to be with Maximilian but decided that she still wanted to see the rest of Europe. So she boarded a train for Paris and spent the long journey convincing herself that she had made the right decision. But once she settled into her cheap Parisian hotel, she knew she had made a mistake. Paris was a terrible place to be alone and an even worse place to be while missing a gorgeous Dutch boy with blue eyes and black hair. The people were cold and they made fun of her accent, and everything around her—the intimate bistros, the parks, the fountains—seemed to be built for couples.

After a few days, she hopped a train for Zurich, then Munich, then Salzburg, and in each place she searched the faces of the people for some kind of recognition, some acknowledgment of her existence, but everyone seemed indifferent.

Once across the Italian border, everything changed.

"Ciao, bella!" a man in a white apron shouted at Maxine the moment she walked into a coffee bar in Genoa, as if she were an old friend he hadn't seen in years. It was like that everywhere she went—restaurants, bakeries, stores, and newsstands. And as she worked her way south, people only got more welcoming, as if friendliness increased in direct proportion to the warmth of the sun and the decay of the buildings.

Rome is where she met Jake. They were staying at the same hostel, but he was with a group of college friends. Each night,

Jake's group would head out to one of the Irish pubs near the train station and get drunk on Guinness, while Maxine spent the night roaming the streets, hanging out at little wine bars, and eating hunks of pizza on the cement benches of the piazzas.

One evening, Jake and his friends were standing outside the door of the hostel, trying to figure out which pub to go to, when Maxine walked out. She ignored the group, as she had for the past three days, and headed confidently down the street, even though she had no idea where she was going. A few seconds later, she felt a tap on her shoulder.

"Hi!" said Jake.

"Hi," answered Maxine, stopping abruptly. She was surprised to have been followed but pretended it was the most normal thing in the world.

"Sorry to bother you, but my friends can't seem to get it together and I've noticed you going out every night by yourself."

"How do you know I'm not meeting someone?" Maxine said, resuming her walk as if she was rushing to an appointment.

"Oh, yeah, sure. You could be," said Jake nervously, struggling to keep up as he searched for the right words. "I mean, you probably are. But on the off chance that you're not . . ."

"I'm not," she said, slowing down the pace a bit so he could catch his breath.

"I'm sorry. I didn't mean to butt in. It's just that you seem to know what you're doing, and my friends—"

"Getting a little tired of the Irish pubs?" asked Maxine.

"How did you know?"

"It's all your friends ever talk about. You'd think all Rome had to offer was beer, and not even Italian beer!"

"I know, I know. It's mortifying."

"So why do you go with them?"

"I guess I'm not as self-assured as you."

"I guess you're not."

"But we go to museums and churches and stuff during the day," said Jake, trying to convince Maxine of his worthiness, following her like an eager, unwanted puppy.

"Yeah, when you finally get up around noon, because you're so hungover. The museums and churches close by then for the lunch break."

"So we go eat at a restaurant, and by the time we're done, it's three o'clock!"

"You eat in restaurants?" she asked, stopping once again, surprised that someone her age would have the means to eat in a real restaurant. The one time Maxine tried doing that, she was horrified by the extra charges for bread and water and angry that the waiter guilted her into ordering three courses and a dessert. The whole experience made her feel powerless, so she vowed never to do it again.

"Um, yeah. Where else would I eat?"

"I've eaten so much bread and cheese over the past month, I think I may be getting scurvy," said Maxine, putting her hand on her forehead like she was taking her temperature.

Jake smiled. "How about I buy you an orange, then?"

Maxine looked at him. "So, what? You want to tag along with me now?" Maxine wasn't sure why she was being so bitchy to this poor guy. He seemed sweet and was actually nice looking, for an American guy. Maybe he just paled in comparison to Maximilian.

"Yes, I do!" said Jake confidently, as if he needed more of a backbone to get anywhere with this girl.

Maxine had planned to check out some new places that evening but decided that she'd take Jake to some of her favorite spots instead. Rather than going down the busy Corso, where cars whizzed by and tourists jammed the sidewalks, Maxine led Jake down a series of narrow, winding roads, where housewives carried the ingredients of their evening meals in blue plastic bags, men stood in wine shops drinking a glass before heading home, and young lovers held hands, stopping every now and then to look in the windows of shoe stores.

When they arrived at Piazza Navona, they were greeted by a vast open space with three fountains lit up, the water sparkling in the moonlight.

"Wow," said Jake.

"You haven't been here yet?" asked Maxine in disbelief.

"No, I have. But not at night."

"Yeah, Rome is totally different at night. You've got to see everything at night."

And so they proceeded to see everything—or almost everything. The Pantheon, the Coliseum, the Tiber—walking the whole way. At the Forum they hopped a fence and sat on a rock that was probably the base of a column thousands of years old.

"Aren't you glad I came along with you tonight?" asked Jake, taking Maxine's hand.

"Maybe."

"Oh, come on. I know you've been checking me out ever since you saw me."

"Are you kidding me?"

"My friends noticed too. 'What's the deal with that loner girl?' they said. 'Does she have a thing for you?'"

"That's very funny, because, actually, you and your friends have been annoying the hell out of me."

"But now you see how wrong you were. Right?"

"Right," said Maxine. "Very wrong."

Maxine thought back to Maximilian, how attracted she was to him from the moment she saw him and how they shared the same passions. Yet there was something so distant about him, like he was an alien from another planet whom she could never truly know.

With Jake it was different. She hadn't been attracted to him right away, and on the face of it they had little in common. He was starting medical school in Boston in the fall, and she had no idea what she wanted to do. But already she felt safe and comfortable with Jake. Already she felt like he was someone she could spend the rest of her life with.

Jake had planned to leave with his friends the next day and head to Brindisi, where they would take a boat to Greece. Instead, he asked Maxine if he could stay with her in Rome and then head south to Sicily. Far from being taken aback by Jake's forwardness, Maxine was impressed with his spontaneity and his certainty that he wanted to be with her.

From that night on, Maxine and Jake never lived apart again.

Maxine had planned on going back to Cleveland and staying with her parents until she figured out what to do, but instead she went to Boston with Jake. From his first year in medical school, Jake was a star, so he was always getting exciting opportunities to study and work in the best hospitals in the country. Maxine was excited to be able to live in so many great places—from San Francisco to New Orleans—but it was impossible for her to hold on to a job for more than a year, making it hard to establish herself and her own career. When she thought about it, she realized that summer in Europe was the first and last time Jake followed her instead of the other way around.

After they got married and Jake finished school, Maxine hoped they'd settle on one of the coasts. But Jake's best offer was at a teaching hospital in Kansas City, so Maxine agreed that's where they should go. She knew not to complain. How many struggling artists had rich husbands to support them? She could take classes, build a studio, and have plenty of time to paint without having to worry about getting a job.

Not only that, Jake started to get invitations from around the world to speak at conferences and seminars, and he always brought Maxine along. Sometimes they would take months off at a time to do charity work in Africa or Southeast Asia.

Yes, it was all pretty spectacular. So what was the problem? The problem was that, at a certain point, they stopped having sex.

Literally—no sex. None.

When Maxine allowed herself to think about when and how this could have happened, she knew the answer right away. It was when she got pregnant with her first child, Matthew.

Jake was a doctor, and he always said how beautiful women were when they were pregnant. But when it happened to Maxine—when her belly ballooned and her ankles swelled and her ass widened and her face got plump and she was constantly chewing on Tums to relieve her indigestion and little patches of brown formed on her face—it all seemed less beautiful to Jake. By the fifth month, he barely touched her, which was fine with Maxine, who felt miserable, ugly, and not at all sexual. Then came breastfeeding. When the weight came off, Jake was ready to go, but Maxine was dry as a bone, so she held him off for six months until she decided to stop, partly because she worried her marriage wouldn't survive.

But while the sex resumed, it wasn't quite the same. Maxine wondered if it had something to do with childbirth, with Jake standing over her as she lay sprawled on a hospital bed, her legs spread and a variety of multicolored tubes hanging out of her. Yes, seeing their son's head emerge from her vagina must have been an amazing experience, but wouldn't that vision change the way he saw that particular body part—no longer a locus of pleasure but now simply a component of a larger baby-making machine?

It was subtle, but Maxine detected the difference right away. Jake kissed her less when they had sex. He avoided looking into her eyes. He developed a preference for doggy style. Maxine thought about saying something to Jake, but they had never been a couple who talked about sex. And what would be the point anyway? Maxine hoped it was only a phase.

Then she got pregnant two years later with Abby. This time during pregnancy, she felt more horny than she ever had in her life, but Jake's abstinence started even sooner—at four months. So she satisfied herself with Jackie Collins's entire oeuvre and a few early-morning sessions on her own when she had the chance.

Maxine breastfed Abby for only three months, figuring it was better to get back to having sex with Jake sooner rather than later. But this time he was even more distant, and they were doing it less and less. Then came baby number three, Suzanne, two years later. By that time, their sex life had become so erratic, so detached, so unsatisfying, that the gradual progression to no sex at all was practically a relief. Besides, they were both too tired to even think about doing it, and it seemed that there was always at least one kid in their bed almost every night.

So there they were, the perfect couple, without the sex. Jake made up for it by jacking up his public displays of affection, as if he wanted the rest of the world to believe they had a loving, healthy physical relationship. He held her hand, rubbed her shoulders, gave her long soft kisses. Maxine's friends would comment on how amazing it was, how Jake was so clearly still madly in love with her, and Maxine would just smile and shrug her shoulders. How lucky she was!

She couldn't bring herself to talk about it with her friends, not even her best friend, Katie, to whom she had always told everything. Maxine couldn't let herself think about it too long either, so she threw herself into parenthood and painting, determined to not only be a great mother but also to find real success as an artist.

And she did.

It started with shows in the best local galleries. Then she began showing in galleries in New York and L.A. Soon, invitations from contemporary museums all over the country started coming in. There were talks with visiting artists and fancy dinners with collectors and glowing reviews in newspapers and art magazines. Finally she had achieved a success in her world that Jake had achieved in the world of medicine.

Maxine knew Jake was proud of her, but there was something missing. As with the sex, he seemed detached. No one else noticed, of course, because he would always be hanging all over her, smiling lovingly and kneading her shoulders. But Maxine could feel it. He just wasn't all there.

Then one night after dinner, Maxine needed the number of the pediatrician's office but couldn't find her cell phone. Jake's BlackBerry was sitting on the kitchen counter; she picked it up. Maxine had never used a BlackBerry before, so she started pressing random buttons. A list of recent text messages came up, and there was only one name. Deirdre.

Deirdre was the newest doctor in Jake's practice. She was a graduate of Brown University and did her residency at the Cleveland Clinic. When Deirdre arrived in Kansas City to start her new job, Jake and Maxine hosted a cocktail party for her.

The first thing Maxine thought when Deirdre walked into the house that night was that she looked like a better version of herself. Deirdre was thirty-two, tall, and athletic, with silky blond hair, flawless skin, and blue-green eyes that seemed to change color like the waters off a Greek island. Maxine was forty-two, short, and slim, with dirty-blond hair, pale freckled skin, and eyes the color of the murky waters off Manhattan. Maxine had always felt she was cute enough, that she actually looked pretty good for a mother of three, but Deirdre's otherworldly beauty set off an insecurity she'd never experienced before.

"That Deirdre is pretty amazing," Maxine said to Jake when they were climbing into bed after the party.

"Yeah, really bright," he said casually. "We were lucky to get her."

"And beautiful. She's very beautiful. I've never seen anyone so beautiful."

"I guess," he said, remaining nonchalant. "I think she's got a boyfriend."

Maxine smiled to herself. She knew Jake found Deirdre attractive—how could he not?—and she appreciated his effort to comfort her with the news of Deirdre's boyfriend. Not for a moment did Maxine consider that Jake would cheat on her. Never. Jake was the most honest, upstanding guy she had ever met, and, despite their issues in bed, she knew he loved her and respected her and would never do anything to hurt her. Sure, she was a little jealous of Deirdre. Who wouldn't be? But she trusted Jake completely.

Until she saw those text messages. Couldn't there be an innocent excuse? she thought. Maybe they'd been going back and forth about a patient. Maybe they were discussing a movie they'd both seen. All Maxine had to do was open one up and she'd know for sure, but she simply couldn't do it. In her heart, she knew what she would find.

Jake had never texted Maxine in his life, and clearly he wasn't texting anyone else but Deirdre. Texting was something young people did, and Deirdre was young. It was something intimate, a mode of communication just for her.

Maxine put down the phone and locked herself in the small bathroom in the finished basement. She sat on the floor for half an hour and cried. Then she got up, washed her face, and went to bed. She slept fine that night, not even hearing when Jake came to bed an hour later.

The next morning, after she brought the kids to school, Maxine sat in her studio, staring at the canvas she had been working on over the last week. She tried to paint but couldn't do it. So she sat on the living room couch and turned on the TV. Regis and

Kelly were interviewing a young movie star Maxine had never heard of. They were talking about the star's parents, her love of french fries, and her next movie. Maxine started flipping the channels until she came to an *E! True Hollywood Story* about Jennifer Aniston.

It was an in-depth documentary with all the crucial details of Jen's life: her rise to fame, her early loves, her marriage to Brad, and the breakup. Maxine was fascinated. More than ever, she couldn't believe all the many parallels between her life and Jen's— the career success, the perfect marriage. And then Angelina came along.

That was it! Deirdre was Maxine's Angelina! Deirdre was more gorgeous, more successful, more intelligent, and she shared a connection to Jake that Maxine never had—medicine.

As she watched Jen's story unfold, Maxine began to feel like she was getting a glimpse of what was in store for her. She wondered if Jen, too, had begun to feel her husband pull away long before their breakup. She wondered if Jen had trusted Brad implicitly. She wondered if Jen knew, deep down, what was coming before it happened.

Most of all, she wanted to see how it would all turn out in the end. What would happen to Jen after leaving the love of her life, the perfect man, her happily ever after? But the show ended before these questions could be answered.

Of course, Maxine felt foolish. Couldn't she find a great literary character to identify with instead of a movie star? A Madame Bovary? An Anna Karenina? A Lady Macbeth?

But who would want to identify with those tragic figures anyway? Better she should relate to the hot chick with the amazing legs, the sunny smile, and the millions of dollars.

So Maxine got up from the TV and went straight to her computer, where she searched for everything she could find about Jen and Brad and Angelina. She read for hours, soon finding other couples to read about and find similarities to. There seemed to be an endless stream of stories and betrayals and lessons to be learned.

Maxine didn't know what she was going to do about her own situation. Would she confront Jake? Would she forgive him? Would she leave him? But maybe she could find the answers somewhere here, online, in the lives of the rich and famous.

Chapter Three

Claudia had a lot of good reasons for hating her husband. Steve had lost his job as a research analyst during a brutal round of lay-offs almost a year ago and hadn't worked since—completely for lack of trying. Friends, family, people on the street, had given him plenty of leads, but somehow he always managed to not get the job. He sat around the house all day—watching TV, playing videogames, and surfing the Net—leaving only to take the girls to school and pick them up from soccer practice. While he usually managed to wash the dishes, he never picked up a mop, cleaned the toilet, or dusted the furniture. He left that to the cleaning woman, who still came once a week, even though they could have used the extra cash.

But what Claudia really couldn't stand about Steve was how he had made her into such a raging bitch.

Not only was she bitchy to Steve, she was bitchy to her daughters, bitchy to her coworkers, bitchy to salespeople, waiters, the mailman, and everyone else she came in contact with. Her friends, who managed to escape the ill will mostly by plying her with alcohol until she loosened up, finally confronted her about it.

"Claudia, we're worried about you," said Katie.

"Worried about what? I'm fine," said Claudia defensively.

"You've just been so . . . high-strung lately," said Maxine.

"I know, I know," said Claudia. "It's Steve. He's making me crazy!"

"It can't be all about Steve," said Annie. Annie was their never-been-married friend. She had no idea what a husband could do to a woman.

"Believe me, it's *all* about Steve," said Claudia.

"Well, whatever it's about, we think you need to talk to someone," said Katie.

So she went and talked to someone. Claudia described to the doctor how the mild annoyance she had been building up toward her husband over the years had lately turned into all-out hate. She told him that Steve was a lazy good-for-nothing whose only ambition was to reach the highest level of Halo. She told him that Steve watched everyone from Rachael Ray to Paula Deen to Emeril on the Food Network but never once got off his ass to make dinner for the family. And, to top it all off, he had thrown himself into Facebook, creating an alternate universe for himself where he wasn't such a pathetic loser.

Yes, the Facebook thing was what really got her. Claudia had joined two years ago because it was a requirement for attending her twenty-year high school reunion, and Steve decided he'd sign up too. For the first year they pretty much ignored it, passively acquiring "friends" but never posting anything or seeking anyone out. But when Steve lost his job, he went on a frenzied friend-acquisition spree, racking up some five hundred friends. His five or so "real" friends would call him up and ask him to go out for lunch or to play a round of golf or have a drink with the guys, but Steve always refused, preferring to stay home and interact online with his five hundred fake friends. Claudia figured he'd rather be the cool, funny Facebook guy than the depressed, boring, unemployed guy who had to be cheered up by his buddies.

Steve was one of those perpetual status updaters, but instead of telling the truth ("Watching Rachael Ray make a turkey lasagna and thinking about the Chinese takeout we'll have tonight" or "Just wondering how many brain cells die from three straight hours of Call of Duty"), he'd write vague, elliptical posts about exotic travel ("Anyone know if it's OK to drink the water in Cambodia?") and philosophers he'd never read ("I'm gonna vote 'no' on Nietzsche's theory of eternal return").

And whenever they went somewhere as a family—a restaurant, the girls' soccer game, the mountains of Colorado—Steve would always be on his iPhone, punching in his status. "Bacon burger topped with brie. Gotta try it!" "Sandy and Janie the big scorers!" "No place better than the Colorado Rockies!" he'd enthuse, even though he didn't seem to be particularly interested in the burger, the game, or the view.

It was bad enough that Steve had sunk so low, but his insistence on making everyone else think he was at the top of the world made it all the worse.

So Claudia stopped going on Facebook. In fact, she began to shun all forms of electronic communication, seeing them as an evil plot to disguise the truth and ultimately prevent real human interaction. At the public relations firm where Claudia worked, everyone used email and instant messaging and texting to communicate, never calling or actually getting up from their desk and speaking directly to their coworkers. Claudia decided she would single-handedly change the corporate culture. So when she got an IM from her boss, who sat in a cubicle two feet away, saying, "Did you look over that press release?" Claudia peeked over the fabric-covered wall and answered, "Yes."

That was how Claudia got over her chronic bitchiness.

After working at the firm for three years, Claudia knew barely a quarter of the two-hundred-some employees. But once she started following her new face-to-face policy, she discovered that there were a lot of cool, interesting people in her office. Like Fred in accounts payable.

"Fred?" she said, peeking into his cubicle. Claudia had emailed Fred frequently over the years but had never taken the trip up to the fourth floor to meet him in person.

"Yes?" Fred looked a bit startled sitting there behind his desk, far from the hustle and bustle of the lower floors filled with account executives and art directors.

"Hi. I'm Claudia from downstairs."

"Oh, yes, Claudia. What can I do for you?"

At first, Fred didn't make much of an impression on Claudia. But when she took a closer look she noticed his beautiful green eyes, and she thought she detected a nicely shaped biceps lying underneath that crisp white oxford shirt.

"One of our vendors has been waiting three months for his check. I figured it must have gotten lost, so I'm bringing up another copy of his invoice."

"Oh. I see." Fred took the invoice from Claudia, still appearing a little confused. "You know, you can just email invoices to me if you want," he said, waving the piece of paper in the air as if it was a useless artifact from a bygone era.

"I know," said Claudia, "but I thought it would be nice to meet you."

"Really?" Fred smiled, exposing a nice straight row of teeth. "Wow. I don't think any of you guys have ever ventured up to the fourth floor. And certainly not just to meet me! I'm honored."

"Aw, shucks, Fred. Don't tell me you have an accounts-payable complex." Claudia stepped into the cubicle and sat on a portion of the desk.

"Well, yeah. I guess I do. You creative types intimidate me." Fred scooted his chair back a bit, making room for Claudia.

"Creative types? Ha! You obviously have no idea what I do."

"Then maybe you can explain it to me sometime," said Fred, his initial shyness beginning to evaporate.

The fact that Claudia didn't wear a wedding ring—she simply didn't like rings—had never posed any problems during her thirteen-year marriage to Steve, since she always had a wall around her that served the purpose of keeping men at a distance. But now that she was opening herself up to new people and being so friendly, she realized that wedding rings can perform an important function.

"Once I figure out what the hell I do, I'll be sure to let you know." Claudia laughed nervously, standing up and backing out of the cubicle. "Well, I should head downstairs. Come and visit sometime," she added, regretting it once she did. Was she leading him on?

That evening Claudia went home in such a good mood, she forgot to transform into her bitchy self for Steve. So for the first time in months, she was actually kind of nice to him.

"Hey, Steve, how's it going?"

Steve looked up from the sofa where he was watching TV, startled by his wife's lack of venom. "Fine?" he asked, not sure whether this was real or some kind of trap.

"Watching the news? That's good." Claudia sat down on the arm of the sofa. "Man, I haven't watched the evening news in forever. Who they got now? Peter Jennings? I love Peter Jennings."

"Um, Claudia, Peter Jennings died years ago."

"That's right. He was just so . . . so timeless. You know? Like he was never going to die. But we all die, don't we? So no point in frittering away our time."

"Look, Claudia, don't start. I was only just sitting here—"

"Oh, no, Steve," Claudia practically shouted. He had totally misunderstood. "I wasn't saying anything about you. Just thinking about life and how it's over before we know it. That's all. You know me. I get that way sometimes."

Steve knew all too well the many moods of Claudia. The contemplative Claudia, the boisterous Claudia, the I'm-having-an-existential-crisis Claudia, the I-hate-everyone Claudia, and, most recently, the I-love-everyone Claudia. Yes, she was moody, but Steve was the one person who was able to handle her wild swings.

Claudia had always been a "handful," as her parents liked to put it. She was outspoken and strong willed and fearless. Growing up in the conservative Midwest, she quickly gravitated to the left. Her parents, who were devout Republicans, insisted that she chose her politics based on the number of potential arguments she could have per capita. In high school she was the editor of the newspaper and used her position to argue her causes. She was always the one standing outside school gathering names on petitions for the cause of the moment, and she was probably the only fourteen-year-old manning the polls on Election Day. Her parents never once praised her for her command of the issues, her initiative, or even her spunk. But the lack of encouragement never deterred Claudia.

She had her heart set on going to Berkeley for college, but her parents insisted they could only afford to send her to an in-state school, so she went to the University of Kansas. Claudia managed to find a sufficient number of liberal, sensitive, artsy types, but none of them seemed to match her temperament as well as the brash football players, the boisterous frat boys, and the pompous president of the Young Republicans club.

Claudia was a striking presence at almost six feet tall, with long brown hair as thick as a Kennedy's and almond-shaped brown eyes. She tried dating a slender boy who majored in ceramics and later the bookish editor of the college literary magazine, but while their intellects were in synch, their bodies weren't.

Every now and then, Claudia and her friends would venture to one of the fraternity parties, partly for the free beer but mostly to gather material for their late-night bitching sessions, where they lamented their lot in having to go to college in the farmlands of Kansas and plotted ways to transfer to Berkeley. One weekend they opted for a luau-themed party where everyone wore grass skirts and leis, but they defiantly did not.

"Hey, baby, wanna get 'lei-ed'?" asked a soon-to-be-wasted football player wearing a blue and yellow sarong and holding up a necklace of fake fuchsia flowers.

Claudia looked at him blankly, considering whether to walk away or attempt a witty comeback that would most certainly go over his head. "Yes, I'd love to get laid," she said, surprising even herself. For a split second she imagined this mammoth man seizing her, sure he could beat a lawsuit with those words ringing in his head, but then she relaxed, figuring she could handle even this meathead.

"Awesome," he said, placing the lei around her neck and walking on.

Claudia smiled.

"What's so funny?" asked another guy, a little smaller than the first but still big, wearing only a grass skirt—his impressive physique on full display.

"You guys," said Claudia.

"Oh, really? You find us funny?"

"Yeah, extremely funny."

The boy paused, blatantly looking Claudia up and down. "You're tall."

"Yes, I am."

"And pretty."

"If you say so."

"I've never seen you before."

"Not surprising, considering about twenty thousand people go here."

"My name's Mike. What's yours?"

"Claudia."

"You want to go out on a date, Claudia?"

A date? thought Claudia. People don't go out on "dates" in college, unless, of course, they live in a frat house. There was something quaint about the notion.

"Sure, why not," said Claudia. And before she knew it, she was giving this stranger her phone number.

Mike called the next day and arranged to take Claudia out that weekend. He picked her up in an old Cadillac convertible and took her to an Italian restaurant with velvet wallpaper and red leather booths. He wore a light blue polo shirt that showed off his bluish-gray eyes, and his thick black hair was still wet. After getting permission from Claudia to order for the two of them, he asked for a bottle of Chianti, fried ravioli for an appetizer, and chicken spiedini.

"I feel like I'm going to the prom," said Claudia.

"Why? You never had a guy take you out before?"

"Not really."

"Most guys, they don't know how to treat a lady."

Claudia was surprised when that first date led to a second, then a third, until finally they were a real couple. She couldn't believe how pliable she was around Mike, how they never argued about anything. He wasn't particularly political or opinionated, but every now and then he'd come out with some stupid remark about commies or welfare moms, and she would just let it go. Why was she suddenly so easygoing? Because she was finally getting laid.

Claudia didn't have a boyfriend in high school, mostly because she towered over everyone. And the boys she hung out with in college didn't appeal to her. With his muscular body and manly good looks, Mike was the first boy she felt sexually attracted to.

Claudia was nervous the night she decided to lose her virginity, but Mike was as adept in bed as he was in a cheap Italian restaurant.

"You sure you want to do it tonight?" Mike asked with a smile, confident that Claudia was ripe for the plucking.

"Uh-huh," said Claudia, enjoying the feeling of letting herself go, of letting someone else call the shots.

Mike was gentle and affectionate but also strong and authoritative. Claudia couldn't believe what she had been missing all those years.

Some of her friends, on the other hand, couldn't quite figure it out.

"I don't get what you see in that guy," said her roommate, Barb. "He's so . . . right-wing."

"Yeah, well, you're not going to get it unless you sleep with him," said Julie, who immediately understood the attraction.

"Why don't we all go out together one of these days?" suggested Barb.

Claudia had been avoiding doing that for months, fearing that exposing the relationship to the outside world could be the end of it. But she could no longer hide Mike from the people who were most important to her.

She decided they'd all meet for a drink at one of the loudest bars on campus, hoping that they could get drunk, shoot some pool, and avoid too much conversation. Everything was going fine, until Barb started getting mischievous.

"So, Mike. Did you know that Claudia was once a member of the Socialist Party?"

Claudia could feel her anger swelling. Why was Barb trying to sabotage her relationship with Mike? But then she caught herself. Barb was only being playful—and honest. Claudia was ashamed. Why was she suddenly so intent on hiding everything about herself? No, she didn't like the feeling of being outed, but maybe Barb was right. Maybe she should just tell the truth.

"Briefly," said Claudia, smiling hopefully at Mike.

"That's all in the past, anyway," said Mike. "Claudia's a different girl now."

Barb and Julie looked at Claudia quizzically. Claudia looked at Mike.

"What's all in the past?" asked Claudia.

"I know you used to be all liberal and stuff. I see the books on your shelf. But you're not like that anymore."

"What makes you think that?" asked Claudia.

"Well I'm pretty conservative, and we never argue. Right?"

"Yeah, well, that's just 'cause I want you to screw me."

Julie glanced at Barb, biting her lip. Barb stared down at her drink. And Mike looked like he was about to cry.

"I'm sorry, Mike," said Claudia. "That wasn't nice."

"No, that's fine," said Mike. "I understand." He stood up. "I think I'd better go now." And he left.

"Oh, God, Claudia, I'm so sorry!" said Barb. "This is all my fault."

"No, it's okay. It had to happen."

She knew it did. But Claudia couldn't help but feel she would never have sex again.

Then she met Steve.

Two years out of college, Claudia was working as a temp at a high-powered ad agency in Kansas City. She was ordered to go to Kinko's, drop off a presentation to be copied, then pick it back up by five o'clock. When she arrived at Kinko's at four forty-five, she was handed a big box of bound booklets. She flipped through them, making sure everything was in order, but noticed one problem: The copies weren't double-sided.

"Excuse me, but I asked for double-sided," said Claudia with barely contained contempt.

"I don't think so, ma'am," said the young boy behind the counter. "I have the order right here."

"I did. I know I did," said Claudia, getting increasingly frantic by the minute.

"Look, ma'am—"

"Stop calling me ma'am!" shouted Claudia, prompting everyone in the store to turn and stare. "I'm barely twenty-three, for God's sake."

"You asked for a lot of things . . . miss. Color, bright-white paper, three-hole punch . . . but not double-sided."

Claudia looked into the boy's pockmarked face and quickly realized she needed to talk to someone else. "Let me talk to the manager."

The boy went to a back office and out came Steve.

Steve wore one of those cheap polyester uniforms meant to tame and subjugate employees, but he wore it with a grace and confidence that said: "Yes, I'll do this for now, but I'm not long for this place."

He walked out from behind the counter and went right up to Claudia, getting as close as he could without appearing intimidating. "Can I help you?"

Claudia gazed up at Steve, who must have been at least six foot five, and decided that if she could not surpass him in height she would surpass him in volume. "I have to get these presentations back to my office in ten minutes, and you people completely screwed them up!"

Steve looked at her patiently, taking a moment to measure his words. "Look . . . I'm sorry. What's your name?"

"Claudia!" she shouted, annoyed that this man wouldn't get to the point.

"Claudia. Let me explain something to you. I'm here to help you. I suggest that the next time you have a problem, you act nicely toward the person who has the power to help you. I would be happy to rerun this order exactly how you want it, and I will get it done as quickly as humanly possible. If you want to continue to waste time by arguing over whose fault this is, go right ahead. Otherwise, why don't we just get started?"

Stunned into silence, Claudia realized that this person had taught her something that could possibly change her life. At that moment, she decided that she had to see this man again. But while Claudia and Steve did see each other again and did ultimately get married, the lesson that he taught her that day faded quickly. No one, not even Steve, had ever bothered to explain the concept to her again. Instead, once Steve and Claudia started dating, he accepted her for who she was, embracing her faults—her temper and her stubbornness—and never once asking her to change.

That was what Claudia appreciated most about Steve, but it was something that she often overlooked. For her part, Claudia wanted to change almost every aspect of Steve. That first day they met, at the local Kinko's, Steve seemed destined for great things. But he never was able to fulfill Claudia's vision of what he could be. Maybe that was why she found his carefully constructed virtual life so repugnant. Why couldn't he live that way in the real world?

Steve always held decent, well-paying jobs at marketing or pharmaceutical or consulting firms, but somewhere along the way any ambition he might have once had mysteriously disappeared. Sometimes Claudia wondered if her own quick rise to the top of her profession was the reason for Steve's lack of drive. She went from associate to account executive to supervisor to vice president in less than a decade, switching firms every couple years as she searched for the most prestige and the highest pay and taking off only three months after the twins were born. Was Steve actually intimidated by Claudia's success? Or did he look at her rising salary as an opportunity to goof off, lose his job, and never go back to work again?

When Claudia met old friends and acquaintances around town, she often wondered whether they were part of Steve's simulated universe. One day, she was making a three o'clock coffee run when she bumped into Heather Murphy, a high school friend of Steve's who had attended their wedding.

"Hi, Heather!"

"Claudia! It's been so long! How are you?"

"Terrific. And you? You look great!"

"Thanks. How's Steve?"

"Oh, you know. The same. Still out of work."

"Really?" asked Heather with a look of puzzlement.

"I thought everyone knew."

"Well, what I know about Steve is mostly from Facebook, and he doesn't talk about work much. I did wonder, since he posts throughout the day."

"Yeah, sorry about that."

"No need to apologize! He's very amusing. I have to say, Claudia, I admire you for being so . . . understanding."

"Well, you know, we're in a recession, so I can't get too mad."

"No, I mean the Facebook thing. Some of the stuff he puts up there . . ."

"Right," said Claudia, pretending she knew everything. "Yeah, I know."

"I mean, I know it's all in good fun, but I don't think I'd want Ned writing that kind of stuff."

"Oh, sure. It's all in good fun," said Claudia.

"And what's up with that Marjorie Gooding chick? Remember her? Every time Steve says anything, she's like: 'Thumbs up!' 'Like that!' 'Ha-ha!' It's kind of nauseating."

"Yes! So annoying!" Claudia exclaimed a little too loudly.

"Well, I wish you'd write something up there sometime. Would love to hear what's going on in your life for a change."

"Oh, nothing much to say at this point."

"Still, I'd love to catch up. Anyway, gotta run. Let's keep in touch!"

When Claudia returned to her desk, without coffee, she considered going online right away to see what Steve was up to. But instead she printed out an old invoice, hopped on the elevator, and pressed the button for the fourth floor.

Chapter Four

Most people Annie knew kept up with old friends through Facebook or Myspace or Twitter. All Annie had to do was open up *The New York Times.*

Annie grew up in New York City, went to a fancy prep school, and studied comparative literature at Yale and business management at Wharton. Along the way, she played hopscotch with a future clothing designer, cheated off the math test of a future filmmaker, smoked her first joint with a future congressman, and made out with a future Pulitzer Prize—winning journalist. But that was just the beginning.

It seemed to Annie that every time she read *The New York Times* she came across at least one name she knew. Once it was a lengthy profile of a guy from her study group at Wharton who'd moved to San Francisco, started an online stock-trading company, sold it for $50 million, then opened a four-star restaurant in Napa, where he was the chef and the entire staff was made up of former drug addicts. Another time she read in the "Vows" section about a girl from her high school who married the son of the ambassador to France, lived in Paris, and wrote a bestselling novel that was about to be made into a major motion picture. One classmate from Yale got written up for potty training her child at only nine months. It seemed that even the stay-at-home moms on the East Coast were overachievers.

At first, Annie found it amusing to be sitting at her kitchen table in the middle of Overland Park, Kansas, getting these glimpses into her past life, but soon the newspaper that she had once admired and treasured for keeping her abreast of all the latest thoughts and trends and discoveries that would have otherwise passed her by became the bane of her existence.

Annie had always been one of those people who was destined for great things. She went to the best schools, excelled at everything she did, even made a name for herself on the junior table-tennis circuit. When she graduated from Wharton, she was recruited by Sprint, and while she was hesitant to come to the Midwest, she felt like she was pioneering terrain that she and her fellow easterners knew nothing about. But after a few years, the charms of being a New Yorker in the heartland wore off, and she became just another marketing director at a massive telecommunications company, sitting in a landlocked state far from the city she once loved.

Meanwhile, everyone else she knew was making millions, creating important works of art, or contributing to the betterment of society—all within a short driving distance of a great beach and a scenic mountain range.

Once she made the mistake of bemoaning her predicament to her mother, who had been against Annie's move to Kansas City from the start.

"Today's paper was the worst," said Annie to her mother one Sunday morning after spending three hours reading an especially hefty issue of the *Times*. "Ron Goldfarb was on page one for discovering a new planet, there was a review of Christine Hepner's new movie in the 'Arts' section, and Scott Anderson wrote an op-ed about spending a year in Spain eating paella. One more story about a former classmate and I was gonna heave my Honey Bunches of Oats."

"So why don't you move back here?" asked her mother.

Annie should have known that would be her mother's response, but she had hoped for some sympathy instead. "Oh, yeah? So they'll put me in the *Times* just for moving back home?"

"You know what I mean. If you'd stayed here maybe you'd be making movies . . ."

"Or discovering planets? Doubt it. I might be eating more paella though. The restaurants here suck."

"I think you're wasting your potential there, Annie."

There were others like Annie all over town, other young talented women from major cities and prestigious colleges who had dreams of making it big in a strange new land. But once they settled in, they began to lose their edge. At first, Annie and these women lived in downtown lofts and trolled the bars and galleries and got tickets to see hip bands, trying to make the city into a place that resembled where they had come from. But, gradually, each one of them married a nice midwestern guy, bought a house in the suburbs, started having babies, and quit their job. All except Annie.

Annie would have liked to say that she consciously chose not to go down that road, that she had no desire to pursue such a traditional lifestyle, but she would have been lying. In fact, she tried hard to find the nice midwestern boy, but in the process kept running into the not-so-nice boys.

She wasted time with a hipster she met at a gallery opening who wanted to get out of town as soon as he could. Later, she graduated to a corporate lawyer she could never seem to lure off the golf course. But the biggest waste of time was Ben Weiner, whom she dated for six years. She met Ben while he was in dental school and they were both twenty-nine years old—ripe for a serious relationship. They immediately hit it off, spending all their time together, saying "I love you," and even hanging out with his family. That's what really did Annie in—the family.

Ben was Jewish, and every Friday night he would go to dinner at his parents' house. Not wanting to exclude Annie from this regular part of his life, Ben always invited her to come along, and she usually did. Ben had four older siblings—two brothers and two sisters—and there were nine nieces and nephews among them. Every week it was a loud, raucous event, but Annie loved it because it reminded her of the large, boisterous Jewish families she knew back in New York.

The best part was how nice Ben's family was to her. Being the only nonrelative at the table, she was always given special attention, but she was never made to feel like an outsider. And because she was so familiar with Jewish customs, the family never had to explain the prayers they said in Hebrew or the traditional foods they ate. Unlike Ben's past girlfriends, Annie always ate the chopped liver and the matzo ball soup and told Ben's mom she made the best stuffed cabbage she'd ever had.

Everything about Ben pointed to a marriage proposal. The only thing that caused Annie concern was the possibility that he wouldn't want to marry a non-Jew, but with his family being so welcoming, Annie figured it must not be an issue. Besides, one of

Ben's brothers was married to a woman named Brittany, with blond hair, blue eyes, and a ski-slope nose, so clearly there was a precedent.

Annie kept waiting for Ben to bring up the subject of their future together, not wanting to be one of those women who had to give an ultimatum. But on her thirty-fifth birthday, she could hold out no longer.

"So I think I'm having a midlife crisis," Annie told Ben over a glass of champagne at their favorite French restaurant.

"Unless you're planning on dying young, I don't think it's a midlife crisis," said Ben, taking a bite of his tuna tartare.

"I guess I'm feeling kind of old. Don't you ever feel that way?"

"Nope," he said, reaching over and taking a spoonful of Annie's French onion soup.

Annie was beginning to think that men in their thirties still believed that they would live forever and felt no rush to get married and start a family. The thirties were the new twenties.

"Okay. Then I guess it's just me," said Annie, thinking this conversation was not going the way she had hoped. She was starting to feel a distance from Ben that she'd never felt before.

"Don't worry, Annie. You're still young and beautiful, and have a long life ahead of you."

"I know," she said. "But, well, I hate to do this to you, and I hate to be this kind of woman, but I have to ask. What do you think about the whole marriage thing?"

"Are you asking me to marry you?" said Ben, trying to make light of it.

"No, I'm asking if you ever think about marriage."

"Well, honestly, I don't," answered Ben. "I know I should, and I know that's what people do, but I just don't think about it much right now. I have time."

He has time? thought Annie. "Really? I didn't think at age thirty-five we were still thinking we had all the time in the world."

"Listen, Annie," said Ben, finally putting down his fork to give Annie his full attention. "The other thing is . . . Well, I thought you figured out that I can't marry a non-Jew."

"Are you kidding me?"

"No."

"But your family—they love me!"

"Yes, they do. They love you. But if they knew you weren't Jewish . . ."

"What do you mean, 'if they knew'?" asked Annie incredulously.

"I think they think you're Jewish," he mumbled, looking down at his plate.

"What?!"

"You know, you're from New York, and you sort of have that accent, and your name is Sax," said Ben, pleading his case.

"Sax with an 'x.' That's different."

"Yeah, but they don't know that."

"They don't know because you never told them! Why, Ben? Why didn't you tell them?"

"I guess it was easier to lie."

"Easier? For whom? You?"

"I just didn't want to go there with them."

"I can't believe this!" Annie looked at Ben as if she was looking at a stranger. "What about Brittany? She's not Jewish."

"She is, actually."

"But I look more Jewish than Brittany! And she won't even eat gefilte fish!"

"Annie, I'm sorry. I thought . . . You never talked about marriage before, never, and I figured that you weren't interested."

Annie broke up with Ben that night, but deep down she knew he was right. Maybe this *was* all her fault. In six years she had almost pathologically avoided the subject of marriage. Maybe she wasn't interested in settling down with someone after all.

Annie wondered if what she really wanted were all the things that came with marriage. Like the house. When Annie moved from New York to Kansas City, one of the things she was most excited about was the prospect of owning a freestanding single-family home. Almost ten years later, with a good job and plenty of money, she decided it was finally time. So she bought a house in an upscale development near her office. With four bedrooms, three and a half baths, and a finished basement, it was much more than she needed, but she couldn't get over the fact that she could have such a huge house for the same amount as a nice studio in New York would cost. Besides, she would be able to host her family and friends if they ever decided to visit her in Kansas City, something that still hadn't happened in almost ten years.

Annie was also tired of hanging out with single people. She was tired of going to bars and clubs and cool new restaurants, tired of shopping for sexy clothes in expensive boutiques, and, most of all, tired of talking about men. It seemed to Annie that no matter the news of the day, whether it be a war, a mass shooting, a mishandled hurricane evacuation, or a significant election, all the single women around her preferred to talk about men. They talked about how to meet them, where to meet them, how wonderful they were, and how horrible they were. More often than not, they alternately characterized men as unevolved infantile bores or as sex objects. And yet it seemed to Annie that these bland pieces of meat took up most of their time and attention.

So she found herself gravitating toward married women. The married women, particularly those with children, had a kind of calm about them that Annie admired. Yes, they appeared frazzled and stressed on the outside as they juggled their jobs, husbands, and kids, but they were free from the inner turmoil that seemed to plague so many single women in their thirties, free from the question mark that constantly hung over their lives.

Her first married friend was Claudia, who worked for the

PR agency that Annie had hired. While Annie had adapted well to the nice, polite, middle-of-the-road midwestern way, she was thrilled to meet Claudia, who with her brash, confident, lefty sensibility seemed to have been flown in directly from New York City.

It wasn't until their fifth meeting at the PR agency's office that Annie finally worked up the nerve to ask Claudia to go out after work. "Would you like to go have a drink?" she asked shyly.

"Um, sure," said Claudia, sounding a bit hesitant.

As they sat at the bar of a nearby restaurant in awkward silence, Annie realized: Claudia must think I'm interested in her. She decided to nip it in the bud right away. "I hope you don't think I'm making a move on you or anything," said Annie. When the words left her mouth she experienced a brief moment of mortification, but that quickly passed when she noticed Claudia's entire body relax with relief.

"Well, yes. I did."

"Oh, wow. Sorry about that."

"No problem. I have to admit, I was a little excited, because I've never been hit on by a woman before. I guess I still haven't."

"So you thought I was a lesbian?" asked Annie.

"To be perfectly honest, I've thought you were a lesbian for a while now."

"Really? Am I butch?" Annie asked, tugging on her long, straight brown hair as if to say: "This is not the hair of a lesbian!"

"No!" said Claudia. "I don't know. There's something different about you."

"What is it?" asked Annie, clutching her face with both hands, turning from side to side so Claudia could see her from a variety of angles.

"Maybe you don't seem to be interested in men."

"It's true, I'm not!" said Annie excitedly, impressed by Claudia's first observation and eager to hear more.

"Like that Jerry guy. All the women in your division are nuts for him. They get all flustered when they talk to him. They can't look him in the eye. But you, you don't seem to care a bit."

"Interesting," said Annie. "You're right. I don't care."

"Maybe he's just not your type."

Annie knew that Jerry was good-looking, had heard women at the office talk about him, but he didn't have an effect on her. Actually, she couldn't remember the last time a guy did have an effect on her. Maybe she was a lesbian. No, it wasn't that. Annie simply wasn't feeling sexual toward anybody lately.

"Maybe there's something wrong with me," said Annie, hoping that Claudia might have some insight into her problem.

"Maybe there's something right with you," said Claudia. "It's always bothered me how women, even the strongest women, let men rule their lives."

"I can't imagine you letting anyone rule your life." Because Annie's face was so delicate and her body so petite—barely five foot four and a mere 115 pounds—she was always in awe of women like Claudia, who was tall and muscular with dark, striking features. Annie knew she was strong and independent, but sometimes she wished her dainty features and frail frame didn't stand in such contrast to her bold personality.

"I never 'let' them, never thought it was happening. But it did," said Claudia.

"Your husband?" asked Annie.

"Definitely."

"How?"

"It's not like he's power-hungry or anything. He's the nicest, most laid-back guy. And that's the worst kind! They seep into your life, your brain, without you even knowing it. And pretty soon everything you do, every decision you make, it's all about them."

"Well, when you're married, isn't that the way it is? Don't they do the same thing for you?"

"No. I don't think so. I really don't," said Claudia. "I think men are different. I don't think Steve thinks and acts with me in mind, because if he did, he'd be doing things a lot differently."

Annie noticed their martini glasses were already empty, so she waved to the bartender. "You want another one? Do you need to get home?"

"Perfect example, right there!" said Claudia, slapping her hand on top of the bar. "Normally, I'd say, 'No, I've got to go home.' Why? So I can make dinner for my out-of-work husband, who's been home all day watching TV and should have dinner waiting for me? Yes, I'll have another drink."

"Great," said Annie. "But I hope I'm not causing any strife—"

"No, no. You're fine. I'm sorry for going on about my husband."

"Please, I don't mind at all. It's actually good for me to hear about it. I've been thinking lately about skipping the whole husband thing."

"Awesome idea!" said Claudia, raising her newly poured martini with three plump green olives.

"There are some problems with the idea though," said Annie.

"Like what?" asked Claudia, with a hyperbolically confused look on her face.

"Well, there's the lack of sex."

"You've got to be kidding me. I had way more sex before I got married!"

"The lack of support?" asked Annie.

"Ha! You'd probably end up supporting him! Financially, emotionally . . . They're always getting their egos bruised, getting deflated, and needing to be pumped up."

"Loneliness?"

"There's nothing more lonely than a bad marriage," said Claudia. Annie noticed the mood change, as if Claudia felt that she had gone too far.

"Oh, wait. I know. Kids!" said Annie, trying to steer things in a different direction. "I think I'd like to have kids."

"Absolutely! I'm all for kids."

"You have some?" asked Annie.

"Two. Twin girls. Twelve years old."

"How cute!"

"You know, Janie and Sandy are better companions than any man I've ever known."

"But having kids on my own? I don't know," said Annie. "It seems like it would be awfully hard."

"It would be. But kids are hard no matter what. And in some ways, raising kids with someone is the hardest. I can't tell you how many fights Steve and I have had over those kids. I've often thought that the whole thing would have been easier if it had been only the girls and me. I don't know. Maybe it's something to consider."

Annie had never thought about having kids in anything more than a vague, someday sort of way, but after her talk with Claudia she became obsessed with the idea. Maybe having a child on her own was exactly what she needed to do. It did seem that everything had been leading up to this—her breakup with Ben, her distaste for men, her attraction to married women with children, and, of course, her buying a huge four-bedroom house in the burbs. Maybe subconsciously she was preparing for this very thing.

Annie was a little taken aback at how impressionable she was, how a drunken conversation with a coworker she barely knew could make her think about changing her life so drastically. But this wasn't the first time. Annie remembered when she got the offer from Sprint and was struggling with the idea of moving to the Midwest. She was living in New York with her parents for the summer, working part-time at her father's law firm and spending the rest of her time going to coffee shops, museums, and half-priced Broadway shows. One beautiful sunny day she decided to take a Circle Line sightseeing cruise around the city. She ended up sitting next to a middle-aged couple from Tulsa, Oklahoma.

"What brings you to New York?" Annie asked.

"Visiting family," said the woman, straightening the straw visor perched on her head. "I'm actually from here."

"Really? And now you live in Tulsa?" Annie was intrigued. Did New Yorkers who moved to the Midwest suddenly develop a taste for wicker headgear, pink polyester scarves, and matching tank top and shorts ensembles?

"I left New York twenty years ago. I love it here, love visiting. But it's so good to leave."

"So you like living in the middle of the country?" asked Annie.

"Sure. It was hard at first, adjusting. I miss all the culture, the big-city feel. And I've never found a decent bagel. But other than that, I love all the space. I like being able to walk down the side-walk without feeling like a salmon swimming upstream."

After that, Annie couldn't walk anywhere without feeling ha-rassed by the crowds that surrounded her. She hated riding the subway during rush hour, when she felt packed in like a sardine. She hated waiting in line at the Museum of Modern Art and hav-ing to stand next to five other people just to look at Monet's *Water Lilies.* She was even annoyed by the apartment where she had grown up and lived most of her life, with its narrow galley kitchen and cluttered living room and no access to the outdoors. Within a week she made her decision to take the job at Sprint—leaving cramped New York for the wide-open Midwest.

It appeared Annie was going to do the same thing with having a baby. After that first drink with Claudia, the two became fast friends, and Annie always took the opportunity to pepper Claudia with questions about her kids. But Annie knew better than to cavalierly make the decision to have a baby. Everything else was reversible—where she lived, the job she took, the man she dated. Giving birth to a child was not.

After a while Annie stopped talking about it with Claudia and began to seriously consider the idea of single motherhood.

At first it seemed that everything about the idea was difficult and sad. She imagined waking up in the middle of the night to a crying baby, with nobody there to nudge and say: "Can you get this one?" She imagined bringing her child to school on the first day of kindergarten and having no one to stand next to arm in arm as she waved goodbye. And when her child was a teenager, who would she worry and wait up with until two o'clock in the morning?

But then she remembered everything that Claudia had said about raising kids with her husband. According to Claudia, Steve slept right through the kids' wailing in the middle of the night and never once got up to feed them. He skipped the first day of kindergarten because he had a meeting he couldn't get out of. And now that the girls were entering their teenage years, Claudia and Steve fought about everything from curfews to dating to whether they should be allowed to wear makeup.

Annie wondered if maybe Claudia was right, that maybe it would be easier to go it alone. Sure, there wouldn't be anyone to help when things were hard or to share in the good times, but there also wouldn't be anyone to argue with or disappoint.

In the end, whether or not to have a partner in parenthood was really beside the point. Annie was thirty-eight years old, and not only was there not a man on the horizon, she hadn't even been mildly interested in one for three years. If she wanted to get pregnant and have a healthy child, she needed to act.

So without saying a word to her friends and family, Annie began researching the process in secret, scouring the Internet for information about artificial insemination, in vitro fertilization, and sperm banks.

For Annie, that was the best part: the digital sperm bank. As a busy executive who hated going to the malls and shopping centers that dominated her surroundings, Annie bought everything over the Internet. Now it felt like she was shopping online for a baby.

She'd go to her favorite site and input her donor preferences: eye color, hair color, hair texture (curly? wavy? straight?), skin tone, height, ethnicity. She could even narrow her choice down to a Buddhist with a master's degree, type A blood, and an interest in linguistics. There were profiles and essays and staff members' impressions to read, and for a price she could see a baby photo, listen to an interview, and look at a personality test. The site even let her do a search based on the celebrity the donor resembled most. There were look-alikes for everyone from Vince Vaughn to Bob Saget, John Travolta to Keanu Reeves, Tom Brady to Stephen Colbert. There were even two versions of Russell Crowe to choose from—a youthful Crowe from his *Gladiator* days and an older version, presumably after the thrown telephone and extra poundage.

Once Annie stopped worrying about hormone shots and midnight feedings and instead concentrated on what her child would look like and which stroller to buy, the whole process seemed a lot more fun and a lot less scary. She felt comforted by all the websites hawking services and products for women just like her, who simply wanted to give birth without having to find, date, and marry a man first. She imagined there were whole legions of women out there thinking about and doing the exact same thing. Then she did a search on Google—singlemom.com, single mothers.org, singlemothersbychoice.com—and discovered there were.

Chapter Five

Sometimes, a cigar is just a cigar, but rarely is a book club just a book club. Most of the time, it's a way to meet people, a way to assuage one's guilt for not being well read, or a way to get out of the house one evening a month. Katie joined this club made up of moms from her kids' school two years ago, right after she broke up with Rob, to take her mind off the divorce and to try to rebuild all those brain cells that had died during pregnancy. Maxine joined because Katie didn't want to go alone. Claudia, whose kids went to the same school as Maxine's, joined a few months later because Maxine told her it would be a night away from Steve. Annie, the newest member of the group, joined because she wanted to meet a whole new batch of married women with kids.

Every four months or so, the book club morphed into something different, depending on who showed up, what books they read, and what kind of refreshments were served. At first, the club was dominated by former English majors who wanted to re-read all the classics and have weighty discussions about character, point of view, and narrative, as if they were back in a college literature seminar. During that period, cheese and crackers and Diet Coke were served. Then a few of the literary types dropped out and were replaced by women who had no interest in Austen, Dickens, or even Updike and instead insisted on books that had the stamp of approval of Oprah, Tyra, Ellen, or some other one-named daytime-television talk-show host who could be trusted not to waste their time. These women upgraded the cheddar and Ritz to fontina and water crackers, and the Diet Coke was replaced with merlot. Then there was a brief self-help phase, with books by everyone from the Dalai Lama to Dr. Phil and refreshments that included raw vegetables and herbal tea.

The latest phase was the confessional memoir, covering everything from drug addiction to incest to domestic violence. This month's selection was about a stay-at-home mom who couldn't stand staying at home with her kids so she arranged play dates in order to get wasted with the other moms. Since Katie was hosting, she decided to serve her special artichoke dip along with her favorite mixed drink—frozen melon balls. But when she brought out a tray of martini glasses filled with the chilled, slushy green mixture, the women looked at her with mild confusion. Katie suddenly realized that her refreshments were probably not appropriate for a discussion about alcoholic mommies, but she set the tray down anyway. After a brief, uncomfortable pause, each woman picked up a glass and started guzzling.

The drinks were downed in roughly fifteen minutes, prompting Katie to go back into the kitchen to whip up another batch.

"Hey, those are awesome," said Maxine as she walked into the kitchen. "Can I get another one?"

Soon after, Claudia came in with Annie following close behind.

"Us too," said Claudia.

"I knew they'd be a hit," said Katie.

"But I'm afraid you might be in here blending the whole time," said Annie.

"That's okay," said Katie. "I don't feel like talking about this book anyway."

"Me neither," said Maxine.

"I didn't even read it," said Claudia.

"Me neither," said Maxine.

"I read the blurb on the back and I think I got the gist," said Annie.

"You guys!" said Katie. "It's a book club. You have to read the book!"

"Nuh-uh," said Claudia, taking a gulp of her drink and chewing on a stray chunk of ice. "I was prepared with lots of comments about this book even though I never read it. I was gonna say that this woman has no business drinking wine while she plays Candy Land with her kids and someone should call Child Protective Services immediately."

"Well, if you read the book you'd know it was a little more complicated than that," said Katie, pulling a piping hot dish of artichoke dip out of the oven. "She's actually a sympathetic character."

"Whatever," said Claudia, taking a cracker and sticking it into the dip.

"Isn't she a blogger?" asked Maxine.

"Who isn't a blogger?" said Annie.

"I'm not and never will be," said Claudia as she finished the last of her melon ball and grabbed another, which was sitting on the wooden serving tray that Katie got for a wedding present. "I can't stand all that spewing. Get an editor, for God's sake." Blog-ging was a sensitive subject for Claudia, who had begun to see her husband as a mini-blogger wannabe, with his incessant unedited Facebook updates.

"I was thinking about starting a blog," said Katie warily. " 'Dealing with Divorce'."

"Catchy," said Annie.

"I know," said Katie. "But then I realized I would actually have to write the damn thing."

"How are you dealing with divorce, anyway?" asked Annie. Annie hadn't known Katie long but was intrigued by this woman whose life had been turned upside down so abruptly and who seemed to have made the transition so effortlessly.

"Great!" said Maxine, who never missed the opportunity to point out Katie's heroic reaction to divorce. "She's amazing. She's like the poster child for great divorces. You know, you really should write a blog, or a book. Why don't you write a book, Katie?"

"Because I'm too busy being the best divorcée ever," said Katie. "Anyway, I'm not going to have any time on my hands now that I'm starting to date."

Katie hadn't had a chance to tell Maxine in private and hadn't meant to reveal her entry onto the dating scene to a larger audi-ence yet, but she was so excited—and a little drunk on melon balls—that she couldn't resist saying something. She also felt like she needed a good pep talk and maybe some advice on what to do. By Katie's calculations, she hadn't been on a real date since her junior prom eighteen years ago.

"What?" Maxine practically screamed. "You're dating?"

"Not yet. We're going out this weekend," said Katie.

"I can't believe it!" said Maxine. "Why didn't you tell me?"

"It just happened," said Katie.

"Who is he?" asked Annie. "How did you meet?"

"Online," said Katie.

"What?!" cried Maxine.

"Oh, God," said Claudia.

"What?" said Annie, giving Claudia a reprimanding look. "Why not?"

"What do you expect me to do?" asked Katie. "Go hang out at a singles' bar?"

"I would have fixed you up," said Maxine, a bit hurt. Because she was eight years older than Katie, Maxine often felt like she needed to take care of her friend. She regularly asked Katie if she could set her up with one of the single dads at her kids' school. Last week she told her about a journalist who had recently separated from his wife of fifteen years. She thought Katie would have leapt at the chance to meet a writer, considering her interest in poetry and all, but she completely blew it off.

"No, thanks," said Katie. "I don't like the idea of getting fixed up. I really want to choose someone on my own."

"I'm sorry for sounding so negative, Katie," said Claudia. "I'm just a little anti-Internet lately. I think it's great that you did it."

"So who is he?" asked Maxine, ready to get over her feelings of rejection and support her friend.

"Well, his name is Ed. He's forty-six—"

"Forty-six!" shouted Maxine, newly incensed that Katie was taking matters into her own hands. Clearly she had no idea what she was doing. "That's kind of old for you, isn't it?"

"An Ivy Leaguer. Went to Wharton for business school. Didn't you go to Wharton, Annie?"

"Yeah."

"I don't think they knew each other, Katie," said Maxine. "He's way older."

"Enough about how old he is! Forty-six is not old!" Katie glared at Maxine.

"Sorry," said Maxine.

"He grew up in L.A.," Katie said calmly, sure that the rest of Ed's résumé would win her friends over.

"Cool," said Claudia.

"Works for some tech company. And he makes at least $150,000 a year but probably way more."

"Do you know how much he weighs?" asked Claudia.

"He's well toned."

"Huh?" said Annie.

"That's how they do it. Athletic, well toned, average . . ."

"So what are you?" asked Annie.

"Average," said Katie.

"Average? You're not average!" Maxine was often frustrated by Katie's self-deprecation, feeling her friend had no idea what an incredible person she really was. For that reason, she didn't trust her to choose a man who was sufficiently worthy.

"I'd rather he be pleasantly surprised than disappointed."

"Are you kidding?" said Maxine. "This old coot hit the jackpot with you!"

"What does he look like?" asked Annie.

"Kind of professorish," said Katie.

"I hope he's not all stuffy," said Claudia.

"No, I don't think so." Katie wondered if she had done the right thing by telling her friends about Ed. She was already feeling a little exhausted by the third degree she was getting. "Should I mix up some more melon balls?" she asked, trying to change the subject.

"Definitely," said Claudia. "So you're not going to get married again, are you?"

"No!" said Katie. "I just want to have sex. I mean, it's been over two years, you know."

"Wow," said Claudia. "I hope you remember how."

"Claudia!" said Maxine. "Don't freak her out."

"I'm kidding! Of course she'll know how. It's like riding a bike."

"I think I might have forgotten how," said Annie. "So much so that I don't even want to do it anymore."

"Really?" asked Claudia. "I mean, I can barely stand my husband and I still want to do it with him."

"I know what you mean, Annie," said Katie. "After a while, I forgot what it was like, and I didn't miss it at all. Then, all of a sudden . . ."

"What?" asked Maxine.

"I don't know. I started wanting it again," said Katie. "It was like I remembered."

"What reminded you?" asked Claudia. "Did you find a sex tape that you and Rob made or something?"

"Ha! No, it wasn't Rob. I definitely don't think about that. I think it was a movie I saw."

"Which one?" asked Maxine.

"*Little Children.* With Kate Winslet," said Katie.

"Yes!" said Claudia.

"You know, when she's sitting on top of the washing machine and he's just banging her, and you can see his cute little tushy going back and forth."

"Oh, my," said Claudia.

"I guess I could relate to that," said Katie.

"Have you done it on top of a washing machine?" asked Maxine.

"No, but I do a lot of laundry," said Katie.

"Maybe you could lure Ed down to your basement and reenact the scene," said Annie.

"This is so exciting, Katie!" said Maxine. More than anything, she was happy that Katie was finally getting out, no matter who the lucky guy might be.

"Or pathetic?" said Katie.

"Are you kidding?" said Claudia. "We're all jealous of you. You're going to be doing it in the laundry room with some hot—"

"Forty-six-year-old," said Maxine. "Oh. Sorry."

"Yeah, well, don't be jealous yet," said Katie. "Anyway, I'm not the one you should be jealous of. Look at Maxine over here. Miss Perfect Marriage."

"Oh, come on," said Maxine. "Don't start with that."

"It's true," said Katie. "I'd be jealous of you if I wasn't so happy for you."

"Thanks, Katie," said Maxine, feeling a little uncomfortable.

"Man, I want to meet your husband," said Annie. "He sounds amazing."

"He is," said Claudia, with a touch of wistfulness. "There aren't a lot of guys like Jake out there."

Annie didn't have to be told that. She knew there weren't any perfect guys. In fact, she had her doubts about this Jake she'd heard so much about. She was skeptical that anyone could really be that wonderful, just as she was skeptical that Steve could really be that bad.

"Excuse me?" came a voice from the kitchen entryway. It was Lilly Weilander, one of the newer recruits to the book club. "People want to know if there are any more drinks left."

"Of course," said Katie. "They're almost ready. Can I give you a refill?"

"Yes, please!" said Lilly, holding out her glass. "I know it's wrong, but after a long day with the kids, sometimes a drink or two does take the edge off."

"Whatever it takes, Lilly," said Claudia. "Whatever it takes."

Chapter Six

Besides the fact that she hadn't gone out on a date in almost two decades, over the past two years Katie hadn't been to a wedding, a fancy dinner, or any other occasion that required her to wear a dress and makeup. So when her five-year-old daughter, Maggie, watched as Katie stood in front of the bathroom mirror in a tight-fitting black dress, her hair freshly curled and sprayed, carefully applying mascara, she asked, "What's happening, Mama?" as if something momentous and terrible was about to take place.

"Nothing, sweetie," said Katie. "Mama's just going out to dinner with some friends."

"Are we coming?"

"No, you're going to Grandma's house."

"You look pretty."

"Thanks, Maggie."

"Is Daddy going with you?"

"No, honey. Daddy's not coming." By now Katie was used to these types of questions from her kids. It wasn't as if they hoped their parents would get back together, it was more a curiosity about the boundaries of their relationship.

"Daddy's never seen you like that."

Katie stopped and looked at her daughter. "Yes, he has. He's seen me like this many times." On second thought, maybe the kids *were* determined to see their parents reconcile.

Katie regularly checked in with her kids about how they were feeling about the family situation. "So, how do you think this whole divorce thing is going?" she'd ask. Frank would immediately respond, "Good!" and Maggie would chime in, "We like it this way!" Sometimes they would list all the pros of having divorced parents, like two homes, two sets of toys, and being able to have a dog at Daddy's house. But Katie wondered if they were simply giving her the responses that she so desperately wanted to hear. She wondered if her kids really did wish for a more traditional home life.

Ed had asked Katie if he could pick her up at her house but obliged when she said it would probably be best if they met at the restaurant. He had chosen one of the most expensive restaurants in Kansas City, a place Katie had never been before.

Katie was fifteen minutes early, so she told the hostess she would wait at the bar. She decided to order a cosmopolitan to help her relax. Because she hadn't eaten the entire day, two sips were all it took to make her feel light-headed and happy. She told herself it didn't matter what happened with Ed. The important thing was that she had finally worked up the courage to go out on a date with a man.

She watched the door as couples arrived and were shown to their tables, until, promptly at seven-thirty, Ed walked in.

Katie recognized the piercing blue eyes and the ruddy complexion, but other than that he looked completely different than his online photos. He had much less hair a slightly bigger belly, and appeared shorter than the five foot eleven he had written in his profile. Still, he looked dapper in his dark-blue suit and pink tie, so Katie decided to overlook the discrepancies.

"You must be Katie," said Ed as he walked over to the bar. He took her hand gently and gave her a light kiss on each cheek. He had a nice smile, and his eyes crinkled in a way that made Katie smile back. She decided to focus on those eyes, welcoming and seductive, and not too much on the balding head and protruding belly.

"You're even more beautiful than your pictures," said Ed, and Katie took the compliment happily, not caring that she couldn't say the same to him. She couldn't remember the last time a man had called her beautiful.

When Katie had first separated from Rob, she was so distraught over the collapse of her marriage that she couldn't bring herself to eat. For weeks, she had to force herself to eat the minimal amount she needed to survive—a handful of nuts, a slice of cheese, an apple. Soon she found herself with a body as trim and light as the one she had in high school. Losing those extra pounds also gave her an abundance of energy, so she went to the gym regularly, which helped her get her appetite back. As a result, she was muscular, fit, and eating better than she ever had. She looked good, and her date with Ed was the first time she was able to take her new body out for a spin.

They were seated at an intimate table for two, a single votive candle glowing in the center. Katie's first cosmo worked so nicely, she ordered another when the waitress came around.

"So, Katie," said Ed. "I hope you don't mind me asking, but what are you looking for from Match.com?"

Katie hadn't prepared for this type of question. She felt like a contestant on *The Bachelor*, being asked if she was "there for the right reasons." Katie had a feeling that "needing to have sex" was not "the right reason" for a woman of her age to go on Match.com, so she figured she should say something more innocuous. "I don't know. I guess I'm looking to meet new people."

"Really?" asked Ed. "You could go to a church social for that."

"Okay. I'm looking to meet single men."

"That's more like it."

"What about you?" Katie asked, determined to move swiftly out from under the microscope.

"I'm looking to meet single women. But, to be honest, I always hold out hope that I might find 'The One.'"

The One? Katie was a bit taken aback by this forty-six-year-old man with graying hair talking about finding The One. Having already found and dispensed with her first "One," Katie no longer believed in that little fantasy. There was "That One," and then there was "The Other One," and maybe, if she was lucky, there would be "Yet Another One."

"Good luck to you now," said Katie, lifting her cosmo and taking a swig.

"Are you really so cynical?" asked Ed.

"Of course not!" said Katie with mock indignation. "Just because I spent my entire adult life with one man, thinking he was the love of my life, and now I'm a thirty-something on a first date with a guy I met online, why would I be cynical?"

"Come on, it's not so bad, is it?"

"Nothing against you!" said Katie.

"Who knows, you might have some fun."

"I'm sure I will," said Katie, who was thinking that she was already having fun. "So what do you think, Ed? Am I 'The One'?"

"Could be."

"Really?"

"Why not? You're beautiful, funny, smart. What more could a guy want?"

What more *could* a guy want? Katie wondered to herself. And yet she was sure that she was nowhere near any man's grand ideal. "Maybe someone without two little kids at home?"

"The kids are a plus for me."

"Then why do you think you never settled down and had kids?" Katie asked, not hesitating to get personal.

"My last serious girlfriend, Jessica, we were together nine years. She didn't want kids."

"So why did you stay with her for nine years?"

"Because I loved her."

"Then why didn't you marry her?"

"Because I wanted kids."

"Hmmm."

"It's complicated."

"I guess," said Katie, trying to process this new information. "Do you miss her?"

"No. We broke up five years ago, but we're still friends."

"Really?" Katie never could understand why a person would remain close to an ex, unless they had children together. Did it mean that there was some unfinished business?

"I usually end up staying friends with old girlfriends. She meant a lot to me, but not anymore, not like that. I see now that she wasn't right for me. Too selfish. And the kids thing. She wasn't very nurturing. You know?"

Katie wondered if all first dates began with a lengthy discussion of a person's ex. She hoped that Ed wasn't going to ask her about Rob, since she had no desire to discuss him. Once their food arrived, Katie managed to steer the conversation to lighter subjects, like where to find good sushi in a landlocked state and whether Martin Scorsese was still at the top of his game.

After two cosmos, a glass of expensive white wine, six raw oysters, one piece of rare tuna, and lobster risotto, Katie was feeling good. She was surprised at how effortlessly the conversation flowed. And she was even more surprised at how attracted she was to Ed. Was it the drink? Or maybe the seafood? Whatever it was, she wondered if, when, and how Ed might kiss her.

After dinner, Katie led Ed to her parked car. "This is mine," she said, wishing she had agreed to let Ed drive.

"I had a wonderful time," said Ed, keeping a respectful distance.

"Me too," said Katie. She could tell that Ed was going to be the perfect gentleman on this, their first date, but she found herself wishing he would grab her and kiss her passionately.

"All right, then. I guess, well, I guess this is it," he said.

Katie could tell that Ed didn't want the date to be over either, so before she could change her mind, she took him by the arm and pulled him close. Then she lifted her face to his and gave him a deep, openmouthed kiss. After about thirty seconds of kissing, she pulled away, looking him square in the eyes.

"Wow," he said, smiling.

"I hope you don't mind," said Katie.

"Not at all."

There they stood, once again, awkwardly wondering what would come next. And, once again, Katie knew it was up to her. "Why don't I follow you to your house?" she said.

"That's a wonderful idea."

Ed lived in a historic neighborhood in a one-hundred-year-old house big enough for a family of six. It was all brick and dark wood and stained-glass windows, furnished with antiques and perfectly neat.

When they walked in and Ed closed the door behind them, they immediately embraced, continuing the passionate kiss from the parking lot. At first, Ed kept his hands primly on Katie's shoulders, but after a few minutes he moved them down her sides. He left one hand on her butt and moved the other up to her breast. As he touched her, Katie felt a profound relief, as if years of tension she didn't even know existed were escaping her body. She could have stayed like that for hours, standing there in the hallway, kissing, his hands moving up and down her body. But after a while he stopped and led her upstairs to the bedroom.

When Katie lifted her dress over her head and stood there in her black bra and panties, Ed seemed overwhelmed by the sight, as if he had never seen a beautiful woman in her underwear before. Ed took off his shirt, revealing a big, hairy barrel chest that Katie found thrilling. She liked Ed's manliness, liked that he looked nothing like Rob.

Before Katie knew it, she was lying on a king-sized bed with Ed on top of her. She looked up at him, his balding head, his broad chest covered with graying hair, his flabby stomach, and she never felt more turned on in her life. She couldn't believe how effortlessly he moved, how he knew exactly what to do. When Katie broke up with Rob—the only man she had ever had sex with—she worried that she'd never be able to have an orgasm with anyone else. After one and a half minutes with Ed, that fear was finally put to rest.

Katie smiled the whole drive home, replaying the scene over and over in her head. It was two o'clock in the morning, and she sped through the deserted streets with the windows open and the radio blaring. Ed had asked her to stay the night, but she thought it best to leave, not wanting to risk losing the magic of the encounter to the morning light.

She fell asleep the moment her head hit the pillow, not waking until ten o'clock, when the phone rang.

"How'd it go?" asked a voice on the other end.

"Maxine?" Katie asked groggily.

"What? You don't know me anymore? What happened?"

"Oh, God. I'm so . . . tired."

"Are you hungover?"

"I don't know."

"So how was it?"

"Good. It was good."

"Yeah? What's he like?"

"Well, he didn't look so much like his pictures."

"Really?"

"Yeah, I think they might have been old."

"That's weird."

"But it's okay. He's very nice."

"Did you kiss?"

"Um, yeah."

"Did you do something else?"

"Um, yeah."

"Katie?!"

"What?"

"What did you do?"

"We kinda . . . did it."

"Oh, my God."

"C'mon, don't freak out. It's not a big deal. I did it. So what?"

"Okay, so what?"

"I know! So that's done. And he probably won't call me ever again. Isn't that how it works?"

"Katie, this isn't an episode of *Sex and the City*. I'm sure he'll call you."

"Whatever. I don't care. I'm just glad I finally did it! I feel so . . . relieved. You know what I mean?"

"Yes, I know what you mean. I think that's great."

"I know. It is great. And I don't care what happens now."

"Good. That's a great attitude. I'm proud of you, Katie."

"Thanks, Maxine."

But as the day wore on and Katie picked up her kids and took them to the zoo, all the while thinking about Ed, she couldn't fool herself any longer. She did care. She desperately wanted him to call that day, and she carried her cell phone in her pocket instead of in her purse, so she'd be sure to feel its vibration. By six o'clock, when there was still nothing, Katie decided she would have to forget about Ed and chalk up the experience to a good lesson learned: no sex on the first date.

When she arrived home and walked in the back door, she noticed the light blinking on her answering machine. Then she remembered. She had never given Ed her cell-phone number. He had only her home number. She rushed to the machine and pressed "play."

"Hi, Katie. It's Ed. I wanted to thank you for an amazing evening. Give me a call. I'd really love to see you again."

It seemed that Ed was no game player, so Katie decided she wasn't going to be one either. She called Ed that same night, right after putting her kids to bed. They talked on the phone for an hour and a half and made plans to see each other the next weekend, when Rob had the kids. Ed called again the next night and they talked for two hours. The next day, Katie came home from work to find a bouquet of red roses sitting on her front porch with a card that said: "Hope you had a wonderful day." Rather than waiting for his call, Katie phoned Ed immediately to thank him. He told her he couldn't wait until Friday night to see her and asked if she would meet him for lunch the next day. She did, and when they were done eating they sat in Ed's Mercedes and made out for ten minutes.

The weekend was filled with nonstop activity. They went to a gallery opening, a tapas bar with live music, a play at the university, and a cocktail party thrown by one of Ed's coworkers. It was also filled with nonstop sex.

Katie was amazed at how in synch they were when it came to sex, how they always wanted it at the same time, how they both knew exactly what to do. There were moments when Katie wondered if she was getting too caught up in the sex, if maybe it was clouding her judgment. But then she thought, no, she really did like him. She enjoyed every minute of their time together, in bed and out.

Katie's only concern was that Ed was going a little too fast. They talked every day. He sent flowers at least once a week. He gave her gifts—CDs, lingerie, small household appliances. Then, after only five weeks of dating, he said it.

"I think I'm falling in love with you," he whispered while they were lying in bed.

Katie looked at him and, before she could catch herself, said, "Me too."

She knew she shouldn't have said it after knowing him such a short time, but it just came out. She wondered if maybe it was real. Maybe he did love her and maybe she did love him. So what was the harm in saying so?

After that, Ed started making references to their future together. He'd talk about trips they would take and cities they might want to live in one day. Once he pointed out the bedrooms that Frank and Maggie would take when they moved in. He even gave Katie a key to his house and the code to his alarm, telling her she should feel free to come and go as she pleased. Katie knew it was crazy, but she couldn't see the harm in letting Ed fantasize. Who knew what would happen?

But all the talk had an effect on her. She had always vowed never to get married again, but listening to Ed and all his plans made her wonder if maybe she had been wrong. Maybe, with the right person, marrying again could be a good thing.

Katie and Ed had been together only two months before he came right out and asked her: "Have you ever thought about marrying again?"

"Actually, I was always pretty sure I never wanted to marry again," she said.

"Have you changed your mind?"

"I don't know. I think I'm more open to the possibilities."

"You should always keep your options open."

"It's kind of strange to me that you never got married, Ed," said Katie. "You seem like you're the marrying kind."

"I guess I am. But when you spend your prime marrying years with a woman like Jessica . . . I guess I missed the boat."

"That's another thing. I don't get why you didn't break up with her. Why you held on if she didn't want any of the things you wanted."

"I don't know, Katie. I was wrong. She was wrong. In some ways, I kind of hate her for that."

"And yet you say you're still friends."

"Right. But, gosh, I haven't even seen her since we started dating."

"Really? How often do you see her?"

"I guess about once a month we get together for dinner or something."

"Well, I have to say I'm glad you haven't seen her."

"Oh, come on, sweetie," said Ed, taking Katie in his arms. "You've got nothing to worry about. She's nothing to me anymore. And, besides, I'm completely, madly in love with you."

Katie didn't really feel like Jessica was a threat. The more they talked about her, the more it was clear that Ed had nothing but contempt for her. Once he showed Katie a picture of her, which further calmed any fears she might have had. Jessica was older than Ed by a few years—practically fifty. She had brassy, fake red hair, her eyes were too close together, and she was noticeably plump. Katie couldn't find one appealing thing about her. When she wondered why Ed kept Jessica as a friend, she figured it must be because he felt sorry for her.

But what made Katie truly secure in her relationship with Ed was how they were always so happy to see each other, how they could talk for hours on end, how they couldn't keep their hands off each other. By their three-month anniversary, the thrill was not only still there, it was stronger than ever.

Every Thursday night at around nine o'clock, when Ed was sure Frank and Maggie were asleep, he'd call Katie to discuss their plans for the weekend. But that Thursday he didn't call. Katie read in bed until midnight, then went to sleep.

The next day at work, Katie waited all day for the phone to ring. At four she decided she'd call Ed. There was no answer, so she left a message.

Usually, when Katie left a message for Ed, he'd phone her back within the hour. But this Friday, the day they were supposed to see each other after a week apart, she heard nothing. The kids were with Rob that weekend, so Katie went straight home after work. There was no message from Ed on her answering machine, no email in her inbox. At seven o'clock she phoned him again. "Hey, wondering where you are," she said on her message.

By ten o'clock, Katie was in tears. She was sure something had happened to Ed. It was the only explanation. Surely he was lying dead on the side of the road. Or perhaps he had been picked up and taken to the hospital, but who would know to call her—the love of his life?

She woke the next morning at six, her eyes red and puffy, and she immediately dialed Ed again. "Ed, please call me. I'm worried."

Katie went online, scanning the local news outlets to see if there were any reports of a fatal accident involving a silver Mercedes and a forty-six-year-old man. After two more hours of crying, she called Maxine.

"He must be dead," cried Katie, not even trying to hold back her tears.

"Katie, I'm sure he's not dead. There must be an explanation."

"What? What is it?"

"I'll tell you what," said Maxine. "Why don't I give him a ring? He doesn't know me, doesn't know my number. So if he's there, he'll answer."

"He's not going to answer for you," Katie shouted. "Why would he answer for you and not for me?"

"I'm just saying, so we can rule things out."

"Fine! So call him!"

Katie hung up and waited. One minute later, Maxine called back.

"Katie? Listen, I'm coming over there."

"What? What happened?"

"Katie, he answered. He answered the phone."

"I don't understand, Maxine," cried Katie as Maxine cradled her in her arms. "I just don't understand."

"Me neither," said Maxine. "It's . . . it's inexplicable. This happens to women. I know. I've heard of it before. Men who seem totally in love, and then nothing. They simply stop calling."

"I've never heard of that," said Katie.

"Well, I have. It happens. And no one has ever figured out why. We'll never know what happened with Ed."

"No!" said Katie, pulling away from Maxine. "I'm not letting this go. I'm going to find out what happened."

By the time Maxine left at around eight o'clock in the evening, Katie had finally stopped crying. She took a shower, got dressed, and put ice packs on her eyes. Then she drove to Ed's house.

Ed's car was sitting in the driveway, and the light on the front porch was on. Instead of knocking or ringing the bell, Katie decided to use the key that Ed had given her weeks before. As she opened the door and walked in quietly, she had no idea what she was going to say or do. She wasn't scared and she wasn't ashamed. She was simply there to find out the truth.

The house was quiet and dark, but Katie could hear music coming from upstairs. As she climbed the steps, she imagined what Ed's reaction might be when he saw her. Certainly he would be surprised. Would he be sorry? Regretful? Angry? She hadn't thought about the possibility of anger, that perhaps he might hurt her. She realized that she didn't really know this man the way she thought she did, didn't know what he was capable of. She imagined that if Maxine knew what she was doing she'd be furious at her, but she kept going nonetheless.

At the top of the stairs, Katie could see that Ed's bedroom door was open and there was a light on. She tiptoed to the doorway and looked inside.

On the bed she saw the back of a woman with a mess of brassy, fake red hair, her plump white ass in the air, with Ed's hairy pink legs sticking out from under her.

After taking in the vision, Katie immediately turned away, tiptoed downstairs, and walked out the front door. She ran to her car and sped away. And as she drove, holding back her tears, telling herself to wait until she was safe at home, she had the dizzying sensation that she was living somebody else's life—somebody one might find on an episode of *Jerry Springer*.

Chapter Seven

Maxine was shocked when Katie told her what she had done, but she also couldn't help but admire her friend for her bravery, her willingness to face the truth, whatever it was. It had been months since Maxine first discovered that Jake was texting Deirdre, and she still had done nothing about it. She convinced herself that there was nothing to do, that it was all probably completely innocent, that if she was to say something to Jake she would be making a fool of herself. Nor would she allow herself to investigate further by looking at the messages or snooping through his emails, since that would irreparably break the trust between them.

Rather than making her distrust Jake, the whole Ed incident made Maxine believe in Jake all the more. She couldn't imagine that the man she'd been with all those years would be capable of something like that. Maxine had to believe in Jake, had to believe in their marriage, because that's all she had.

Still, she had to admit that her marriage was in trouble. Not having sex was not okay. So she decided if she could fix the sex part, maybe everything else would fall into place.

Engineering a night alone with her husband was not easy with three kids, a full-time nanny, and the ever-present chance that Jake would get called in for an emergency. But Maxine succeeded valiantly, carting the kids off to various friends' houses, giving Cindy the nanny the night off, and conferring with Jake's partners to ensure they could cover for him in case something came up.

It had been a long time since Maxine had tried to seduce Jake, but she remembered what the key ingredients had to be. First was the lighting. Jake was probably the only physician west of the Mississippi who personally supervised the decorating and lighting design of his waiting room. He couldn't stand stark overhead lights, except of course in the operating room, and was particularly keen on candles. So Maxine filled the kitchen, dining room, and bedroom with candles, the unscented kind so they wouldn't bother Jake's allergies.

Second was the food. Jake was partial to French food, particularly dishes containing an animal or a body part that wasn't routinely consumed by human beings, such as snails, frogs, lamb pancreas, and cow intestines. Not having the stomach for personally cooking such things but being perfectly willing to eat them, Maxine ordered from a nearby French restaurant, which was Jake's favorite.

Last was Maxine's attire. She debated whether she should wear a dress—something slinky and sexy and red, Jake's favorite—or whether she should skip the preliminaries and go right for the lingerie—also something slinky and sexy and red. She decided on a red silk low-cut top with jeans and heels, in hopes of looking ready—but not overly eager—for sex.

One of the great advantages of being married was not having to endure the awkwardness, embarrassment, or rejection that occurred mainly in newly budding romances. Married couples were so well attuned to each other's needs and desires that the oft-quoted line, "Not tonight, honey, I have a headache," was seldom uttered. It was usually more like: "Yes, I know you have a headache, I know you're in a crappy mood, and I know that you'd much prefer watching a rerun of *Friends* to having sex with me." Those married men and women who were willing to ignore all signals and urge their partner to put out, knowing full well they didn't want to in the least, were so used to the constant refusals that the rejection didn't really hurt them anymore.

Maxine decided that one of the reasons she and Jake had gone so long without sex was that she had always refused to put herself out and risk rejection. If the subtlest of gestures—a brush against his thigh, an extra button undone on her blouse—didn't work, she would back off before Jake got the idea she was interested in something he might not be willing to give. Maxine realized that would no longer work. So she decided to pull out all the stops, to make it clear to Jake exactly what she wanted and deal with whatever his reaction might be.

When Maxine heard Jake's car enter the garage, she made sure she was casually but attractively perched on a kitchen stool, her face lit by a candle, a glass of red wine on the counter, the latest *New Yorker* open in front of her.

"Hey there, beautiful," said Jake as he walked in. Jake had a way of saying such things routinely, so tonight, when Maxine truly did feel beautiful, hearing it was a disappointment.

"Hi!" said Maxine with a smile, intent on keeping the mood happy and light.

"No kids, huh? What's the occasion?"

Maxine had considered making something up, telling Jake this was the anniversary of their first kiss or something, but then she decided to go with the truth. "No occasion. It's been a while since we've been alone. I thought it would be nice."

"It is nice," said Jake, giving Maxine a friendly kiss on the cheek. "What's for dinner? I'm starving."

"Escargot, sweetbreads, and crème brûlée for dessert."

"Wow! Come on, what's going on? Did you wreck the car or something?" Jake asked, smiling and wrapping his arms around Maxine from behind.

With Jake's body pressed against hers, his warm breath on her neck, Maxine suddenly felt foolish for ever doubting him. "No, I didn't wreck the car. I just wanted to do something special for you."

"You're the best, Maxine," he said, squeezing her tight and kissing her on the top of her head. "Come on, let's eat!"

Maxine was actually a little nervous as they sat down to dinner, wondering if they could hold a real conversation without resorting to the topic of their children. But after a glass of wine and a few bites of escargot, she and Jake were eager to catch up on all that was going on in their lives. Jake told her about an article he was writing for a medical journal about ulcerative colitis. Maxine told Jake about her show in Los Angeles that was opening next month. They talked about the upcoming midterm election, about a documentary Jake had seen on capital punishment, about their need to decrease the family's carbon footprint. They both lamented the fact that they hadn't taken a trip abroad in a long time and threw out ideas for places they wanted to go, like Egypt, Peru, and New Zealand. Maxine marveled at how energized she felt, how a single, intimate meal could do so much to reinvigorate her marriage. Best of all, she could tell that Jake felt the same way. He, too, had a sparkle in his eye and an excitement in his voice that she hadn't seen or heard in a long time.

Maxine brought out a special bottle of cognac and led Jake to the couch for a drink. At first they sat a good three feet apart, still talking about their grand plans for the future. Then Maxine moved in close. She took Jake's drink out of his hand and set both glasses down on the coffee table. She turned back to him and leaned in for a kiss. It was a nice, long, languorous kiss, tender and gentle, not urgent and passionate. Maxine pulled away and said, "I love you."

"I love you too," said Jake.

Still looking in Jake's eyes, Maxine reached over and undid his pants. She put her hand inside and leaned in for another kiss. As she massaged Jake through his underwear, Maxine thought back to the way this process used to work in the past. As best as she could remember, after two long kisses and some firm massaging, Jake was usually ready to go. But now nothing was happening. She kept working away, but after a few minutes she started to feel foolish. It was like trying to start a car with a dead battery, repeatedly twisting the key but hearing only the defeated wheezing and sputtering of an engine that wouldn't turn over.

All the while, Jake sat calm and placid, content to allow Maxine to continue for as long as she wanted. But then, perhaps sensing her frustration, he said, "I think I'm tired, honey. Maybe we should just go to bed."

"Just go to bed?" asked Maxine, backing away and looking at him incredulously. "We always just go to bed. This is not normal, Jake."

"Maxine—"

"No, Jake! We have to deal with this. We don't have sex. Not normal."

"Maxine. We're tired. We're busy. We have kids. It's very normal."

"Not this long. People find a way," said Maxine. "Look! Right now. We can do it right now, and we're not!"

"I had a long, hard day and I'm tired," said Jake. "Then we had a big meal, a bottle of wine, cognac."

"So? Some people get turned on by good food and wine. You used to!"

"It's not that I don't want to, Maxine. Sometimes . . . it just doesn't work. I can't get it up."

"Really? And what about Deirdre? Can you get it up for her?" The words came out in a rush, as if they had been waiting to come out for weeks.

"What are you talking about?"

"You know what I'm talking about," said Maxine, even though she wasn't at all sure herself.

"No, Maxine, I don't."

"I'm saying that I think you and Deirdre are having an affair."

"Are you crazy?" said Jake, looking at Maxine in complete disbelief.

"I saw your text messages," she blurted.

"You read my text messages?"

"No, I saw . . . accidentally . . . a list . . . all from Deirdre!"

"And did you read any of them?"

"No, I wouldn't do that."

"You wouldn't. Great. So you see a list and make assumptions," said Jake, regaining his calm. "Well, maybe if you had read them, you'd see that they are completely innocent."

"Why are you texting her?"

"Because that's the way she likes to communicate! She's young—"

"Yes, very."

"And she prefers texting. So we text."

"About what?"

"About patients!"

"Really," said Maxine sarcastically. Since when do doctors consult each other via texting? she thought.

"Yes, really." Jake pulled his BlackBerry out of his pocket, pressed a few buttons, and handed it to Maxine. "Why don't you read them?"

Maxine took the phone and clicked on a message randomly. "IBS" was all it said. Completely ignorant of the secret language of texting, Maxine wondered what IBS could possibly mean. I be sad? I be sleepy? I be sexy?

"IBS," she said angrily, pretending that she knew exactly what that meant and had caught him in the act.

"Right," said Jake. "Irritable bowel syndrome. Next?"

Frustrated, Maxine threw the phone into Jake's lap. "Just leave me alone, Jake," she said.

She climbed the stairs, went into her oldest daughter Abby's room, and threw herself on the bed facedown. More than anything, she wished she and Jake were not alone in the house. She thought about going and collecting her children from their various sleepovers and installing them in their rooms but quickly realized she couldn't do that at midnight.

Of course Jake had a logical explanation for his texts with Deirdre, thought Maxine. He had a logical explanation for everything. He was a doctor, after all. So rational and logical. It made Maxine sick. Deep down, she felt that all the explanations about why they didn't have sex and why he was heavily texting a gorgeous, young, brilliant colleague were covering up what was really wrong with their marriage. Maxine had always thought of herself as smart and perceptive and intuitive, but she couldn't figure this one out. Jake was stonewalling her, thought Maxine. He was hiding something. Now she was finally ready to find out what it was.

Maxine and Jake almost never fought, and in their twenty years together, they had never slept in separate beds while under the same roof. But after that night, Maxine could not bring herself to sleep next to Jake. So after the kids went to bed, she closed herself in her studio to work and fell asleep on the futon in the corner. When the kids asked why she was sleeping in her studio, she told them she had to work late for a new exhibit and didn't want to wake up Daddy when she came to bed in the middle of the night.

Rather than working, Maxine spent most of her time on the computer, perusing her favorite gossip sites, paying particular attention to the articles about cheating spouses. She noticed how whenever a "news" outlet reported that a star was having an affair, a vociferous denial always followed, with a representative assuring everyone that the star was still happy and devoted to their partner. Then weeks, even months later, it would eventually come out that the cheating really did happen and the star really was leaving their beloved. Maxine couldn't understand why people needed to prolong the inevitable, why they needed to deny the truth. She figured that when someone was caught cheating, it was simply human nature to leap to one's own defense and fight the charges.

For that reason, she concluded that Jake's denial was completely meaningless. And so she decided to take her investigation elsewhere, to the other source of the possible affair: Deirdre.

Maxine knew that Jake and his colleagues frequented a particular coffee shop when they needed a break, so one morning she took her computer there and sat down, determined to wait until Deirdre showed up. She chose a day when she knew Jake had back-to-back surgeries, but she didn't care if he did walk in. She no longer cared what Jake thought.

After four hours, Deirdre finally arrived at one o'clock. She ordered a coffee and a sandwich and sat down at a table near the door without even noticing Maxine.

Deirdre was the kind of woman who could wear the most boring clothes—beige slacks, a white shirt, black pumps—and still look glamorous. Her shoulder-length blond hair was cut straight across, with no particular style, but it was thick and shiny and had a natural bounce whenever she moved her head. She wore no discernible makeup. Her eyes had such a lovely shape and her skin was so luminous that mascara or blush would have been a distraction.

Maxine packed up her computer as if she was leaving and headed toward Deirdre's table. "Deirdre?"

"Hi, Maxine! How are you?"

"I'm great! Came in to do a little work on my computer."

"Are you here to see Jake? I think he's in surgery."

"Oh, no. I was in the neighborhood and thought I'd hang out for a while before I get the kids from school. Sometimes I need to get out of my studio, you know what I mean? Well, I guess you don't really know what I mean, since you don't work in a studio. Although maybe you do. Don't tell me painting is another of your many hidden talents!" Maxine knew she sounded like a babbling idiot, but wasn't quite sure how to stop.

"No, I'm no artist," said Deirdre, seemingly unfazed by Maxine's rambling. "By the way, I went to see your show at the Red Gallery a couple weeks ago. It was amazing."

Maxine thought it strange that Deirdre would take the time to go to her show. Was she checking out the competition? "That's so nice of you to go see it."

"Oh, I love that stuff. I wish I took advantage of the culture in this city more often."

"Who'd you go with?" Maxine regretted the question the moment it came out, especially when she saw Deirdre's confused look. But, she thought, isn't that why I'm here, to ask the tough questions? For the first time, Maxine wondered what exactly she hoped to learn from Deirdre. Did she think there would be a confession?

"I went with a friend," answered Deirdre.

"I know how hard it is to make friends in a new city," said Maxine. Without waiting for an invitation, she pulled out the empty chair across from Deirdre and sat down. "I'm glad you're meeting people."

"People here are very friendly."

"Yes, they are. Especially when you're as beautiful as you!" Deirdre smiled shyly.

"I'm sure you hear that all the time," said Maxine.

"No, not really," said Deirdre.

"I know, you're right," said Maxine, who was never shy about highlighting people's attributes. "Maybe it's because I'm an artist. I appreciate beauty. And I don't think there's anything wrong with pointing it out."

"Well, that's nice of you to say," said Deirdre. "But it still makes me uncomfortable."

"That's better than being vain," said Maxine. "I'm always telling my girls how beautiful they are, but sometimes I worry it'll go to their head."

"I don't think so," said Deirdre. "Girls are so critical of themselves, I think it's great that you tell them they're beautiful. As a kid, I was always so hard on myself. And my parents weren't very . . . complimentary."

"Really?"

"They were kind of cold. They expected a lot of me but never gave me much encouragement."

"That's too bad," said Maxine. She felt sorry for Deirdre. Then she wondered if Deirdre was now looking for approval from an older man—a father figure.

"It's okay. I managed all right."

"You certainly did."

"But I admire the way you and Jake are with your kids," said Deirdre. "They're so well behaved and so happy. They clearly come from a loving home."

Then why do you want to break it up? thought Maxine. From

one minute to the next, she couldn't figure out how to read this woman. "So you're getting along well with the other doctors?"

"Oh, yes, everyone's been so wonderful."

"I hope Jake's been helpful," asked Maxine, hoping a direct reference to Jake would bring something out.

"Yes, definitely. They all have."

Interesting, thought Maxine. Deirdre seemed to be avoiding talking about Jake. If there was nothing going on, wouldn't she want to praise him a bit?

"Because I know firsthand he can be difficult," said Maxine.

"Really? You two seem to have such a perfect marriage."

"Oh, God," moaned Maxine, a little too annoyedly.

"I'm sorry," said Deirdre, confused about what she might have said wrong.

"No, it's just, I get tired of hearing that," said Maxine. "No one has a perfect marriage."

"You're right," said Deirdre. "I'm sorry. I shouldn't have said that."

"It's okay. It's funny, people don't seem to want to admit how hard marriage is. Including me. I've always been happy to perpetuate the notion that I have a perfect marriage. Or maybe I just really believed I did." Maxine wasn't quite sure why she was saying this to Deirdre, whom she not only barely knew but who was quite possibly having an affair with her husband. But then she thought maybe this was exactly whom she should be opening up to. Besides, she couldn't help but like Deirdre.

"I know it's hard!" said Deirdre. "I saw it with my parents. Look at me. I'm in my thirties with no prospects in sight. I'm obviously not anxious to get married."

"I often wish I had done it your way. Not get married so young and instead establish myself first. I feel like I did everything for Jake during those first years."

"But then you might not have those three gorgeous children," said Deirdre. "You have to look at them and know you made the right choices."

Maxine was touched by Deirdre's words. She always thought about her children when she questioned marrying so young, always thinking that she wouldn't trade them for anything. But it meant a lot to hear such reassurances from someone else, especially someone who had taken the opposite path.

"Thanks, Deirdre," said Maxine. "That means a lot to me."

Maxine left the coffee shop not knowing any more about her and Jake's problems than she did before. But what she did learn was that Deirdre was a truly lovely woman, and she wouldn't have blamed Jake a bit for falling in love with her.

Later that evening, Maxine got an email from the Los Angeles gallery that was showing her work in a few weeks. The owner wanted to know if Maxine would be willing to come out for a week before the opening to help set up the exhibit and do interviews with some local magazines. They offered to buy her a first-class ticket, put her up at the Chateau Marmont, and pay all of her expenses. Without figuring out how the kids would get to and from school, without checking her calendar or talking to her agent, and without asking Jake, Maxine replied, "Yes!"

Chapter Eight

Claudia's heart started racing when she stepped off the elevator and headed toward Fred's desk. Her palms were sweating too, dampening the invoice that she clutched tightly in her hands. She thought about turning back but pushed herself forward. It's no big deal, she said to herself. You're just checking on an unpaid invoice. No, that's not all, she thought. Claudia wanted to be honest with herself. You want to say hi. Maybe chat. There's nothing wrong with that.

When Claudia arrived at Fred's desk and saw his empty chair, she wasn't relieved. She was disappointed. She was surprised at how much she wanted to see him again. She turned around and went back to her desk, wondering how she'd get through the last two hours of the day.

As she stared at her computer, Claudia suddenly remembered that she needed to go to Facebook and see what Steve had been writing. It was something she had always avoided because she didn't like seeing that side of Steve, the Steve who made stupid jokes and embarrassing comments and laid out his life for all to see. Now she had to worry that something more sinister was going on. What could he have put up there that would make his friend Heather say all that?

She logged on to her account and went to the "News Feed" page. Claudia had only about fifty friends, so half of the posts had Steve's little half-inch photo next to them. His most recent entry was that day, an hour ago, posted from his cell phone: "Is it weird that I wish I were in high school again?"

Yes, that is weird! Claudia thought to herself. You wish you were in high school again so you can go back to being the football star and the straight-A student and the girl magnet instead of the loser adult you turned out to be. But two of Steve's friends responded with a "like this," and one, who had a picture of Homer Simpson as his photo, commented: "I'd rather skip to college so I don't have to get a fake ID."

Claudia scanned down the page, looking for something provocative among the photos and video clips and links to articles. Just as Heather had said, Marjorie Gooding could be relied upon to give Steve a vote of approval for almost everything he wrote. After one posting, they engaged in a long back-and-forth exchange.

"Why does it annoy me so much when people say they are going 'leaf peeping'?" wrote Steve.

"Same!" exclaimed Marjorie.

"Oh, good. I thought maybe I was being a curmudgeon."

"You, Steve? Never!" exclaimed Marjorie. Claudia wondered if Marjorie said anything without an exclamation point.

"So what is it about that phrase that's so annoying?" asked Steve.

"'Peeping.' It's a very annoying word!"

"I think it's that you don't peep at beautiful fall foliage—you look at it, stare at it, take it all in," wrote Steve.

"Exactly!" exclaimed Marjorie.

Claudia didn't understand why Steve and Marjorie had to carry on this little conversation in front of all their friends. Couldn't they have just contacted each other directly? Did they think they were being so witty that everyone needed to see? Then she wondered if they *were* contacting each other directly. Claudia noticed Marjorie's thumbnail photo, which showed her with a riotous grin and her big chest sticking out of a tight yellow T-shirt.

Then Claudia found more posts from Steve:

Check out these classics from Henny Youngman:

My wife was at the beauty shop for two hours. That was only for the estimate.

She got a mud pack and looked great for two days. Then the mud fell off.

She ran after the garbage truck, yelling, "Am I too late for the garbage?" "No, jump in!"

Okay, thought Claudia, ugly-wife jokes. These didn't bother her too much, since she was never one to be insecure about her appearance. But then she saw this one: "My wife and I have the secret to making a marriage last. Two times a week, we go to a nice restaurant—a little wine, good food. She goes Tuesdays, I go Fridays." For Claudia, that one hit a bit too close to home.

Claudia wondered if this was the type of stuff Heather was talking about. She scrolled down, looking for more, clicking on "Older Posts" every time she reached the bottom. But at a certain point there were no more. She couldn't read anything older than a week ago. Claudia wasn't sure what to make of all this. Going through a week of posts, she didn't find anything terribly incriminating but enough to make her wonder what else there might be.

Because she hadn't gone to Facebook for so long, Claudia had never really wondered about Steve's other life there. But now that she had caught a glimpse, she realized how much she didn't know about his world.

When she walked in the door that evening and saw Steve sitting on the couch, watching TV, he looked like a complete stranger to Claudia. Before, she thought she knew so well what was going through his head. Now she wasn't so sure.

"Hey," said Steve, not looking up from the TV.

"Hi," said Claudia. Normally she would go check on the girls, maybe lie down on the bed for a few minutes before figuring out what to do for dinner. Instead, she walked over to the couch and sat down next to Steve.

"Whatcha watching?" she asked.

"CNBC. *Mad Money.*"

They sat quietly and watched commercials until the show resumed. An ad for macaroni and cheese came on, with a mother doling out heaping bowls of the steamy fluorescent-orange noodles for her eager children. Wondering what he was thinking, Claudia stole a glance at Steve, who was seemingly mesmerized. Would he write something on Facebook about it? "Why do they have to make macaroni and cheese so orange?" he might write. Then Marjorie would respond, "I know! Food should never glow in the dark!!!" Claudia remembered that there was a time when she and Steve would sit on the couch watching TV and make comments to each other and laugh about what they saw. Now she felt like she was no longer a part of his life, that a comment or a joke to her would be a waste. Now all he wanted to do was gather material and run to the computer or his cell phone, where he could share his thoughts and feelings with a larger, more appreciative audience.

The show came on, and a short, bald man immediately started yelling and gesticulating at the camera. Claudia was so stupefied by his antics, she couldn't concentrate on what he was saying. Steve continued to stare blankly at the screen, so Claudia decided to make some conversation.

"Didn't this guy get in trouble for starting the economic down-turn or something?" asked Claudia.

"Well, he didn't exactly 'start' it," said Steve, looking at the TV. "I guess you could say he contributed to it somewhat."

"So then why is he still on the air?"

"He didn't commit any offense. I guess some people think he has something to say."

"I hope you're not taking any of his advice," said Claudia.

"No, Claudia. I'm not taking his advice," said Steve, with a touch of exasperation.

"What? I'm just saying—"

"Fine. It doesn't matter anyway," said Steve, finally turning his head to look at Claudia. "We don't have any money to invest."

"I know we don't."

"So then why did you ask if I was taking his advice? Why do you do that?"

"Do what?" asked Claudia. "I only wanted to make sure—"

"Right, you only wanted to make sure," said Steve, turning back to the TV.

"Look, Steve, don't start making this my fault. I didn't say any-thing. I didn't do anything. I'm trying to protect what little we have."

"It's not that bad, Claudia."

"Well, it will be soon. Sorry if I worry about it. I worry, okay? I worry about our future, the kids—"

"And you never miss an opportunity to let me know."

"Maybe I think if I bring it up enough you'll do something about it," said Claudia.

"Great. Here we go again. I'm not doing enough."

"No, you're not."

"I send résumés and make calls every day."

"And then you sit on your ass."

"What should I do?" asked Steve. "I can only make so many calls and send out so many résumés."

"Maybe you could get a job?"

"Huh?"

"Just a job! Why not spend your time working instead of sitting around? Why not get a job at Starbucks?"

"You want me to work at Starbucks?" asked Steve, struggling to maintain his composure.

"Why not? At least it's something."

"And how I feel—my self-respect—doesn't matter."

"I would think getting out and doing something would help your self-respect."

"Really? You think me in a green apron taking coffee orders from my friends and neighbors and former colleagues will help my self-esteem?"

"I don't know anymore, Steve," Claudia said wearily as she got up from the couch. "But I have to say, your self-esteem is not at the top of my list of priorities right now."

The next day at work, Claudia found herself unable to think of anything but Fred. She thought about going back up to the fourth floor but couldn't bear the thought that he might not be there again. And even if he was there, what would she say? What did she want? She thought it might be nice to go to lunch with Fred—just as a friend—but how would she work up the nerve to ask? How could she ask without it sounding like a come-on?

Claudia decided the best thing to do was to email him. No awkward conversation, no stammering before responding, no embarrassing rejection. She could construct a carefully worded invitation, and he could take his time composing a response without being caught off guard.

"Hi, Fred," she wrote. "In the interest of corporate unity, peace, and understanding, would you like to go to lunch and learn about what we 'creatives' do? I have a craving for Sasha's Sushi but hate going there on my own. How do you feel about raw fish?"

Claudia hit "send" and prepared herself to wait a long time for a reply. But after three minutes, her computer dinged.

"Hey, Claudia," wrote Fred. "Yes, as I said the other day, I would love to hear about what you creatives are up to, if only to ensure that you are truly earning your keep. And I, too, love Sasha's Sushi. (I don't know about you, but I find a love of raw fish to be a rare quality here in KC.) What time?"

As she read Fred's email, Claudia's heart began pounding. How would she possibly sit through a whole sushi lunch with him? she wondered. She couldn't remember the last time she felt so nervous and vulnerable but liked it.

"How about 12:30?" wrote Claudia.

"Great," answered Fred. "See you down in the lobby."

Claudia stuffed her purse with company brochures and literature, just in case Fred really did want to learn more about what she did all day. When the elevator doors opened onto the lobby, she saw Fred standing there, tall and lanky with his crisp white shirt and slate-gray pants. Fred was probably in his early forties, but he had a full head of thick black hair, no trace of belly fat, and an unlined face.

"Ready?" said Fred, without a bit of nervousness. Claudia was grateful for how easy he was making this.

The restaurant, which was only half a block from the office, was packed. "Should we sit at the bar?" asked Fred.

"Sure." As Claudia walked toward the bar she quickly scanned the room, looking for a familiar face, but didn't find one.

"You come here often?" asked Fred as he pulled out a chair for Claudia.

"Not so much. But I love it. They say the owner is some Russian guy."

"Sasha," said Fred. "You don't know Sasha?"

"You mean there really is a Sasha?" asked Claudia.

"Of course. That's the name!"

"I thought they called it that because it sounded good," said Claudia. "See, that's the thing about us creative types. We assume that nothing's true. That everything's marketing."

"Wow," said Fred. "That's kind of a scary world you live in."

"Very scary."

"I come here a lot, so Sasha's my buddy," said Fred. "When you're a single guy who doesn't cook, you tend to make friends with a lot of restaurateurs."

Hearing Fred come right out and call himself "single" sent a wave of dread through Claudia's body. She couldn't allow one more minute to pass without letting Fred know she wasn't single.

"Well, when you're a working married gal with two kids and a lazy husband, you tend to make friends with the pizza-delivery guys."

Claudia searched Fred's expression for a sign of surprise, disappointment, or even annoyance, but saw nothing.

"Lazy, huh?"

Claudia smiled to herself. Fred could have easily said, "Husband, huh?"

"That's not very nice, I know," said Claudia. "It's just that he's out of work with a lot of time on his hands. I mean, he could go out and learn how to make sushi!"

"Is he Japanese?" asked Fred.

"No."

"I don't like sushi unless it's made by a Japanese person."

"In a restaurant owned by a Russian," said Claudia.

"Yes."

"All right, then I won't invite you over for sushi night at my house."

"Fine," said Fred. "It would probably be kind of awkward anyway, with your husband and all."

"I can't have a friend who's a man?" Claudia asked innocently, although she couldn't think of one male friend she'd had since getting married.

"I find that women my age don't usually want to make friends with single men," said Fred. "Usually they're married and their husbands don't take kindly to the idea. They kind of treat me like I have the plague."

"It might help if you were less good-looking," said Claudia. Now that she had established her marital status, she felt safe in making such an observation.

"That's nice of you to say," said Fred, a little embarrassed. "But I don't think that's it."

"Sure it is," said Claudia. "The women are afraid that their husbands will be threatened by you. And they're also afraid that they'll be tempted by you."

"Really?" said Fred with pretend fascination. "So why then would it be okay for you to be my friend?"

"Steve—my husband—he's not the jealous type. And me—I've never had a wandering eye."

"That's good to know," said Fred.

"If you don't mind my asking, why aren't you married?"

"I don't mind. I was married, actually."

"Kids?" asked Claudia.

"No," said Fred.

Claudia could tell Fred didn't want to take the discussion any further. "So here's to trusting husbands and faithful wives," she said, lifting her glass of water.

Fred lifted his glass and said, "I'll drink to that."

The next day, Fred invited Claudia to lunch. And the next day, Claudia invited Fred. Soon there were no more invitations. The two simply always had a default lunch date. Sometimes one of them brought leftovers from home but always enough to share with the other. If Claudia had a lunch meeting or was too busy to take a break, they would meet for an afternoon coffee.

Claudia hadn't spent that much time with one person since college, but Fred was so easy and fun to be around. From their first lunch date, they clicked. The conversation always flowed, but when there was a moment of silence, they waited it out comfortably, without a trace of self-consciousness. It was obvious to both that they found each other attractive, even remarking freely on each other's good looks. But it was okay, because Claudia had made it clear that she was a loyal wife who was simply going through a rough patch in her marriage, and Fred was a single guy simply wanting to have a female friend his own age.

In fact, Fred even counseled Claudia about her marriage, telling her things she could do to improve the strained dynamic.

"Don't bring up the fact that Steve's out of work," he told her. "It doesn't help and only aggravates the situation.

"If you don't have something nice to say, don't say anything at all," he advised. "Just go to your room and relax until you can be civil.

"And maybe you should try lowering your expectations a little," he said. "Then you won't constantly feel disappointed."

Claudia took Fred's advice and it worked. She and Steve had stopped fighting and were actually getting along pretty well. But Claudia felt like it also had something to do with the fact that she now had Fred in her life. She felt calmer and happier and more hopeful. And even though their relationship was platonic, she enjoyed having a man to interact with—to joke with and spar with and discuss common interests. She was able to let go of her anger and dissatisfaction with Steve because she got fulfillment from Fred.

One day, Claudia came home early to find Steve at his computer, his Facebook account open. From a distance she could see that he was having a lengthy exchange with someone but couldn't tell who. So she decided to try something.

"Steve? Would you do me a favor?"

"What's up?"

"I meant to pick up some cereal and milk on my way home but completely forgot. Would you mind running to the store?"

"Sure," said Steve. Claudia noticed that he clicked on his MSN home page without logging out of Facebook, then closed his laptop.

The moment Claudia heard Steve's car pull out of the driveway, she ran to the computer. She figured she had at least fifteen minutes—five minutes to the store, five minutes in the store, and five minutes home. She opened the laptop and pressed the space bar. Then she clicked on the "back" button and found herself in Steve's Facebook account. And there she was: Marjorie Gooding.

"That must be so hard for you, Steve," was Marjorie's last message.

What was so hard for poor Steve? wondered Claudia. She didn't have the patience to read the entire string from the beginning so she went right to Steve's last comment.

"Claudia's definitely been better, not on me so much. So I don't feel so angry like I used to, so pissed off at her. But now I feel . . . just empty, like nothing. I don't feel anything, you know?"

Claudia scrolled up, scanning the ten or so messages that preceded this one. Her eye was caught by the words "Café Bella," a coffee shop a few blocks from the house.

"Maybe we should meet at Café Bella sometime?" wrote Marjorie. "It would be nice to talk in person for a change."

"I've got a job interview Thursday morning," wrote Steve. "Maybe after that? I'll give you a call."

He has a job interview? thought Claudia. Why didn't he say anything to me?

Claudia stared blankly at the rest of the conversation but couldn't bring herself to read any more. She knew what she was doing was wrong and knew she had to stop. Yes, part of her wondered what else lingered in Steve's inbox. But another part of her didn't want to know.

On Thursday, Claudia suggested to Fred that they go to a Mexican restaurant about fifteen minutes away by car, in a neighborhood neither had been to before. They rarely drove to lunch, partly to save time and partly because there were plenty of places to go within walking distance of the office. But sometimes either Claudia or Fred had a hankering for a certain type of food or they simply felt like they needed to get away.

"Where'd you hear about this place?" asked Fred as they sat down.

"There was a review in the paper last week," said Claudia. "They said the tamales are amazing. And the margaritas are to die for."

Fred looked at Claudia and smiled, tilting his head in mild disapproval. That was one thing about Claudia and Fred's lunches: No one ever drank. Somehow, they both implicitly knew that going down that road would lead to no good.

"Oh, come on," said Claudia. "Just this once, I promise. I love margaritas, and the article said these are the best!"

"Okay," said Fred. "Just this once. But I want the Gold. On the rocks. With salt."

"You got it," said Claudia.

The first drinks went down so easily and so fast—before their food even arrived—that they decided they needed another one to accompany their tamales and enchiladas. Not until their sopaipillas and café de olla arrived did they really start to feel a buzz.

When they got into the car, Fred paused before putting the key into the ignition. "Hmmm. I still feel a little tipsy. Maybe I shouldn't drive."

"Me too," said Claudia.

"You see?" said Fred, smiling. "You are naughty!"

"I know." Claudia smiled. "I'm sorry. Sort of."

"Let's sit here for a minute," said Fred. "Maybe it'll wear off."

" 'kay," said Claudia, leaning her head back on her seat, facing Fred.

Fred also put his head back against the seat, sank down low, and twisted his body to face Claudia.

"I'm drunk," said Claudia.

"You're a lightweight."

"You are too, buddy."

"I know," said Fred.

After a minute of silence, Claudia said, "I like you."

"I know," said Fred.

"You know?" said Claudia, lifting her head slightly in indignation.

"Yes, I know," said Fred. "I like you too."

"Duh," said Claudia.

They sat for a moment, looking at each other and smiling.

"Fred?"

"Yes?"

"I'm dying to kiss you."

"Really?"

"Yeah."

They sat for a moment, looking at each other, no longer smiling.

Claudia leaned in close to Fred. She smelled his hair. Then she smelled his neck. Then she brought her mouth close to his and kissed him gently on the lips. She pulled back and looked at him. Then she went in for another kiss. This time, Fred responded. They sat in the car and kissed for about fifteen minutes.

"What time is it?" asked Claudia.

"Two-thirty," said Fred.

"I want to go to your place," said Claudia.

And Fred said, "Okay."

Chapter Nine

It was fun for Annie to use the online sperm bank's searchable database to create her own wonder child—randomly choosing straight hair over curly, blue eyes over brown, Welsh ancestry over Irish. But when it came right down to it, she couldn't stand the idea of weeding out prospective donors so mindlessly. What if the man who was meant to be the father of her child was hidden within the less-than-five-foot-five range? Besides, she had heard that height was inherited from the mother. So Annie was forced to methodically go through hundreds of profiles, essays, and statistics in her quest to find the perfect man.

Then there was the problem of defining what the "perfect man" was. Was he a blond-haired, blue-eyed Viggo Mortensen? A dashing and confident George Clooney? A sly and silly Ben Stiller? Annie was reminded of the first time she walked into Bloomingdale's as a child, of being completely overwhelmed by all of the departments, all of the choices, all of the different personas she could create for herself there.

Annie's dilemma was crystallized one day when she found herself stuck on two prospective donors who could not have been more different.

Donor No. 59873—whom Annie referred to as Rick—was twenty-eight years old, six foot three with thick light-brown hair, an athletic build, and a 3.8 grade point average. He was in his last year of business school. He played varsity basketball in high school but his favorite sports were tennis and golf. He went to Northwestern for college and majored in economics with a minor in political science. He hoped to make it big in the business world and then one day run for public office. He spoke Spanish, played piano, loved to cook, and had traveled extensively through Europe. His favorite foods were Thai and Italian. The places he most wanted to travel to were Vietnam and Kenya.

Donor No. 43009—whom Annie referred to as Bob—was twenty-two years old, five foot ten with dirty-blond hair, an average build, and a 2.7 grade point average in his last year of college. He played pickup basketball and handball but didn't play organized sports. He was an art major, aspiring to be an illustrator of children's books. He spoke only English, played a little harmonica, and had never traveled outside the United States. His favorite foods were steak, peanut butter, and mangoes. He hoped to one day travel to Mexico to see the Mayan ruins.

Rick was a star and knew it. According to his personal essay, he was raised by doting parents who always told him he could be whatever he wanted to be. He considered himself confident, outspoken, and brave in the face of adversity, even though he'd never really had any. Under "Staff Impressions," they wrote that Rick was charming and friendly and always asked staff members about their lives and how they were doing.

Bob had modest goals and was comfortable with himself. He wrote that his parents probably could have been more encouraging and affectionate, but he loved them anyway. He was shy and uninterested in politics, tending more toward quiet activities such as reading and listening to music. The staff wrote that Bob was sweet and thoughtful, with a lovely smile.

In his note to the child who would be born of his sperm, Rick wrote: "I am honored to have played a role in giving you life, and I hope my genes serve you well. I wish you a happy, healthy, successful life full of fun and adventure."

Bob wrote: "No matter what life might throw at you, always know that you can handle it. Maybe someday you will read one of my books and you will like it and you will think that you have a special connection to the author—because you do."

Bob or Rick? It was like during the presidential election, when everyone asked: "Which candidate would you rather have a beer with?" Basing one's choice of a president on whether they'd be a good drinking buddy was ridiculous, thought Annie. But when it came to fathering her child, it seemed like a relevant question. Who *would* she rather have a beer with?

At work one day, Annie received an email from a familiar name—Jeff Briggs. "Hi, Annie," he wrote. "Remember me? I'm doing some consulting work for Sprint. You still there? Would love to get together. Jeff."

Ah, yes, thought Annie. Jeff Briggs. Too big for his britches was what she always thought of when she heard that name. But a nice enough guy. Annie hadn't seen any of her old Wharton classmates in years.

"Hey, Jeff," she wrote. "Of course I remember you. Gimme a call when you get in and I'll show you the town." Show him the town? thought Annie. Jeff's firm was based in New York. She always dreaded having to show New Yorkers around Kansas City. The snide remarks, the Dorothy references, the where-are-the-cows comments.

They agreed to meet at an Italian restaurant near Sprint, located in one of the high-end shopping centers that had recently sprouted up all around the campus. These establishments were like little oases amid the eight-lane roads and endless parking lots and treeless fields of Overland Park, their plush, elaborate, dimly lit interiors a welcome contrast to the stark landscape outside.

Annie recognized Jeff Briggs right away, not because he looked the same as he did in school but because she could instantly pick out a misplaced New Yorker among a sea of midwesterners. She didn't know what it was about him exactly, whether it was the suit, the haircut, the briefcase, or the way he stood at the bar with an air of nonchalant discomfort. Annie wondered if she still looked like an out-of-place easterner or if she had taken on the characteristics of a Kansan.

"Hey, Jeff."

"Annie!" he said, giving her a hug. Jeff stood a good eight inches over Annie, so she had to raise herself as high as she could on her tiptoes to reach him. "Wow. It's been so long." He took a moment and looked into her eyes, as if he was taking in all that had happened to her since they last saw each other. Then he put his hand on her back and guided her to the hostess desk. "Come, they've got a booth waiting for us."

Of course Jeff had already negotiated just the right table with the hostess, thought Annie. But she wasn't annoyed by his assertiveness. It felt good to be with someone who so willingly took control of the situation.

"This is kind of weird, huh?" said Annie as she slid into the booth.

"Why weird?" asked Jeff.

"I don't know. When's the last time we saw each other? Graduation?"

"Didn't we see each other in the city that summer?" said Jeff. "We met at that bar in the Village with Grace and Peter."

Jeff had dated Grace, Annie's roommate, for a few months, and Annie had dated Peter, Jeff's roommate, for a few weeks.

"That's right," said Annie. She remembered that night, how she'd ignored Peter and drunkenly flirted with Jeff and worried that Grace was mad at her. "And now here we are in Overland Park, Kansas."

"So who do you keep in touch with?" asked Jeff.

"A few high school and college friends. No one from Wharton."

"Really? You should join our class on Facebook. Everyone's up there."

"No, thanks."

"Annie! When did you get to be so antisocial?"

"I'm not, but it's hard maintaining friendships so far away. I really don't go back east much at all."

"I understand."

"I guess you keep up with the old crowd?" asked Annie.

"Pretty much. They're a good group. And very helpful when it comes to recommendations and all that."

So which is it? thought Annie. Are you keeping in touch as friends or are you holding on because you think they can help you advance in your career? Annie knew she was being too tough on Jeff. He was just playing the game like everyone else. Maybe she was mad at herself for letting all those connections go— connections that could have one day gotten her somewhere.

"What about Grace? She's one person I wish I'd kept up with," said Annie.

"She was at Merrill for a while. Then she got married, had two kids, and now stays home and writes a blog."

"She's a blogger?" asked Annie in disbelief. Now that her old friend had joined the ranks of the blogerati, Annie wondered if she'd have to start taking the whole thing seriously. "What does she blog about?"

"Something about kids—eating, sleeping, bad Mommy, good Mommy. I don't know. I can't keep track of all that stuff."

"I guess you don't have kids," said Annie.

"I've got two but I'm not interested in dissecting every last detail of child-rearing."

"I hear ya, babe!" said Annie.

"I mean, when my kids were really little, I couldn't believe the amount of time other parents spent discussing their children's sleeping patterns, eating habits, and pooping schedules."

"How old are your kids?"

"Four and six. Now all anyone talks about are piano lessons and soccer games and what schools they'll go to and what we need to do to get them into Harvard."

"Sounds fun."

"Oh, I can't complain," said Jeff.

"Sure you can," said Annie.

"I mean, things are good. I still have a job, we've got a great place right in the city. But what about you, Annie? Tell me what's going on in your life."

Annie was always surprised when a man asked her about herself. Most men she knew would go on and on about themselves and never ask her a single question. She remembered this about Jeff. How attentive he could be. Curious. He always made her feel like she was the most interesting person in the room.

"Well, I also have a job—certainly not a given these days. And a nice place—not in the city."

"Where is it?"

"I'm actually just about half a mile from here," said Annie. "Oh, you would die if you saw it. It's a big hulking mass of stucco in a subdivision right off a golf course."

"Really?" asked Jeff. "You play golf?"

"No. I don't use the golf course. In fact, I don't even use three-quarters of the house. I've got all these bedrooms and like four bathrooms and a rec room in the basement and I don't need any of it."

"So why'd you get it?"

"Because I could," said Annie. "You know how in New York, it's all about space and how much square footage you have and everyone's always complaining that they don't have anywhere to put anything? I guess I'm rebelling against all that."

"Well, I think that's great. Next time I'll bring the whole damn family and we can stay with you!"

"Of course!" said Annie, trying to picture Jeff, his lovely wife, and his two kids taking over her nice, quiet, well-ordered home.

"Just kidding."

"But you could!" she reassured him. Maybe it would be kind of nice to have houseguests.

"Thanks. My little boy would want to poop in all of your bathrooms."

"There you go, talking about pooping again," said Annie.

"Sorry," said Jeff, smiling. "You always make me feel so comfortable, Annie."

"You know us midwesterners, we're so down to earth."

"So now you're a midwesterner?"

"Kind of. I think I'd feel out of place in New York now. Maybe that's why I don't keep up with our classmates. Maybe I'm a little intimidated by all their wealth, fame, and success."

"Oh, come on," said Jeff. "It's not like everyone is so rich and famous. Most of us are struggling to get by like everyone else."

"Well, maybe not like everyone else."

"Of course, you're right."

"I do wonder sometimes," said Annie, "about what I left behind. About what might have happened if I'd stayed."

"That's only natural," said Jeff. "But it seems to me like you've got a good thing going here, Annie."

"Thanks. But I'm sure it must seem incredibly provincial to you."

"Not at all," said Jeff. "My work has me going all over the country, so I see what's out there. My friends in New York, they don't know the difference between Kansas City and Oklahoma City."

"Is there a difference?" asked Annie.

"If you'd ever been to Oklahoma City, you'd know," said Jeff. "I think this is a great place to live."

"It's not so bad."

"Remember what it's like in the city? Everything is so hard. Sometimes it gets to me. Then I come here and I'm tooling around in my BMW convertible—"

"Doesn't your company know we're in a recession?"

"They feel sorry for sending me here, so they try to make up for it with perks."

"Little do they know you love it here!" said Annie.

"I do! I love how easy it is to park and how you can walk into a place like this without reservations."

"It's not Del Posto."

"Who cares? I don't like al dente anyway."

"So move here," suggested Annie.

"Part of me would love to," said Jeff. "But I can't see myself ever living anywhere but New York. It's, like, not an option."

"You can do whatever you want, Jeff."

"Maybe I'm just not as strong as you."

Much to her surprise, Annie enjoyed her evening with Jeff. It was fun being out with a handsome, smart, funny guy who wasn't a snob and actually listened to what she had to say. Even though she knew men like Jeff were not flooding the streets of New York, she began to long for the city in a way she hadn't in years.

Annie imagined that if she had stayed in New York, she might have married a guy like Jeff. They would have had two kids and talked about pooping patterns with their friends and researched preschools together. They would have hired a nanny so she could keep working, and every Thursday they would have met for a nice lunch at the Gotham Grill or Pastis.

Annie knew it was much too late for all that. She had made her decision and she had to live with it. But maybe she was being too quick to completely discount the idea of moving back to the city. Maybe she hadn't fully morphed into a midwesterner. No, she couldn't start over, but she could create a different life for herself there. She could find a job with a cool Internet start-up, hang out with some of her old friends from school, maybe even date some nice divorced guy with two kids of his own.

Annie rarely called her mother, instead waiting for her to make her weekly call. But suddenly she felt an urge to talk to her, maybe even float the idea of going home, if only for a fact-finding mission.

"Annie? To what do I owe the pleasure?" said her mom in a vaguely accusatory way. Maybe this was why Annie never called.

"Nothing," said Annie. "Just calling. What's up?"

"What's up? A lot is up, let me tell you!"

"Yeah . . ." said Annie. If she didn't insert a "yeah" or an "uh-huh" or some other indicator that she was listening and wanted to hear more, her mother would pause and wait for it.

"Well, your sister is going nuts trying to find a new school for Sally—"

"Why? What's wrong with her old school?"

"Too much teaching to the test, that's what she tells me. I don't even know what that means. Do you?"

"Yes, it's—"

"So now, instead of sending Sally to public school for free, she's looking at private schools that cost twenty-five thousand a year, and that doesn't even include book fees!"

"Wow," said Annie.

"Meanwhile, Roger is expecting a pink slip any day now, so how they think they're going to come up with that kind of money is beyond me."

"How's Dad doing?" asked Annie, trying to change the subject. She loved her sister but hated hearing her constant trials and tribulations.

"Your father? He's suing the co-op board!"

"Huh?"

"Oh, something about the maintenance fees going up too fast. He's still mad about the whole kitchen-remodel thing. Anyway, now that he's not practicing anymore, he's always looking for someone to sue, and the board president is such a schmuck he just couldn't resist."

"Well, as long as he's enjoying himself," said Annie, mimicking what her mom always said.

"Exactly! So what about you, Annie? Any news? Any boys?"

Annie knew that the only kind of news her mother was interested in was boy news. "No boys," she said. But then she decided to add, "An old friend from Wharton is in town and we had dinner."

"Really!"

"He dated Grace."

"Oh, I love Grace. So who is he? What's he do?"

"Don't get too excited, Mom. He's married with two kids."

"Well, you never know . . ."

"You never know what? He might get a divorce? Is that what we're hoping for? I can be a homewrecker?"

"No, Annie, of course not. But maybe the marriage was already on the rocks."

"No one's on the rocks. Everybody's happy. Anyway, we had a nice time."

"Well, good. You know, I've been hearing about so many eligible men lately! I mean, just the other day Margaret told me that Jimmy Hunter is getting a divorce."

"Jimmy Hunter from high school?"

"Of course—you know another Jimmy Hunter? Anyway, and then I also found out that the new guy in 3C is single. Forty years old and never been married!"

All this talk about expensive elementary schools, antagonistic co-op boards, and pink slips from Wall Street investment firms was starting to make Annie feel queasy. What was she thinking? Did she really think she could move home and create a fabulous New York life for herself without also enduring the constant indignities of the big city, not to mention the relentless matchmaking of her mother?

"I'm going to have a baby!" Annie blurted out. She'd had no intention of telling her mother about her plans, had even been thinking that maybe she would abandon the idea. But somewhere inside she felt the need to say it, to make it real, to end her wavering.

"What? You're pregnant? Oh, my God."

"No, Mom, I'm not pregnant. But I want to get pregnant."

"Well, of course you do, dear! We all want you to get pregnant! And as soon as you find a nice boy you can start trying right away!"

"No, I'm not going to find a nice boy. I'm going to have a baby on my own."

"Oh, please, Annie. This is too much. Please tell me you're kidding."

"I'm not, Mom. I've already looked into sperm donors."

"Sperm donors! You're going to have a baby with some stranger?"

"Mother—"

"At least let me find a nice man to give you his sperm. Could you let me do that for you?"

"No, Mom. You can't do that. It's okay." Annie was starting to feel a little sorry for her mother. How hard it must be to hear your daughter tell you that she had given up on finding a husband and was instead going to buy a jar of sperm from an unknown donor, squirt it into her body, and give birth to a child whom she would raise on her own in a colorless subdivision of Overland Park, Kansas, a thousand miles away.

"Oh, Annie. Are you sure about this?"

"Yes, Mom. I'm sure. Really, I can handle this."

"Annie, I have no doubt you can handle this. Of all my kids, you're the one who can handle anything."

"Thanks, Mom. And I've got a great donor all picked out. I think you'd like him."

"Yeah? What's he like?"

"Supersmart, handsome, ambitious, charming . . ."

"How do you know all this?"

"They tell you. It's all online."

"So I guess you know what you're doing."

"Yes, I know what I'm doing."

"All right. I'm behind you, Annie. One hundred percent."

One conversation with her mother and Annie had committed herself to having a baby. Not only that, she'd finally settled on a sperm donor—Rick. It seemed so obvious once she began describing him to her mother. He was perfect, the kind of guy girls dream of bringing home to meet their parents. If Annie couldn't bring Rick home with a ring on her finger, at least he could father her child.

Annie still had a soft spot for Bob. There was something about his profile that was so endearing. She had to admit, Bob seemed more sincere than Rick. More modest, more real. But how could she choose modesty and sincerity over brains and ambition? And who was to say that her child wouldn't be all of those things anyway? She was sincere and modest. She could give those qualities to her child.

Two weeks later, Annie went to see her gynecologist, who told her that she was in great shape. In fact, it was possible that Annie would need no interventions to get pregnant—no hormones, no egg harvesting, no in vitro fertilization, just squirt it up there and wait. The doctor told her to move forward on getting the sperm, and she would take care of the rest.

That evening after work, Annie sat down at her computer, logged on to the sperm bank's website, and input Rick's number. She had already read his profile many times, pored over his personal essay, dissected the comments of the sperm bank's staff members, all of whom seemed to have a crush on him. She knew with all her heart that Rick was the right choice. She was no longer nervous or apprehensive, no longer had any doubts. She was filled with excitement that she had made a decision and was moving forward into a new stage of her life.

Next to Rick's profile was a big red button that read "purchase." How many times had Annie clicked on just such a button to buy a sweater, a book, or skin cream? Now she was about to purchase a baby online.

She clicked.

Immediately the screen turned gray and a little white pop-up window appeared. "We're sorry," the text read. "This donor has retired from our program. Vials from this donor are no longer available. We do not expect to have any more vials from this donor in the future. Please visit our extensive database so you can choose a different donor. Thank you."

Annie stared at the screen. This must be a mistake, she thought. She went back to the previous page and clicked again on the "purchase" button. Once again, the pop-up window appeared.

Annie could feel her throat tightening, her palms sweating, her heart racing. She was devastated—more than at any other time in her life. Never had she felt so distraught, not even when she broke up with Ben Weiner.

The whole point of this plan was to be in control, not to have to depend on a capricious man to create the life she wanted. And yet here she was, being told by her computer that the man she had chosen so meticulously to be the father of her child was no longer available.

Why had Rick "retired" from the program? Was he too busy building his empire to go to an office in Olathe, Kansas, and jack off into a cup? Did he feel like he had already given enough of himself, that he didn't want to bring one more of his offspring into the world? Was he afraid that he'd be walking down the street one day and see hordes of little Ricks staring up at him?

Annie had reached a point where she felt she knew Rick, that she had a real connection to him. Maybe if Rick knew about her, he would feel the same way. Maybe he would reconsider and want to give away his sperm one more time. But how? How could she reach out to an anonymous sperm donor? How could she find him in a greater metropolitan area of two million people?

Annie didn't know what she was going to do, but she knew she had to do something. She would not allow the thoughtless choices of a man to once again spoil her plans.

Chapter Ten

At the end of the last book club, Katie, Maxine, Claudia, and Annie had decided it was time to cut out the middleman—they would simply join a wine-tasting club instead. A work colleague of Claudia's had told her about a club that met the first Thursday of each month at a local wine shop. For a nominal fee, they could taste up to eight wines, nibble on exotic cheeses, and listen to experts talk about things like bouquet, oxidation, and tannins.

None of them had ever been to a real wine tasting before, so they sat at the end of the long wooden table and watched as the ten other people swirled, sniffed, sipped, and spat their wine.

"I'm not spitting out my wine!" whispered Claudia in hushed horror.

"Why are they doing that?" asked Katie. "Gross!"

"They're afraid they're going to get drunk if they don't," said Maxine.

"I don't think there's any chance of that," said Annie. "Not with these teeny portions."

"I know," said Claudia. "Can't we get a whole glass?"

Claudia fell silent as the shop owner walked by and poured a small splash of wine into each person's glass.

"I think you'll find this one has a lovely oaky finish," said a man standing at the other end of the table.

Katie tipped back her glass and shook out the last drop. "I'm finished. Pass the cheese."

"Maxine, grab that bottle there," said Annie.

"No way!" said Maxine. "I'll get in trouble!"

"This is ridiculous," said Claudia. "Whose idea was this anyway?"

"Yours!" said Maxine, Katie, and Annie simultaneously.

"Okay," said Claudia. "Don't worry. I'll take care of you." She waited until the shop owner walked into a back room, then reached over Maxine and grabbed an open bottle. She quickly filled their glasses. "Drink fast. I don't want them to get suspicious."

"This is pathetic. I would have gladly just paid full price for my wine." Maxine never understood people's delight in getting things for free—the free chocolate chip cookies on Midwest Airlines, the free samples of spanakopita and granola bars and chocolate truffles at Costco, the free appetizers during happy hour that were always lukewarm and stale. But then again, she was rich, so she knew better than to say anything about it.

"Yeah, but this is so much more fun!" said Claudia with a big smile.

"Why are you in such a good mood?" asked Katie.

"I don't know. Aren't I always?"

"No," said Maxine, Katie, and Annie simultaneously.

"Well, then, lucky you, I'm in a good mood tonight!" Claudia knew she ought to temper her jollity, but she didn't feel like holding back.

"What happened?" said Katie. "Did Steve get a job?"

Claudia tilted her head and gave her a look of mild disbelief.

"Did he make dinner?" asked Maxine.

"Did he close his Facebook account?" said Annie.

"Why do you think it has to be about Steve?" said Claudia. "I do have other things in my life, you know."

"Yeah, like working for me," said Annie. "When are you going to have that proposal finished?"

"Don't be such a taskmaster." Claudia had been allowing herself to miss a few deadlines and produce less-than-stellar work, because she knew Annie would give her a break.

"I swear," said Annie, looking at Maxine and Katie. "She's been such a slacker lately."

"Claudia, a slacker?" asked Katie.

"Listen, there are more important things in life," said Claudia.

"All right, then," said Annie. "But don't get mad at me when I have to fire your ass."

"Do what you gotta do," said Claudia with a shrug, but she wondered if maybe Annie was more displeased with her work than she'd thought.

"Wow," said Maxine. "She's not only happy, she's downright Zen."

"I've got a new attitude," said Claudia.

"Me too," said Katie. "But I wouldn't exactly call it Zen."

"Oh, yeah?" said Annie.

"More like pissed," said Katie.

"Like drunk?" asked Claudia.

"Like off," said Katie. "Pissed off."

"Oh," said Claudia. "That's usually me."

"Are you still upset about that guy?" asked Annie.

"Oh, no," said Katie. "I'm not upset. More like embittered."

"What a jerk," said Maxine.

"But it's not even about him," said Katie. "It's more like . . . like, what's the point? What's the point of dating and love and relationships and all that crap? It's such a bunch of bullshit. There's no such thing as love. It's just lust. I knew that before, but I let myself forget."

"Come on, Katie," said Claudia with uncharacteristic sincerity. "You don't really believe that."

"What do you mean?" Katie said to Claudia. "You don't have love *or* lust!"

Claudia stifled a smile, remaining silent. She knew that if she opened her mouth she'd likely say something that would give herself away.

"I don't have love or lust!" said Annie excitedly.

"The only one who has any love around here is Maxine," said Katie. "And lust too. She's an aberration."

"Oh, cut it out!" said Maxine, as she reached for another bottle of wine and filled everyone's glass, not even bothering to wait for the shop owner to leave the room. "I'm so sick of hearing about how in love I am. How do you know?"

Annie, Katie, and Claudia looked at one another in disbelief, then took a big gulp of wine.

"What's going on, Maxine?" asked Katie.

"Nothing, nothing. Don't worry, everything's fine." The last thing Maxine wanted to do was get into the whole Jake thing. No, she didn't want to hear about how great her marriage was, but she didn't want everyone to know how bad it was either.

"You sure about that?" said Annie.

"I'm sure," said Maxine. "In fact, I've got great news. I'm going to L.A. for a gallery opening. A whole week. All expenses paid."

"That's amazing!" said Claudia.

"What are you going to do with the kids?" asked Annie.

"I don't know. Jake'll deal with it."

"I'm impressed!" said Katie.

"I've had the chance to do stuff like this before, but I always said no because of the kids and Jake and everything else I have to do. But enough. I'm going. And they can all fend for themselves."

"They'll be absolutely fine," said Claudia.

"I just want to get away!" said Maxine.

"Don't we all," said Katie.

"Not me," said Claudia.

Katie, Annie, and Maxine all turned and looked at Claudia.

"What?" said Claudia. "I'm happy, remember? And Zen!"

"What is 'happy' anyway?" asked Annie.

"Happiness is getting laid—consistently and well," said Katie.

"Then I guess I'm not happy," said Annie.

"Me neither," said Maxine. She couldn't help herself. And then, of course, came those looks of concern from her friends. "Oh, come on. Do you really think it's all a bed of roses for me?"

"Kind of," said Claudia.

"Well, it's not," said Maxine. "Look, I don't want to talk about it right now, okay?"

"I was happy for a couple months with Ed, but then the asshole started screwing his old girlfriend," said Katie, trying to get Maxine off the hook by changing the subject.

"So why are you so happy, Claudia?" asked Annie. "Is there something you're not telling us?"

"In that department, Steve's always been pretty consistent, if not earth-shattering."

"You know what, Katie?" said Maxine. "I'm starting to think you might be right about this. Maybe that is what happiness is all about—a good, consistent fuck."

"Maxine!" said Claudia. "Keep it down! I think the whole table heard that."

"Whatever," said Maxine. "Like they've never heard that word before?"

"Not from such a classy, sophisticated lady," said Katie.

"So this concept poses somewhat of a dilemma for me," said Annie.

"How's that?" asked Katie.

"Well, I'm sort of banking on the idea that happiness comes from the result of sex, not the sex itself."

"Happiness is babies?" asked Claudia.

Annie shrugged.

Claudia, Katie, and Maxine burst into laughter.

"What?" asked Annie, a little shocked. "Your kids don't bring you joy?"

"Of course they do, Annie," said Claudia. "And, you know, you could very well be right about this. It's just, well, kids are hard. It's not unadulterated joy."

"I know that," said Annie. "But neither is good sex."

"If it's really good it is," said Katie.

"All right, well, I'm going with the baby."

"What are you talking about, Annie?" asked Maxine.

"I've decided to have a baby." Annie was enjoying telling people about her plan—first her mother and now her friends. Contemplating it and researching it all alone on her computer in the dark of her home office made the whole thing feel secretive and sinister. Saying it out loud made Annie realize that, while it was an unusual choice to make, it was something to be joyful about.

"Wow, that's . . . great!" said Claudia.

"Are you going to get inseminated?" asked Katie.

"That's the idea," said Annie. "My doctor thinks it should work fine. There's only one problem."

"What's that?" asked Claudia.

"Well, I've been scouring this online sperm bank for months, scoping out the perfect donor, and finally I settle on one. Really, he's perfect. Everything about him. It's hard to say, I just feel right about this guy. So I'm all set to make my purchase—"

"Visa, MasterCard, or PayPal," said Claudia.

"Be quiet, Claudia!" said Maxine.

"And I click on the 'Buy' button and this window pops up. They ran out of the guy's sperm."

"No way!" said Katie.

"I guess a lot of other women thought he was perfect too," said Claudia.

"Now I feel like I can't move forward with this," said Annie. "It's like I found the father of my child and I can't bring myself to consider anyone else."

"I don't blame you," said Katie. "Why should you?"

"I mean, the guy presumably still has plenty of sperm, unless he's dead or someone chopped off his penis," said Annie.

"And why shouldn't you be able to get some of it?" said Katie.

"Well, it's not as if his sperm is public property," said Maxine.

"I know," said Annie. "But it was on the market before, and it seems like what's another vial or two."

"I'm sure the guy just stopped contributing because he got too busy or something," said Claudia. "I bet if he knew about you, he'd be happy to give you a bucket of his sperm."

"That's exactly what I was thinking!" said Annie excitedly.

"So, what? You're going to track him down?" asked Maxine.

"Maybe," said Annie. "But how? It's all confidential."

The four women sat in silence, thinking.

"You need access to the sperm bank's files," said Claudia.

"How do I get that?" asked Annie.

"You need a spy," said Katie.

"Like bribe someone who works there?" asked Annie.

"That's an idea," said Katie.

"But then what happens if you bribe the wrong person and they report you to the authorities?" Maxine pointed out.

"I don't know," said Claudia. "Bribing someone to get the name of a sperm donor might not be a prosecutable offense."

"Okay, so let's say through some incredible stroke of luck she manages to get the name of the guy. Then what? How does she get his sperm?" asked Maxine.

"I ask him for some?" suggested Annie.

"Maxine, you're being kind of negative about this," said Katie.

"I'm sorry, but I have my doubts," said Maxine. "And maybe I'm a little wary about the idea that this guy is the only possible sperm donor. I just don't believe in that anymore. I don't believe there's one person out there, whether to marry or to be the father of your children."

"I hear what you're saying, Maxine," said Annie. "I don't really believe that either. In this case, though, I don't feel so much like I'm seeking out the father of my child but that I'm seeking out my child. Like, my egg plus this guy's sperm, whoever he is, is what will make my baby, and if I go with some other guy, I won't have the baby I'm meant to have, I'll have some other baby. You know what I mean?"

"Sort of," said Maxine.

"I know it sounds crazy and doesn't make a whole lot of sense. But I have this feeling that all this is happening because of some stupid fluke of timing, like if I had only made a decision and ordered his sperm a week or two earlier, it would all be different."

"I understand what you mean, Annie," said Katie.

"Don't worry," said Claudia. "We'll help you however we can."

"Thanks, guys," said Annie.

"And if the plan to find him doesn't work, I can always get you some sperm while I'm in L.A.," said Maxine. "Brad Pitt, maybe?"

"No, he's a cheater," said Annie.

"It'll be tough to find someone faithful in L.A.," said Maxine. "Particularly someone who's also willing to give a strange woman a jar of his sperm."

"It's okay, we'll find this guy," said Claudia.

"Rick," said Annie. "I call him Rick."

"We'll find Rick and we'll get his sperm and we'll make a beautiful little baby for Annie," said Claudia.

"And then," said Maxine, "we'll find her a good, consistent—"

"Shhhh!"

Chapter Eleven

After the Ed debacle, Katie was mad at herself more than anything. She had gone into the whole online-dating thing just for fun, never wanting anything serious. But then she got swept up in all Ed's talk of love and spending their lives together. He set her up, then promptly knocked her down.

Katie never could figure out what Ed's motivation was. He didn't have to pronounce his love for her in order to get her into the sack—she was ready and willing. She wouldn't have even minded if he had wanted to see other people—all he had to do was say so. Then why did he do it? Was it a sadistic game for Ed? Did he get a perverse thrill from making women think he couldn't live without them and then suddenly deciding he never wanted to see them again?

While the whole nasty experience was disconcerting, as a true member of the Oprah generation Katie was determined to learn something from it. The lesson was simple: She would never let herself get in that situation again. Katie didn't feel like she had to once again give up on men. What she had to do was keep them at a distance while getting what she wanted from them. The moment they started talking about love and commitment, that would be the end.

Katie was ready to get back in the saddle, but she wasn't about to go on Match.com again. The last thing she wanted was a perfect "match." She didn't want to find Mr. Right, she wanted to find Mr. Wrong, so that it would be easy to leave him when the time came.

Katie loved craigslist. She'd found her job at the bank there, bought a new dining room set there, and found a guitar teacher for her son, Frank, there. She remembered seeing a "personals" listing but had never thought to check it out. So she went online and immediately found the perfect thing for her—a section called "casual encounters."

Casual, that's just what I need, thought Katie, and with a few simple clicks—so much easier than Match!—she had a lengthy list of potential dates, all written in that familiar blue typeface and all posted that very same day.

But when she started reading them, she sensed something fishy. "Want some Thursday morning fun?" read one. "Party with me tonight," read another. Things seemed to move a lot quicker here, thought Katie, noting that the men wanted to get together at very specific times. She read on. "Young stud looking for hot MILF," "Seeking NSA—Eager to Please!" MILF? NSA? Katie had no idea what these acronyms could mean and didn't think she'd find them at Dictionary.com. "Lonely housewives: If you wanna get off, cum over to my house." Finally, Katie was getting the message.

But while she understood that this was not the place for her, she couldn't help but click on some of the entries. First she tried the ones that had a little orange "pic" next to them. "My wife leaves the house at 7:00 for work. Want to come over at 8:00 and get nasty with me?" Underneath was a single picture. A penis. Katie quickly hit the "back" button. She tried another. Before she could even read the words, she looked down at the picture. Another penis. This one, however, was attached to a headless torso. She tried one more time. "I'm a busy lawyer who likes to cum home for lunch. Want to join me and we can eat each other?" There were three pictures: a man in a suit next to a car, a naked man lying on a couch, and a man lying on a bed holding his penis.

For the first time in her life, Katie felt like she had stumbled into a scary online universe. How could this be? she asked herself. How could there be all these pictures of penises just a few clicks away from the armoires and apartment rentals and job postings for babysitters?

Katie closed her browser and promptly deleted her history, hoping to erase any remnants of her excursion into "casual encounters."

Surely there must be something in between a soul mate and a sex toy, thought Katie. She searched and searched until she found a local site called DateKC.com. "A safe, comfortable way to meet nice people near you," read the tagline, which seemed to be speaking directly to Katie. Safe, comfortable, nice—exactly what I'm looking for, she thought. She started to randomly click on profiles and immediately liked what she saw. The pictures were more spontaneous than they were on Match—less posed. And there wasn't a naked body part in sight. As she read on, she noticed no references to finding "The One" or "Ms. Right" or even "Somebody Special." Everyone seemed to be in it for a good time— but not too good.

The profiles on DateKC.com were much sketchier than those on Match.com, with no talk about jobs or salaries, height preferences or body type, religious or political leanings. There was an understanding that such things didn't matter much if you weren't looking for a long-term relationship. Instead, people concentrated on their favorite hangouts and activities and whether they were University of Kansas or University of Missouri fans.   ,

Wanting to find someone closer to her own age this time, Katie immediately zeroed in on a cute guy of thirty-two who looked much younger. "Making the best of it in KC" was his headline. "Wishing for the mountains of Boulder, beaches of LA, bars of NY. But I'm here, so why not have fun?" Katie liked this guy's philosophy. She liked that he wasn't so provincial as to think that Kansas City was the center of the universe, that he was aware of what the rest of the country had to offer. But he wasn't wasting his life away wishing for something else.

"Ever try sledding down Suicide Hill? Lounging at the Prairie Village pool?" wrote Katie. "And Mike's Pub isn't bad." She had never actually been to Mike's Pub, which was about a half mile from her house, but she had heard it was a happening place.

Five minutes after sending her email, Katie received a reply. "Mikes? No way . . . thats my home away frm home. Never cu there . . ."

Uh-oh, thought Katie. How would she get out of this one? "Used to go there a lot, not much lately," she answered.

"Wanna meet somtime?" he wrote back two minutes later. "Nice pics . . . btw."

"OK," agreed Katie, thinking it was a little odd that she had made a date without even knowing the man's name. "I'm Katie."

"O sorry . . . im dave," he wrote. "How bout thurs . . . haphour?"

Haphour? Katie wondered. Happy hour! she figured out after fifteen seconds, embarrassed that it took her so long. She imagined this guy was on his phone, using the texting lingo that was like a foreign language to her. Katie decided that if she was going to hang with a younger crowd, she couldn't be afraid to look stupid. She also decided that she would never, ever type "cu" or "btw," no matter whom she was dating.

"Every hour is happy for me. Which are the happy ones at Mike's?" she wrote back.

"@6?" replied Dave.

"At six," Katie spelled out defiantly.

Wow, that was fast, she thought. Then she began to worry that maybe DateKC was just a kinder, gentler version of craigslist. But, no, these were the type of people she was familiar with, the same ones she knew in high school and college, the ones she saw at the bank every day. She was pretty sure they weren't hosting intimate sex parties at their homes during their lunch hour.

Rob wasn't able to babysit on Thursday night, so Katie called her backup sitter, Jenny. After getting laid off from her job as a copy editor at *The Kansas City Star,* Jenny decided to go to nursing school. She had heard that nursing was recession-proof.

"Thanks for coming so early, Jenny," said Katie as she opened the door.

"No problem. You going on a date?" asked Jenny, looking Katie up and down.

Katie widened her eyes and motioned to Maggie, who was watching TV in the other room.

"Oh, sorry," said Jenny. "Meeting your work friends, right? Where you going?"

"Mike's Pub," said Katie.

"Mike's? Really?" said Jenny in disbelief.

"What?" asked Katie, concerned. "What's wrong with Mike's?"

"Oh, nothing. Sorry. It's just that I hang out there. You know, it's kind of . . ."

"Young? Am I too old to go there?" Katie suddenly felt like a fool, going to the same bar where her twenty-three-year-old babysitter went.

"No! Katie, I'm . . . surprised, that's all. Come on! I see people in their thirties there all the time!"

"Oh, God, Jenny. What am I doing?"

"You're fine, Katie. I mean it. But, you know, I would maybe . . . wear something different."

Katie looked down at her faded jeans and her maroon V-neck cotton shirt. She thought she had done well, not too dressy, not trying too hard. "What do you mean?"

"Well, the jeans, they're a little . . . old? And maybe a bit high-waisted."

"Oh," said Katie.

"And the shirt—kind of blah."

"I was trying to be nonchalant."

"You succeeded."

"Jenny, I don't have anything else!"

"Hey! Why don't you wear this?" said Jenny, pointing to her own outfit. "I just got these jeans at Lucky. You wear twenty-eight, right?"

"Yeah, I guess."

"And this top would be perfect!" Jenny was wearing an emerald-green silky shirt with a plunging neckline and puffy short sleeves.

"Really?" asked Katie, not sure she could pull it off.

"Definitely. You'll look fab."

Katie walked into the bar feeling like an impostor. She imagined that everyone saw past the shiny shirt and the overpriced jeans and knew that she was just a mom who would have to wake up at six the next morning to make peanut butter and jelly sandwiches for her kids' lunches. But no one gave her a second glance, so she strode in confidently, searching the crowd for her date.

Katie immediately recognized Dave, who was sitting on the end of a large semicircle-shaped booth with four other guys and three women. When she caught his eye he smiled, jumped up from his seat, and walked over to her.

"Katie?"

"Dave."

Dave took Katie's arm and gave her a kiss on the cheek, and as he did she noticed everyone at his table watching and smiling.

"I hope I didn't interrupt anything," said Katie, nodding her head toward the table.

Dave looked over his shoulder, then turned back to Katie. "Them? That's just the gang. Or part of it anyway."

"You've got a big gang," said Katie.

"Safety in numbers, I guess," said Dave. "Come on, let me get you a drink." He nabbed two stools at the bar and motioned to the bartender, who came over immediately. "What'll you have?"

"Vodka tonic?"

"One vodka tonic, and a Boulevard Wheat for me."

"Oh, I guess I should be drinking beer, huh?" said Katie, feeling like this was the beginning of a long line of social faux pas she would be making that evening.

"Are you kidding?" asked Dave. "You should drink whatever you want."

"Look, Dave, I'll be honest with you. I've never been to Mike's Pub in my life, I've got two kids at home, and the last guy I dated was more than ten years older than you." Katie felt relieved. She needed to be out with it, and if Dave didn't like it, so be it.

"Cool," said Dave, nodding his head. "So what's the problem?"

"Nothing, I guess," said Katie.

"Awesome."

Katie couldn't keep her eyes off Dave's friends sitting in the booth nearby, and they couldn't keep their eyes off her. "I feel like I'm being watched," said Katie.

"Who? Oh. Sorry. It always happens when someone new comes on the scene."

"Who are they?"

"The guys are mostly college friends. The girls . . . I think we met them here."

"They're younger, right?"

"Yeah, I guess."

"And you probably dated them all, right?"

"Yeah, I guess," said Dave, smiling.

"And you probably still hook up sometimes, right?"

"Not so much," said Dave, putting on his most sincere face. "I'm trying to branch out. That's why I did the Internet thing. They all think I'm crazy."

"Really?" Katie was surprised to hear that online dating was still taboo within Dave's circle of friends.

"Yeah, no one I know does that."

"Interesting."

"We just meet people at bars."

Katie figured that these young people thought Internet dating was only for desperate divorced moms and dads who didn't have the time, energy, or patience to sit in a crowded bar and find someone to hook up with. It was probably a source of pride that they had the stamina to drink heavily and stay up late in a smoky bar rather than taking the easy way out by using a searchable database in the comfort of their own home.

"I felt like I wanted to meet someone else, someone different," said Dave.

"Well, you got it!" said Katie.

"Yeah. I like you."

"Already?"

"Sure, why not? You're cool."

"So you're looking to get out of Kansas City?" asked Katie.

"Yeah, someday. But I gotta make some money first."

"What do you do?"

"I'm a videographer. You know, corporate stuff, events. I even do weddings if they pay me enough."

"That's great."

"It's okay. I'd rather be making movies."

"And I'd rather be writing novels."

"Really? You're a writer?"

"No. But I guess that's what I would have wanted to be if I didn't get married at twenty-two."

"Whoa! Twenty-two?"

"Yeah, I know. Sounds like it should be illegal."

"Man," said Dave, shaking his head in disbelief. "I'm thirty-two and I can't imagine getting married."

"I'm sure you can't," said Katie with a smile.

"I mean, what's the point?"

"There is no point," said Katie. "Well, maybe if you want kids it might be a good idea. But guys don't have to be in any hurry."

"Yeah, we're lucky, huh," said Dave. "You know, you're cool. I never heard a woman talk like that. All of them want to get married. Even the divorced ones. They get divorced and then can't wait to get married again. What's up with that?"

"Maybe they think that's what's expected of them. That being married is what they're supposed to be and if they're not they're a failure," said Katie. "Maybe they think that if they just date, they'll keep getting older and the guys'll stop coming around. And one day they'll end up all shriveled up and alone."

"I guess you've thought about this once or twice," said Dave.

"Yeah, once or twice."

"So why don't you care about that stuff?"

"Because I learned from my marriage. I learned that marriage isn't that great, even though society tells you it's the be-all, end-all. And as much as women try to lock in a man by getting married, shit happens. There are no guarantees."

"Awesome," said Dave. "You should teach a course or something. Or write a book!"

"Now, there's an idea."

After two more drinks and two hours of talking, Dave asked Katie if she wanted to go to a different bar on the other side of town and listen to some live music. Katie suggested they go to his place instead.

Dave lived in one of those massive beige-colored apartment complexes that Katie always passed by and wondered, Who lives there? The units were well-kept characterless boxes, each with a balcony and a corresponding parking place. Dave's was furnished with the bare minimum—a sofa, a TV, a bed. Nothing on the walls, no knickknacks, nothing that might reveal his personality. In the corner was a shelf piled high with video equipment and a desk with two computers and stacks of papers, folders, and books.

Katie couldn't help comparing Dave's place to Ed's, which was elegant and grand. Everything about Ed was grand—the way he wined and dined her, the flowers and gifts, the early professions of love. But she liked the feeling with Dave—low-key and not the least bit showy. She felt safe in his easygoingness. She could tell that he, too, felt comfortable, particularly after she shared her philosophy on dating and marriage. They were both on the same page. Neither wanted anything more than some casual camaraderie.

"You want something to drink?" asked Dave, walking into his galley kitchen.

"Sure," said Katie, sitting down on the brown and yellow plaid sofa that looked exactly like the one she had in college, something she had picked up for twenty dollars at a garage sale.

"I just have beer," he said, handing Katie a bottle and sitting down next to her.

Katie took a drink and wondered how long it would take Dave to kiss her and whether she would have to make the first move. She smiled at him, took another drink, and before she could put her bottle down, he was leaning in for a kiss.

It was a good kiss, thought Katie, but not the best. Not quite as good as Ed. Dave was a little too forceful, a little clumsy with the tongue. She put her bottle on the floor and placed her hands on Dave's shoulders, guiding him in for another kiss. This time she held him back a bit. When he poked his tongue in her mouth, she slowly leaned away. "Like this," she said, and proceeded to gently kiss him on his lips, using her tongue sparingly, teasingly.

Dave imitated her movements, and after a few minutes they were perfectly in synch. Katie pulled away and smiled.

"Thanks for the lesson," Dave said.

"Sorry," said Katie.

"No, it's great," and he leaned in for another kiss.

He started to take off her shirt but got stuck on the buttons on the back. Worried that he might rip Jenny's blouse, Katie reached around and unbuttoned it herself. After she peeled off her jeans, she started undressing Dave. Once he was naked, he immediately climbed on top of her, ready to go, but she pushed him down and said, "Wait."

It kept going on like that, Dave pressing forward, Katie pushing him back. She placed his hands where they needed to be, slowed down the pace, all the while giving him verbal cues like, "Right here," "Gently," and "Not yet."

It was a lot more work than it had been with Ed, but it turned out the same in the end. Katie wondered if she was wrong to have taken on the role of teacher with Dave, whether she should have just sat back and let him do what he wanted. But after they were done, the first thing Dave said was, "Thank you."

"You're welcome, I guess," said Katie.

"That was amazing," said Dave. "I never had a woman show me like that, tell me what she wanted. You're good."

"You too," said Katie, although she thought to herself that he would probably be much better after a few more sessions with her.

And he was. Over the next few weeks, Katie and Dave got together every Thursday, meeting at Mike's Pub and then going to his place, and each time it got better and better. Still, the best part was that they stayed casual. For the first time, Katie understood the meaning of friends with benefits. More than anything, she felt like Dave was a good friend who was gradually learning how to satisfy her needs.

Not only that, but Katie also got to know Dave's buddies from the bar. At first she and Dave remained apart, sitting at their own table when they met and leaving after about an hour. But after a few times Katie suggested they join Dave's friends, and Dave happily agreed.

Seeing Dave interact with his male friends was like watching a particularly well-written sitcom, with their running jokes, bizarre catchphrases, and silly non sequiturs. Katie also liked the girls in the group, even though they were all about ten years younger than she was. At first, these young women were wary of Katie, who seemed effortlessly confident and sure of herself, able to chat and joke with Dave and his friends without needing their attention or approval. But soon they began to see her as kind and genuine—maybe even someone to learn from.

Katie liked hearing their tales of dating and hooking up, especially the dramas that took place within the group. She learned that each girl had dated each guy over the past couple of years, and now they were all circling back for another round. She discovered that Dave was the first of the group to venture out onto the Internet and start dating someone else. Katie was told that because everyone liked her so much, they were all considering following suit.

Katie got along best with Henry, Dave's best friend. While Dave was sweet and a bit on the earnest side, Henry was more sarcastic and mischievous. He was also a big flirt.

One night Katie found herself sitting alone at a table with Henry while Dave and another friend shot a game of pool in the next room.

"Alone at last," said Henry.

"I thought they'd never leave," said Katie with a smile. She thought nothing of playing Henry's flirty game, since she was sure nothing would come of it.

"So you're a mom," said Henry.

"That I am," said Katie.

"Very cool."

"Not really. There are a lot of us moms out there."

"Yeah, but not as hot as you."

Katie smiled shyly and looked down at her drink.

"What? You don't think you're hot?"

"It doesn't matter what I think, it's what the guy thinks, right?"

"Well, I'm a guy, and you're hot."

"Thanks, Henry. That means a lot to me," said Katie sarcastically.

"Actually, you know what you are? You're a MILF."

Katie remembered reading that on craigslist and not having the slightest idea what it meant. "What does that mean?"

Henry laughed.

"No, come on. What does it mean?"

"It means 'moms I'd like to fu—'"

"Stop!" shouted Katie. "Don't say it!" and she covered his mouth with her hand.

"What? You've never heard that before?"

"No! Of course not. Where would I have heard that?"

"I bet a lot of guys are thinking it when it comes to you."

"Stop it, Henry."

"Dave also told me other stuff about you."

"Oh, yeah? What did he tell you?"

"He said you're very 'experienced.'"

"Uh-huh." Katie was surprised that Dave would talk about her in that way, but she'd learned not to put anything past a guy anymore.

"He said you know exactly what you're doing in the boudoir. He said he's learned a lot from you."

"Really. Dave said that. I find that odd."

"You know guys talk about that stuff."

"I guess."

"Don't girls?"

"Yeah."

"You probably tell all your girlfriends about me, huh?"

"Why would I tell them about you and not Dave?"

"Because I'm the one you'd rather be going home with," said Henry. Then he leaned in as if he was going to kiss her but instead sniffed the side of her neck.

Katie pushed him away. Then she noticed Dave and two of his friends heading back to the table.

"Hey, baby," said Dave, sitting down next to Katie.

Squished in the booth between Henry and Dave, Katie felt like she was going to suffocate if she didn't get out. "Excuse me. I've got to go to the ladies' room."

Before Dave could get up, Katie pushed her way out of the booth, tripping over his leg. She practically sprinted to the restroom, went into a stall, and sat there for five minutes, trying to decide what to do. She wanted to leave but didn't want to make a scene.

Suddenly Katie's phone began to vibrate. It was a text from Dave.

"u ok?"

"Yeah," she wrote. Then she decided she wanted to tell Dave right away, before Henry said something stupid. "Henry made a pass at me."

After a few seconds, she got another text. "O . . . sorry."

"Can we go now?" she wrote.

Back at Dave's house, Katie told him what happened.

"Typical Henry" was his response.

"Are you mad?" asked Katie.

"No."

"Really?" said Katie, not believing him.

"Honestly, Katie, this is what we do."

"This is what you do?"

"Well, not exactly like Henry did it, but . . . you know, I've slept with girls who my friends have gone out with."

"While they were going out?"

"I don't know. It's kind of sketchy."

Katie paused to process all this. "I think things are different now than when I was dating."

"Maybe. So do you like Henry?" asked Dave.

"Yes, I like him. I wasn't thinking about sleeping with him."

"But now you're probably thinking about it."

Katie stayed silent.

"Look, Katie. I've done this before. People in our group, we're not all caught up in relationship stuff. Bottom line, I can go either way. I like you a lot. I want you to be happy about this. Whatever you feel comfortable with."

Katie was having a hard time following Dave's rambling. "So you're saying, if I want to sleep with Henry I can, and we can still keep seeing each other."

"Yes."

"And if I want to just be with you, that's okay, too."

"Right."

"And you don't care one way or the other."

"You got it."

That was what really got Katie. Dave didn't care one way or the other. She could sleep with his best friend or not, either way, no big deal.

And wasn't that exactly what she wanted—a "casual" relationship? Every time Katie tried to be "casual," she always seemed to get caught up in the traditional relationship trap of wanting longevity and exclusivity. Maybe this was exactly what she needed to do to ensure that she wouldn't become dependent on Dave. Besides, he clearly wasn't dependent on her.

"All right, then. If you don't care, let's just go for it." The moment the words came out, Katie worried that Dave would suddenly become crestfallen, that he would regret the whole arrangement.

But without another word, Dave moved closer to Katie and slid her blouse off her shoulder.

The next day, Katie got a text from Henry while she was at work. "Meet me 2nite?"

"Cant," she wrote back. Katie still hadn't figured out how to write an apostrophe with her outdated phone.

"Wen?" wrote Henry.

"Tomorrow. Meet me at Russillos at 7." Even though she knew Henry didn't make much money as a Web designer, she decided she'd make him take her to a nice dinner before anything happened.

Katie was surprised at how awkward dinner was. Henry was nervous and didn't seem to know what to do. He kept asking her if everything was all right. Their conversation was stilted and strained. Katie figured he was probably so used to meeting women at bars and hooking up, he didn't know how to handle himself in such a formal situation. But when they got back to his place, an apartment in a complex almost identical to Dave's, he relaxed.

After they had sex, Katie had to admit it was the best she'd ever had. Henry had it all—Dave's good looks and Ed's skills in bed. And because they had been flirting for a couple of months before getting together, the buildup was intense.

The next day, Katie got a text from Dave. "Wen can I cu?" Dave almost never texted Katie and never asked to see her outside of their standing date for Thursday at the bar. Henry must have told him they had gone out the night before, thought Katie. Dave must be stepping up his game.

"Thursday?" she texted back.

"Sooner" was his reply.

And so it went from that day on. Katie started receiving endless texts from Dave and Henry, maneuvering to see her more and more. Surprisingly, they still wanted to meet at Mike's, knowing full well the other would be there, but they both acted as if nothing had changed. When Dave invited Katie, she was careful not to give too much attention to Henry, and vice versa. But sometimes she forgot which one had invited her, not sure with whom she'd be going home that night. So she'd have to sneak into the bathroom and check her text messages to try to figure out who her date was.

Katie's one night out a week quickly changed to two, three, sometimes even four. Rob was taking the kids more and more, but she still had to hire Jenny to babysit, shelling out sixty dollars a pop. And she'd often arrive at work the next morning tired and hungover.

One evening, as Katie was getting ready to go out, Frank came into her bedroom and plopped onto the bed.

"You're going out again?" asked Frank.

"Yes," said Katie.

"Who's babysitting?"

"Your father. You're going to spend the night at his house."

Frank sighed.

"What, Frank?" said Katie, turning away from the mirror to look at her son.

"Nothing."

"Are you sure?" she said, turning back to the mirror.

"Who are you going out with?"

"Friends."

"What friends? Maxine?"

Katie thought for a second about lying to Frank but figured it could come back to haunt her. "No, other friends."

"You sure are seeing your friends a lot."

"It's good to have friends. You have friends."

"I don't see them as much as you."

"You see them every day at school."

"Whatever."

Katie finished putting on her makeup and went to sit on the bed with Frank. "Don't you want me to have friends?"

"Yes. But I also want you to be with us."

"I'm not with you?"

"Not that much."

"Really?"

"Kind of."

"Well, this weekend we'll do something special, okay? We'll see a movie and go out for Chinese food. Does that sound good?"

"Yeah," he said glumly.

"Frank?"

"Yes."

Katie wondered whether Frank knew more about what she was up to than he let on. He was only seven years old, but kids were different these days. And like his peers, Frank was more adept at technology than Katie. Could he possibly have gone onto her computer and seen something he shouldn't have? Might he have looked at her text messages behind her back?

The next morning, since she didn't have to bring the kids to school, Katie got to work half an hour late. When she arrived, she found a pink Post-it note on her desk from her boss, Francine. "See me when you get in," it said. Katie couldn't remember ever being summoned into Francine's office during her two years of working at the bank.

"Hi, Francine," said Katie, standing meekly at the door.

"Come in, Katie," said Francine.

"I'm sorry I'm late. But I—"

"No big deal."

Katie liked Francine, who was always laid-back and understanding. They had even gone out for lunch together a few times and often discussed their kids, who were exactly the same age.

"I can't imagine this is going to come as a big surprise, Katie, but due to the economic downturn, the bank is having to let some people go."

At that moment, Katie wanted to get up and go. She knew what the next sentence would be and didn't want to hear it. "Oh, God," she said.

"I'm sorry, Katie. Just so you know, we're having to lay off Janet and Sam too. I've already told them."

"Did I do something wrong, Francine? I know I've been late a few times recently. I've been kind of under the weather—"

"No, Katie. You've been a great employee, but we had to make cuts and . . . well, let's just say the decision was not based on job performance."

Intellectually, Katie knew that the bank was struggling. She also knew that Francine liked her. Even in the past few weeks, with Katie's questionable work habits, Francine had been as friendly as ever. But Katie couldn't help but feel like this was happening now because she was being punished—punished for being a bad worker, punished for being a neglectful mother, and, most of all, punished for being a slut.

Chapter Twelve

From the moment her trip began, from the drive to the airport to the plane ride in first class to walking into the Chateau Marmont, Maxine was in heaven. The anticipation of spending an entire week all alone in a beautiful, luxurious hotel a thousand miles from home was beyond thrilling. It left her feeling like a woman reborn. Throughout the day, it was as if she were having an out-of-body experience—watching herself from above. She didn't recognize this other woman, who appeared to be husbandless and childless and consumed with herself. Before, she probably would have found such a woman selfish and self-centered. Now she embraced her.

When Maxine entered her room she immediately shed her clothes, climbed into bed, and turned on the TV, flipping through the channels. She finally settled on a movie about love and chance encounters, which she figured was the theme of roughly half of all movies in existence. After it was over, she took a hot bath, emptying every perfumed bath product she could find into the tub. When she got out she wrapped herself in the plush hotel bathrobe and relaxed on the settee by the window.

It was getting dark, and she thought she should probably call the gallery to confirm her appointment for tomorrow morning but decided not to. Then she thought she should call Jake and let him know she'd arrived safely—or at least text him.

Yes, before leaving for L.A., Maxine had called Sprint and asked to add texting to her cell-phone service. She realized that if she hoped to compete—whether it be in the world of art or marriage—she would need to have all the necessary tools at her disposal. But at that moment Maxine didn't want to use even a detached form of communication like texting with Jake.

What about the kids? she wondered. Would they want to hear from her? They were probably happy with their various friends and activities. Better to just leave them be. Instead, she called up room service and ordered a bottle of champagne, a shrimp cocktail, and a cheeseburger. After she was done eating, she climbed back into bed, settled on a rerun of *Friends,* and fell asleep.

The next morning, Maxine was picked up by a Town Car and brought to the Susan Shackelford Gallery. Riding in the car with a wet bar at her side and a chauffeur in a gray suit and hat in front of her, she wondered how the gallery could afford all this. Weren't they struggling in the bad economy like everyone else?

When she arrived, Maxine was greeted at the front desk by a slender, boyish young man named Ted.

"You must be Maxine Walters," he said. "Susan will be right down. Can I get you something while you're waiting?"

"No, thanks." Maxine looked around the gallery and saw her paintings scattered around the room, some leaning against the walls and some already hung. She liked this series, which she called "Farm." It was full of cartoonish renderings of pastures, cornfields, barns, tractors, cows, and other farm animals. She'd never done anything so completely midwestern, and here she was about to show it for the first time in Los Angeles.

"We're hoping to get everything hung by tomorrow," said Ted. "And Susan definitely wants your input."

"Great."

"I love your stuff," said Ted. "It reminds me a lot of Wayne Thiebaud."

"Oh, no, no, no," said a woman in a red suit as she walked down a staircase. "Thiebaud is much too . . . obvious. I think she's more Diebenkorn. A mixture of the abstract and figurative. Thiebaud completely lacks Ms. Walters's expressionist bent."

Maxine couldn't believe that she had already been compared to two of her favorite artists within thirty seconds of her arrival.

"Hello, Maxine," said Susan, holding out her hand. "So nice to finally meet you."

"My pleasure," said Maxine. "It's a thrill to be here."

"I see you've met my assistant, Ted. He'll be attending to all your needs. I hope you've found your accommodations adequate?"

"Oh, yes," said Maxine. Did Susan really think she wouldn't find the Chateau Marmont adequate? Maxine figured this woman, with her three-thousand-dollar suit and three-hundred-dollar haircut, was probably the type who would find something wrong with the most perfect of places. She wondered where the vaguely European accent was from.

"Good. We like to keep our artists happy."

"So do you always bring artists in for their openings?"

"As much as we can. Although I should say we tend to favor certain of our artists. I can already tell you'll be one of those."

"I hope so," said Maxine, trying to be modest but not too self-deprecating. She could tell Susan Shackelford liked confidence.

"No question about it," said Susan. "Ted, how many of Maxine's works have already been bought?"

"More than half," said Ted.

"Seriously?" said Maxine.

"I was shocked," said Susan. "You've definitely hit on something, Maxine, and I want to take advantage of it. Your work is bold and different but not too outlandish. Frankly, people can justify the purchase as not only collecting but decorating. I'm afraid in this difficult market, we must consider such things."

Maxine wasn't quite sure how she felt about being told her paintings were decorative, and she could tell Ted was a little uncomfortable with the remark.

"I mean, dead pigs floating in formaldehyde are hot in flush times, but we're in a recession now," said Susan. "People are looking for lower price points and art that works in their homes."

"Of course," said Maxine.

"But I have a feeling that those prices will be going up if we keep selling like this," said Susan, who offered her first smile. "Ted, I've got to jump on a call. Why don't you and Maxine take a walk through the gallery and show her what we're thinking in terms of positioning?"

After a few hours of going through Maxine's paintings and discussing the merits of multiple sequences, Ted suggested they go out for lunch. He took her to a nearby vegetarian restaurant filled with people wearing high-priced designer sweat outfits and sipping on soy lattes and yogurt smoothies.

"I love L.A.," said Maxine as she dug into her tofu scramble. "Everybody's so relaxed and healthy."

"Relaxed?" said Ted. "That's just part of the façade. They're all nutso."

"Where are you from?" asked Maxine.

"Bloomington, Indiana."

"How'd you end up here?"

"I went to UCLA film school and decided to stay. I didn't want to be gay in the Midwest."

"Makes sense. So what happened to filmmaking?"

"I worked as a production assistant for a while, but I hated feeling like I and everyone else in the entire city was in the film business. I guess I wanted to be different."

"Do you like working for Susan?"

"Yeah, she's great. A little annoying at times but a good person."

"It was awfully nice of her to bring me out here."

"She wasn't trying to be nice. She knows her clients like to meet the artist at the opening. So, really, you're doing her a favor."

As Maxine looked up from her plate, she noticed a woman out of the corner of her eye carrying what looked to be a script. In a room full of thin, pretty women, this one was thinner and prettier than all of them. "Oh, my God!" she practically shouted, as if an armed gunman had entered the restaurant.

"What?" asked Ted with alarm.

"That's . . ." said Maxine, gesturing with her head over Ted's shoulder. Ted began to turn around, but Maxine whispered, "Wait! Don't look!"

"I have to look!" said Ted, carefully turning around as if he was searching for a friend. "Calista Flockhart?"

"Oh, my God!"

"She comes in here all the time," said Ted, turning back to his lunch.

"That's so cool!" exclaimed Maxine, still staring at her with wide eyes and a big smile.

"Maxine, I never would have pegged you as a star worshipper."

"I'm not! I . . . well, okay, I do have a thing about celebrities."

"That's kind of weird, don't you think?"

"No! Maybe? Listen, I'm confident enough in myself to admit it. But I'm not a worshipper. It's not like I think they're better than everyone else. They're just . . . different. Like a different species."

"That's true."

"I'm fascinated with them in a sociological way. You know?"

"You want to study them," said Ted.

"Yes! In their own natural habitat."

"Well, you're staying at the right place. Didn't you see any at the Chateau Marmont?"

"No. I ate both dinner and breakfast in my room, so I haven't been out much."

"Don't worry, you will. Maybe I can even get us into a party this weekend."

"Really? How?"

"My boyfriend's an agent. Knows all those people."

"That would be amazing."

"You crack me up, Maxine."

Maxine wondered if she was wrong to let Ted in on her secret, but she liked and trusted him. "Don't say anything to Susan about this, okay?"

"No worries."

When Maxine returned to the hotel that evening, she went to the gym, took a long shower, and had a massage in her room. Afterward, as she sat in her robe, still smelling of almond and lavender, she thought about her family back home for the first time all day.

She had texted Jake that morning, letting him know that everything was fine. Then he left two voice messages during the day, but Maxine couldn't bring herself to call home. She wanted to talk to the kids, wanted to tell Matthew about her chauffeur-driven limo ride, Abby about Susan Shackelford's expensive red suit, and Suzanne about her almond-scented bubble bath. But as much as she wanted to hear her children's voices, Maxine didn't want to hear Jake's even more. So she texted him again: "Sorry not to call . . . been busy busy busy. Going out tonight. Hugs and kisses to kids. Will call soon."

Maxine then turned to the other thing that was occupying her mind: going down to the hotel bar and looking for more celebrities. Seeing Calista Flockhart at lunch was like taking a hit of marijuana. It felt good, and now she wanted more. Not only that, but she wanted the stronger stuff. She wanted movie stars—the bigger the better.

Maxine blew her hair dry and put it in a high ponytail, because someone once told her she looked younger that way. She put on a gold lamé strapless dress that she had bought ten years ago in Berlin for one of Jake's medical conferences and a pair of four-inch-high strappy sandals. Then she headed down to the plush red bar, taking a seat that gave her a full view of the room.

She couldn't remember ever having sat in a bar by herself before but decided she didn't care what anyone thought. She didn't bring reading material so she could look busy, didn't keep her cell phone out for some strategic texting. She just sat and nursed her drink, unafraid to blatantly watch and observe.

Maxine thought back to her earlier sighting, trying to figure out why it thrilled her so much. When she saw the pretty little starlet, she immediately remembered all the details she knew of her life—her marriage to the older Harrison Ford, the adoption of a child, the talk about a possible eating disorder. Maxine realized that she knew more about Calista Flockhart than about anyone else in the restaurant, even the person sitting across from her. The actress seemed more real than everyone else—like a massive dose of hyperreality. All the images Maxine had seen of her, the articles she'd read, the television shows she'd watched, came rushing back, allowing her to form an intense vision of this person she'd never met.

Hollywood was supposedly the land of make-believe, fake and phony, superficial and shallow. But to Maxine it felt so much more real than Kansas City. Back home, the people Maxine saw every day appeared flat. She was rarely given a glimpse into the complexities of people's lives, except for those of her good friends. Everyone interacted on the most superficial of levels, carefully presenting themselves to others.

Maxine used to log on to her Facebook account and read the news feed, searching for a real glimpse into people's lives. But everything seemed so labored over—so unreal.

The stars also tried to carefully construct their personas—using Facebook and Twitter and publicists and stylists to ensure they came across in exactly the right way—but they were constantly failing. As much as they tried to control the image, a tabloid or a photographer or a gossipmonger would destroy it all.

After a while, Maxine stopped going to Facebook to observe the constructed lives of her friends and acquaintances and instead spent all of her time trolling for information about the stars.

Deep down, Maxine knew she should probably feel shame about her obsession. But the more she understood it, the more she could justify it. In a world of pretense and fakery, she was simply looking for some unbridled truth.

So when Maxine looked over at a table of people in their twenties being particularly boisterous, she suddenly felt that familiar charge. She was sure she recognized a few of them from one of those dramas geared toward teens on one of those upstart networks she never watched. They wore flamboyant clothes, smoked cigarettes, and had large bottles of premium liquors scattered about their table.

"Nicky's wasted!" shouted one girl, who looked far more wasted than the other girl she was pointing at.

"Shut up, bitch!" said Nicky.

At that point, Maxine realized that the fact that these young-sters were famous didn't automatically imbue them with the pro-foundly satisfying hyperreality she craved. First, she knew noth-ing about them. Second, she didn't want to know anything about them.

"Come on," said the boy who had his arm around Nicky. "Let's go up to Ashton's party."

Ashton, thought Maxine. There could be only one Ashton.

"No way," said Nicky. "I heard it's all Demi's friends. Bunch of old folks."

Perfect! thought Maxine.

"Well, I'm not hanging around with you losers," said the girl who was drunker than Nicky. "I'm going."

When this girl, who Maxine thought was one of the stars of the mystery show, got up, the others all got up too. Maxine quickly pulled out a twenty-dollar bill, placed it next to her drink, and discreetly followed them.

Two elevators arrived simultaneously and the group split up. Maxine went in the one with Nicky, her boyfriend, and two other girls. The boyfriend pressed the button for the penthouse floor. Then all four of them looked over at Maxine as if to say, "Where do you think you're going?"

"That's my floor too," said Maxine with as much confidence as she could muster, but she knew she wasn't convincing.

Nicky gave her a withering look and then rolled her eyes.

When the elevator door opened and the two girls started to exit, Nicky conspicuously held them back and said to Maxine, "After you."

"Thanks," said Maxine disdainfully. She hated Nicky and was sure she was not famous in the least.

Maxine decided to go left. When she turned the corner, the hallway was filled with people. Doors to several rooms were open, people spilling out, leading Maxine to think there were multiple parties going on. But which was Ashton and Demi's?

Maxine squeezed through the masses of people, trying to choose which room to go into. She settled on the one that seemed the most crowded. As she pushed through the entryway into the living area, she felt like she was back in college, making her way through the basement of a fraternity. Music was blaring, smoke filled the room, empty bottles and glasses were scattered everywhere, and people were packed in like sardines. Maxine was disappointed to find no one even remotely recognizable. But she continued on, thinking that there must be some inner sanctum, some terrace or salon where Ashton, Demi, and their closest friends were hanging out.

After scouring the entire suite and then doing the same in two others nearby, Maxine decided there was nothing there to find. If there were any stars present, they weren't lending any otherworldly magnetism to the proceedings. These were just parties like any others. Maybe the guests were dressed a little better, the alcohol they were drinking was a little more expensive, and the joints they were smoking were a little higher quality, but they were regular old parties just the same.

Maxine felt stupid. People had brushes with fame all the time and never had any grand epiphanies because of it. Did she think seeing a star would somehow make a difference, give her the answer she was looking for?

The next morning before going to the gallery, she decided she'd better call Jake. It was ten o'clock his time, when he was usually in the middle of surgery, but he answered right away.

"Hi," Jake said. Maxine was amazed at how he could convey a delicate mixture of happiness, surprise, and annoyance in one syllable.

"Hey, I'm sorry it's taken so long to call."

"It's okay. I realize you're busy."

Maxine knew it was crazy to think she couldn't have called him sooner, and she knew he thought the same thing. So she decided she'd leave it at that. "How're the kids?"

"Fine. Having fun. Lots of playdates."

"They're probably psyched I'm gone."

"I don't know that they're psyched," said Jake. "But they're enjoying the change of pace. I'm sure you are too."

"Yeah, I have to say I am."

"Good. You deserve it."

"Thanks. Thanks for taking care of everything. I appreciate it."

"No problem. You've done it for me many times."

"Well, you've also got a medical practice to run."

"It's fine. So what's going on there?"

"Just getting ready for the show, you know. The gallery's beautiful, the owner's really nice. It's great."

"Look, Maxine. I know things haven't been so great between us lately. But it doesn't help that you keep avoiding me. I wish you would talk about it."

"I'm sorry, Jake, but talking with you doesn't help. I don't feel like you ever tell me anything."

"What am I not telling you? I tell you everything."

"I don't want to get into this right now."

"Right, of course. You never want to get into it."

"I think maybe I need some more time. To figure things out."

"That's fine, Maxine. Take your time," he said, his annoyance coming through clearly.

Maxine could tell that Jake's seemingly limitless amount of patience was getting close to running out, but she didn't care. "Thanks, Jake," she said, as if he really was being understanding. "Tell the kids I'll call them when they get home from school."

After she hung up, Maxine thought about calling Katie. There was so much to tell her—about the gallery, the hotel, and everything that was going on with Jake. But she knew that once she started talking to Katie, reality would set in. She didn't want anything to pull her out of her new mind-set, not even her best friend.

Maxine spent the next few days preparing for her show, giving interviews to magazines and newspapers, and having meetings with some of Susan's clients. While she had certainly had bigger career successes before, Maxine couldn't remember spending so much time and energy on self-promotion. It was all about her, and she had to admit she liked it.

It wasn't so much that Maxine craved attention, it was more that she felt like a prisoner who had just been freed. She hadn't even realized that she was a captive of her own life, and only when she stepped completely out of it could she see it.

Like so many women she knew, Maxine had tempered her devotion to her career and her drive for success because of her family. It was something she did willingly, without a second thought. But then she saw the way Jake never had to do that. In fact, his career thrived because of his family, not in spite of it.

But it wasn't the kids. Yes, the kids demanded her time and attention and love, but they were not the culprits. Maxine believed it was Jake and his needs that sucked the life out of her.

When opening night finally arrived, it all felt otherworldly to Maxine. She kept thinking that it was like her wedding day, when she was the center of attention and it was the beginning of something momentous. But her wedding day was the time when her life became subsumed by Jake's. This night felt more like Independence Day.

It was like a scene out of a movie, and she was the star. Everyone there looked like extras, whose hair and makeup and outfits had been designed by an art director. People drank premium champagne out of glass flutes, and waiters in tuxedos passed around skewered meats, crab cakes, and toasts topped with sour cream and caviar. The lighting in the room was soft and flattering, but the paintings were illuminated with stark spotlights. All those brightly colored cows and barns and tractors appeared odd next to the cool gray suits and black chiffon dresses, but the contrast made them all the more unique and beautiful. Ordinarily, Maxine felt that people rarely noticed the art at an opening. But this night, people seemed mesmerized by the paintings—and by her.

Susan and Ted kept bringing people over to meet her, and everyone showered her with praise, particularly the men. Maxine was usually shy when it came to male attention and had never mastered the art of flirting. She didn't like the idea of people paying attention to her because of her appearance. But she did like getting recognition for her talent.

Susan brought over one man in his late forties wearing a pinstriped suit. "This is Brent Halliwell," she said. "He insisted on meeting you, Maxine." Then Susan turned around and left.

"Nice to meet you," said Maxine, who after meeting roughly thirty people and drinking roughly three glasses of champagne had shed all of her nervousness.

"Amazing work, Ms. Walters. I told Susan I wanted some to hang at my office, but she told me everything's sold out."

"Really?" said Maxine, knowing already that it was all sold. "Please, call me Maxine."

"I hope you'll consider doing some work for me on commission."

"I'll definitely consider it," she said, smiling.

"Where are you from?"

"Kansas City," she said confidently. At some point during the evening, being from the Midwest had become a badge of honor. A number of midwestern transplants had even come up to her and declared their love of the flatlands.

"Fascinating."

"Not really," said Maxine. "But it does provide some inspiration."

"Absolutely," Brent affirmed. "Sometimes I think I've got to get out of L.A. just to get some perspective."

"Well, if you're ever in my neck of the woods, give me a call." Maxine felt like she was twenty again and traveling around Europe, inviting everyone she met to come visit her back home.

"Maybe I will," he said with a bit of surprise. He paused for a moment and gave Maxine a quizzical look, as if he was trying to figure out whether she was coming on to him.

But she wasn't. Brent, like all the other good-looking, well-dressed, successful middle-aged men in the room, reminded Maxine of Jake. They all knew how to charm and flatter their way into your heart at the beginning, but soon enough, whether it took minutes, hours, days, or longer, it would become all about them.

Maxine noticed Ted approaching, arm in arm with what looked like a carbon copy of himself—a short, slender, cute boy in his twenties wearing a tight silk shirt and jeans. "Excuse me," she said to Brent. "I need to consult with Ted for a minute. It was nice to meet you."

"Hey there," she said.

"Maxine, this is my boyfriend, Bill."

"Bill and Ted!" she exclaimed a little too loudly. When neither reacted, she added, "*Bill and Ted's Excellent Adventure?* The movie?"

"Yeah, right," said Ted distractedly.

"Nice to meet you, Maxine," said Bill, extending his hand.

"Listen, Maxine," said Ted. "I've got some great news for you."

"What, baby?" said Maxine, putting her hand on Ted's cheek. "I don't know if anything could make this night any better."

"I think this might," said Ted, smiling. "Bill just told me that he was invited to another party tonight."

"Oh, no, you're leaving already?" said Maxine.

"It's at Jennifer Aniston's house," said Ted.

Maxine's expression went blank. She looked at Ted as if he had told her somebody had died. "Don't joke about that," she said sternly.

"I'm not joking, Maxine."

"And I suppose you're telling me that I can go with you."

"It's a big party," said Bill. "I already talked to my client and told him about you. He said it would be no problem for you to come. He's putting us on the guest list."

Ever since Ashton and Demi's party at the hotel, Maxine had put celebrity sightings out of her mind. She had decided that it was silly, a waste of time, and would never provide any kind of satisfaction. But this was different. This was Jen. And she would not be a party crasher but an invited guest. Most of all, tonight she was feeling like a star herself. Yes, she would go, because she would be going as an equal.

Chapter Thirteen

It was a feeling Claudia had never experienced before—being incredibly happy and utterly guilt-ridden all at the same time for the very same reason.

Fred was like a revelation to Claudia. He made her feel excited yet also gave her a profound sense of comfort and peace. He was funny and smart and handsome but completely modest and unassuming. She could tell him anything, and he always had a wise, measured response. And it was the best sex she'd ever had.

But Claudia had always prided herself on being moral, so she was keenly aware that what she was doing was wrong. She understood that people fall out of love, that they become attracted to somebody else. But she never understood why those people didn't come clean and tell their partners the truth rather than sneaking around behind the other's back. Now she understood.

Claudia figured out that the reason people cheat is because it's less scary than breaking up.

She wanted to be with Fred, to explore what they might become. But she wasn't quite ready to give up on Steve. Maybe things wouldn't work out with Fred. Maybe her problems with Steve were only temporary. How could she just throw away thirteen years of marriage? How could she break up her family? It would be foolish to leave Steve simply because of Fred. But it would also be foolish not to get to know Fred, who gave her joy she'd never felt before.

And thus Claudia became an adulteress.

In order to live comfortably in her new role as a cheater, Claudia had to also become a self-deluder. She constructed an elaborate rationalization for what she was doing, which included: It was better not to tell Steve and hurt him; Steve was probably doing the same thing with Marjorie; Steve wasn't really there for her; her happiness was important too; and everything would turn out fine in the end.

But the best way for Claudia to keep those shameful feelings at bay, oddly enough, was to spend as much time as she could with Fred, who somehow always made her forget her errant behavior.

They continued their daily lunch dates, but now they added twice-weekly jaunts to Fred's place. Claudia also invented a new client, which she mentioned to Steve soon after beginning her affair. This client was a big client. This client was very demanding. She would have to work late sometimes, and she would have to work weekends. Steve was unfazed.

Claudia's kids, Sandy and Janie, were another story.

They already didn't like the fact that their father was the stay-at-home parent and their mother was the breadwinner. They got along with Steve fine, but at twelve years old they wanted their mother around. So Claudia did her best to make up for her frequent absences by taking them shopping and buying them lots of expensive clothes, making sure they were outfitted with the latest in cell phones, and going to soccer games whenever she could.

One Sunday afternoon Steve and Claudia went to the girls' game together. Steve set up his folding chair, pulled his baseball cap low over his face, and took out his cell phone. Claudia watched as Steve's thumbs raced furiously across the miniature keyboard; he never looked up at the game, even when the crowd cheered. Finally she walked away in disgust. She wandered along the edge of the field until she found another mother she knew and liked.

"Hey, Betty," said Claudia. "Beautiful day, isn't it?"

"Gorgeous," said Betty. "Nice to see you out here."

"I wish I could get to these more often," said Claudia dejectedly.

"Oh, don't worry about it. You're lucky."

"Well, I feel bad. I know the girls get disappointed."

"They have Steve," said Betty, motioning toward Steve's down-turned head and giving Claudia a wry smile.

"Yeah, right," said Claudia, smiling back.

"What is he doing on that phone?"

"Facebook."

"Seriously?"

"Yup."

"I don't get it," said Betty. "What's the attraction?"

"I guess it's easier for him to relate to people online than to actually have to talk to people here."

"I'm not so scary, am I?"

"You know, you might ask him about work or something and he'd have to tell you he's unemployed."

"Well, everybody already knows that," said Betty.

"Yeah, but he can fool himself into thinking you don't."

"I see."

"So how's George?" asked Claudia.

"The same, you know how it goes," said Betty wearily. "The only time we ever seem to speak to each other is when we're trying to figure out who takes to soccer, who takes to baseball, and who takes to piano lessons. Unless of course we're arguing about money, and then we speak a lot to each other. Loudly."

"I know what you mean, Betty," said Claudia. "Have you guys tried getting out together every now and then?"

"We saw a counselor last year who told us to have a weekly date night. So we'd go out to a fancy dinner, have nothing to say to each other, and wind up with an enormous bill at the end. Not fun."

"Betty," said Claudia, trying not to sound overly sympathetic.

"Claudia," said Betty. "Don't tell me it's so much different at your house."

"Of course it's not," said Claudia. But then she thought about Fred, her antidote to all the indignities of marriage, her savior, possibly her future.

Claudia looked out over the emerald-green field and imagined if Fred instead of Steve was there with her. She pictured herself standing with Fred's arm around her shoulder, the two of them watching the game, cheering the girls on, and every now and then turning to each other and smiling at their good fortune.

It was the first time Claudia had ever imagined Fred in a "family" situation, and at that moment she realized that she wanted more from their relationship than she had thought. But what—what did she want? Did she want to divorce Steve and marry Fred? Would Fred become a stepdad to Sandy and Janie? It all seemed so perfect, and Claudia was wary of such perfection. But maybe everything really could turn out right.

After the game, Claudia and Steve took the girls out for pizza. As Claudia sat there, trying to look present and involved, all she could think about was when Monday morning would finally arrive, when she would be able to see Fred again. As she stared blankly at Sandy, watching her mouth move and her eyes dance as she recounted a particularly thrilling play in the game, Claudia suddenly felt a wave of guilt. How could she neglect her children like this? She felt as if she was putting all of her love and attention and energy into her relationship with Fred, and she had nothing left for her daughters. It wasn't right. Maybe the only answer was to break it off with Steve and bring Fred more fully into her life.

When Claudia arrived at work at eight-thirty on Monday and logged on to her computer, there was already an instant message from Fred waiting for her.

"Missed you," it said.

"Me too," she wrote back.

"What's for lunch today?" he wrote.

Claudia thought for a moment. "What's in your fridge?" She knew she wouldn't be able to sit across from him at a restaurant, not being able to touch him, to hold his hand.

"Ah, I see. You want to get me in the sack."

"No, no. There'll be none of that," wrote Claudia. "I just think you make an amazing omelet."

Of course, Claudia knew there would be plenty of "that," and it happened the minute they stepped into his place. Claudia's desire for Fred was so achingly strong, sometimes she worried that was all there was to it. She remembered her college boyfriend Mike, how she overlooked everything about him because the sex was good. She knew how sex could make you think a guy was better than he really was.

But the more she considered such a concept, the more she knew that Fred was the real thing. Yes, she wanted to make love to him in a way she'd never felt before, but she also felt such a deep affection for him, respected him, liked him. She knew she would never have done this—cheated on Steve and lied to her family and friends—unless Fred was truly special.

"That was good," said Fred as they lay on his bed.

"It's always good," said Claudia dreamily.

"We work well together," he said. "Like a well-oiled machine."

"Ooh. That's kind of naughty."

"What can I say?"

"We do work well together," said Claudia. "Maybe we should start a business."

"Like what? Porn?"

"No, dummy. A real business. I meant we'd make a good team."

"We do make a good team," he said, leaning over and giving her a long, passionate kiss.

When he pulled away and lay back down, Claudia thought: It might not be just sex for me, but could it be just sex for him?

"It was hard not seeing you this weekend," she said.

"I know. Why didn't we see each other again?"

"Soccer game."

"Right."

"It was actually kind of nice. Beautiful day. The girls were amazing." Claudia hesitated. "I sort of wished you were there." Once the words came out, she was glad she'd said it. She was tired of holding back.

"Well, that would have been kind of awkward, wouldn't it?" said Fred.

Claudia was disappointed. She'd wanted him to say, "Me too."

They sat for a couple of minutes in silence. Then Claudia turned to Fred and said, "Sometimes I think about doing stuff like that together."

Fred remained silent, staring up at the ceiling.

Claudia didn't want to let it go. "Do you ever think about that?"

Fred faced Claudia. "Honestly, I haven't let myself think about that," he said. "I mean, you're married."

"I know," said Claudia, glancing away. "I guess I'm just fantasizing. Maybe I'm imagining it to see how it feels." Then she turned back to Fred. "It feels good."

Fred looked Claudia square in the eyes. He seemed to be

thinking, working something out in his mind. She watched him closely, as if she could somehow decipher his thoughts from his expressions. She noticed his eyes becoming red and moist.

"I can't," he finally said.

"You can't what?" Claudia said worriedly. Fred looked like he was about to cry.

"I can't let myself imagine what it would be like to be with you," he said, blinking away the oncoming tears.

"Fred," said Claudia, reaching out and putting her hand on his shoulder. "You can. I . . . I'm seriously thinking about . . . leaving Steve. I know it's scary and it's a huge move, but I can't pretend anymore that everything's okay with him. And . . . I can't ignore my feelings for you. I've never felt—"

"Claudia," said Fred, trying to stop her from saying any more. "It's not just that. It's not just that you're married."

"What do you mean?"

"I mean, it is that you're married, but it's also . . ."

"Also what?" Claudia said, her voice rising with impatience.

"The fact that you cheated," Fred said, a little too loudly, a little too harshly. "You're cheating on your husband, Claudia. You're lying to him. Every day."

This time, Claudia's eyes began to well up. She looked at him silently, then said, "I thought . . . you understood."

"I did understand. I do," he said. "I understand what you're going through."

"Then why are you making me feel bad about it?" asked Claudia, the tears falling down her cheeks. "How can you even be with me if you hate me so much?"

"I don't hate you. I . . . I love you." At that, Fred reached out to Claudia and pulled her close.

They lay there quietly, their arms wrapped around each other. After a few minutes, Claudia said, "Then what's wrong?"

Fred pulled himself away. "Claudia, when we first got together,

I wasn't thinking. Like you, probably. It just sort of happened. We were drunk. We fell into it. And then we kept going. It felt so good, I didn't want to stop."

"Me too," said Claudia.

"So I kept pushing everything else out of my mind."

"Me too."

"But now that you're talking about a future together . . . it makes me realize that I could never really be with you."

"Why?" Claudia said.

"Because I could never trust you."

"Oh, God," she blurted out, the tears once again flowing.

"I never told you, Claudia, the reason my wife and I broke up. It's because she cheated. She cheated on me."

"Oh, God," Claudia repeated, now sobbing uncontrollably.

"I know I should have told you, and then maybe this wouldn't have happened. When we were starting to get close, I should have told you and I could have stopped it. I could have said, 'Let's wait. Let's wait till you and Steve break up, because this could be something real.' But I didn't."

"Why didn't you?"

"I don't know. I just didn't have the self-control," he said. "And . . . well, maybe . . ."

"What?"

"Maybe there was a part of me that wanted to see . . . see if you would do it. See if you'd actually go through with it and cheat on Steve."

"You were testing me?"

"Maybe I was," said Fred. "I'm sorry, Claudia. But you don't know what it's like to be lied to by someone you love. It's something I'll never get over. I don't know that I'll ever really trust anyone again."

Claudia had never had an easy time crying in front of others, particularly men. But at that moment she allowed herself to cry like she never had before. Maybe it was because she felt closer to Fred than she had with any other man. Or maybe it was because she knew she'd never see him again.

She cried out of sympathy for Fred, for all the hurt he'd endured and for all the hurt he was destined to endure. And she cried out of sympathy for herself, for losing the one thing she wanted, simply because she had wanted it too badly.

It was starting to get dark outside when Claudia woke up, Fred sleeping close beside her. She wondered if maybe she'd dreamed the whole thing. But then she got up and looked in the mirror at her puffy, tear-streaked face, and she knew it was real.

As she quickly put on her clothes, Fred woke up. "Claudia," he said dreamily, his eyes still half closed. "Come here. We should talk."

"I have to go," she said, putting on her watch. "It's late."

"But—" Fred said weakly.

"I'll see you tomorrow," she said, grabbing her purse and running out the door.

But if there was one thing Claudia knew for sure at that moment, it was that she would not be seeing Fred tomorrow. She would not go in to work. In fact, she might stay out the whole week. Maybe she'd never go back.

When she walked outside and saw Fred's car sitting in the driveway, she remembered. She had driven with Fred and left her car at work. She started running the three blocks to a nearby coffee shop, where she would have a cab pick her up.

As she waited, her phone rang. It was Fred. He must have realized that she didn't have a car and wanted to give her a ride home. She silenced her phone.

Claudia waited twenty minutes for the cab to arrive, and when she got inside she felt like she was in a foreign city. People who had to call cabs in their hometown—where they should have friends and family to transport them in times of need—were usually up to no good, she thought.

It was only now, at the end of her affair, that Claudia was able to fully grasp the extent of her treachery. Riding in the backseat—her shirt untucked, her hair disheveled—watching the sky turn from a blazing red to a soothing purple, she realized that this moment, more than any other that came before, would be the most significant moment of her life. Getting married, having babies, taking a job—these were all external things. Her affair with Fred was different. That was something that not only changed her life but changed who she was. There was no going back. She was now an adulterer. She was someone who could never be trusted. And the more she tried to keep her deception to herself, the more she would reinforce the portrait of herself as a liar.

When Claudia arrived home, Sandy was standing at the door to meet her. She asked her mother, "Why did you take a cab?" and Claudia responded, "My car broke down at work." Another lie. "Why didn't you call Daddy?" Sandy asked. "Work paid for the cab anyway, so I didn't want to bother Daddy," Claudia told her daughter. Another lie. "You look weird, Mom," said Sandy. "I think I'm coming down with the flu," said Claudia. Another lie.

Claudia went to her bedroom, took off her clothes, and climbed into bed. She was exhausted. And she couldn't bear to hear one more lie coming out of her mouth.

When Steve came in to check on Claudia later that evening, she told him she wasn't feeling well. True enough, she thought. She told him that she wasn't going to work tomorrow and asked him if he would take the girls to school.

"Of course," he said sympathetically. "And I'll try to make myself scarce, so you can get some rest."

"Thanks, Steve."

Claudia woke up at eight the next morning. The house was silent. She couldn't remember the last time she woke to an empty house. She shuffled to the bathroom and splashed cold water on her face, hoping to get rid of some of the puffiness. But her eyes remained slits of brown sunk deep in her blotchy red face.

Steve had made coffee, so she took a cup and sat down at the kitchen table. She texted her boss, saying she needed a personal day. Then she sat for a moment staring at the front page of the paper—something about the city's embattled mayor and his meddling wife, who wouldn't leave his side, even when he went to the bathroom. She took a sip of her black coffee, then got up and went back to bed.

She awoke at noon. She went to the bathroom. Her face was still unrecognizable. She checked her phone. Fred had called five times since she left his house. Claudia began typing out a text to him. "Please don't call. I'm OK." No, she thought. I'm not okay. She deleted that part. "Going to take some time off," she wrote, then hit "send."

No more lies, she thought to herself. But is this how it would be? Vague statements that skirted the truth? She no longer had anything to lie about, now that her affair with Fred was over. But not owning up to what she had done, wasn't that just another lie? She would have to tell Steve. The question was how, and when.

She would write him a letter. Claudia sat down at her computer and began to type: "Dear Steve, I had an affair with a coworker. Claudia."

She sat and stared at the words. Yes, it was the truth, but it lacked contrition, sympathy, heart.

Procrastinating, Claudia opened her personal email account, which she hadn't checked in weeks. Most people emailed her at work, so this account was filled with spam. She skimmed the list and noticed a Facebook friend request. She usually accepted these requests automatically, not even bothering to look at the profile of the person who was requesting to be her "friend." But this one was different. It was Jocelyn, her best friend from junior high, whom she hadn't seen for twenty years.

It almost never happened that Claudia received a friend request from someone she truly liked, truly cared about, truly wanted to reconnect with. She accepted and then clicked on Jocelyn's name. As she perused her old friend's photo albums, a message popped up.

"Hi, Claudia! So glad you responded! I've been thinking about searching for you for so long but never seemed to get around to it. Actually sort of surprised you are even on Facebook. Doesn't seem like your kind of thing. Just to catch you up on my life, I moved to Denver 15 years ago with my husband and 3 boys. Don't work anymore, stay home with the kids. Felt weird at first, but now I'm good with it. Getting back into pottery. Remember that throwing class we took? Loved that. Anyway, let me know what's going on with you. Great pic, by the way! You look terrific!"

As miserable as Claudia was, she couldn't help but smile, thinking about Jocelyn. She had been Claudia's first real friend. During their three-year friendship, they were inseparable at school, talked on the phone every night, and spent almost every weekend together. But in ninth grade, Claudia went on to the public high school, while Jocelyn's parents sent her to a private Catholic school. They tried their best to maintain the friendship, but after a few months, they simply didn't have the strength to resist the pull of their two separate worlds. Claudia always felt it was a shame not to have kept up with Jocelyn, thinking they could have stayed friends into adulthood.

After reading Jocelyn's message, Claudia wanted to reply. "You're right, Joce, Facebook is not my thing. But hearing from someone like you makes it all worthwhile. So great to see your face after all these years, and your family is beautiful. How do you like Denver? Better than KC, I bet. Update on me? Where to begin . . . Still here, also with husband and kids. Twin girls. I work in PR."

Claudia stopped. What was she doing? Why was she writing this bullshit? Yes, it was all true. So why did it seem like more lies?

"Remember our 7th grade history teacher, Mr. Roberts? How we tortured him?" she wrote. "He quit teaching after that year, and I always blamed myself. Sometimes I see him around town and I wonder if he recognizes me, if he hates me for what I did. I don't know. I guess I'm feeling kind of guilt-ridden these days. Bad worker (playing hooky as we speak), bad mother, bad wife. Really bad wife. Just ended an affair and still haven't told Steve. Can you believe that? Remember how we used to hate Mr. Seidel because we thought he was having an affair with the French teacher? Well, here I am, pulling a Seidel. Do you hate me? I hate myself. Sorry. Love, Claudia."

Without even reading it over, Claudia clicked on "Share."

Then she sat and stared at the screen. Claudia knew Jocelyn was still online, because she could see her name in the corner of her screen. How would she respond? Or maybe she wouldn't respond at all.

Claudia got up and made herself a cup of tea. Then she sat down in front of her computer and waited some more. Then she noticed Jocelyn's name had disappeared. She wasn't going to respond, at least not yet. Oh, well, thought Claudia. No harm done. Jocelyn was far away in Denver, wondering how she could have been friends with such a crazy lady.

Then a message popped up. But it wasn't from Jocelyn. It was from Marjorie.

Marjorie? Steve's little cheerleader? Claudia didn't remember ever friending her.

"Uh, Claudia? I think you might have made a mistake. Did you mean to post that message as a status update? Seems kind of personal. You might want to delete. Just go to the right and click on 'remove.' Marj."

"Oh, God," said Claudia.

Chapter Fourteen

Annie had gone far in her career, and that achievement could be attributed to one thing: When she took on a project, she gave it everything she had, and she didn't let up until she reached a successful conclusion.

So when it came to the project of finding Rick and getting a sample of his sperm, Annie would do the same thing. She set about it with her usual methodicalness: outlining a plan, drawing up lists, recording her every move.

The first thing to do was to figure out the best way to get Rick's information. One option would be to steal it, either by physically breaking into the sperm bank or getting someone to hack its computer system. Annie did not want to run afoul of the law, so she quickly rejected those ideas.

That meant she would have to get one of the bank's employees to give her the information—but who and how?

She calculated that the best thing to do was target the lowest-level employee who had access to the bank's computers. Ideally, this person would be young, female, not highly educated, low paid, and newly hired, so she would not have much of an investment in her job or her employer. The obvious choice was the receptionist.

"Good morning, Olathe Cryobank."

Annie smiled. The woman on the other end of the line had a soft, high-pitched voice. She sounded friendly but also a little weary, probably having a hard time getting back into work mode on a Monday morning after a weekend partying with her friends.

"Hello. May I ask to whom I'm speaking?" said Annie, trying to sound professional yet accessible.

"This is Jill."

"Hello, Jill. My name is Annie Saunders." She figured she'd better not use her real name, in case Jill tried to Google her. "I'm a writer with *JoCo* magazine." Another made-up name. There were so many magazines out there, Annie figured she could get away with saying hers was a hard-to-find print publication that still had no Web presence. "I'm doing an article on local sperm banks and was wondering if I could talk to you about Olathe Cryobank."

"Should I put you through to the director? I think she's in a meeting right now, but—"

"No, that's okay. Actually, I was hoping to first get an employee's perspective. You know, someone who's on the front lines, talking to customers every day, someone who really knows what's going on there." Of course it was preposterous that Annie would want to talk to the receptionist and not the director, but in an age when everyone—particularly the young—thought of themselves as minor celebrities in their own little worlds and had Twitter accounts with "followers," just like the John Mayers and the Kim Kardashians, Annie hoped that this girl would readily believe she could be the focus of the article.

"Cool," said the girl, coming to life for the first time. "Yeah, I could tell you lots of stuff about this place. You know, the inside story."

"Excellent," said Annie. "Do you get a lunch hour? I was thinking perhaps we could meet for lunch."

"I usually take an hour at noon."

"How about we meet somewhere near you?"

"There's an Olive Garden nearby," suggested Jill. "I love that place."

"Fine, then, let's meet there at noon. I have on a black suit."

"I'm wearing a bright pink shirt. Can't miss me."

Annie would have liked to give Jill the royal treatment by taking her to a fancy, upscale restaurant, but she knew of no such places in Olathe, Kansas, and, besides, Jill seemed perfectly happy to get a free all-you-can-eat pasta meal at the Olive Garden.

Annie spent the first twenty minutes of the lunch asking Jill about her life as if she were a famous Hollywood personality, and Jill was only too happy to be the focus of Annie's attention. She told Annie about growing up in a small rural town in central Kansas and her decision to move to the "big city" to attend junior college. She spoke about her friends and boyfriends and how she missed her family back home, and Annie diligently took lots of notes. Then, finally, she asked Jill about working at the sperm bank.

"Well, I've only been there, like, four months, but it's a pretty good place to work. The people are nice and all, but sometimes I get sick of all the phone answering and the data entry."

"Data entry?"

"You know, putting in the information of the donors. They

write everything out by hand and I have to input it. Pain in the ass. Sorry. I keep telling them they should automate—"

"Absolutely, they should automate," agreed Annie.

"I know!" said Jill, as if Annie had just introduced the idea for the first time. "They should have computers for the guys to sit at and it would be so much easier!"

"I bet you must have a lot of good ideas like that," said Annie.

"Oh, I do. Like, for example, they always ask me to give my impression of the guys, but, like, I only get to say hello–goodbye, no talking. So I think they should let me sit down with each one and talk to them so I can really give my impression. You know what I mean?"

"Yes! And I bet you could give a great snapshot of what the guy is actually like."

"Definitely. But I guess they don't want me sitting down with these guys and getting to know them. They maybe think I'll try to get a date out of it or something."

"Oh, now, that's ridiculous. You would certainly never do that!"

"No, I guess not. But I must say, they've got some real hotties coming in there. And it's funny to think they're in those little rooms looking at porno and doing their business. You know what I mean?"

"Yeah, that must be kind of weird."

"Kind of. But you know, I'm sure I'll meet my soul mate some-day," Jill said dreamily. "And I don't think it'll be after he jacks off into a cup. Sorry."

Annie couldn't help but like Jill, and she was starting to feel guilty about what she was doing. How could she take this innocent young thing, fresh off a central Kansas farm, toiling away input-ting the vitals of sperm donors into a database, dreaming of one day meeting her soul mate, and fool her into betraying her em-ployer and risking her future?

"Of course you'll meet your soul mate someday," said Annie. "Don't settle for anything less."

"You say that, but I see all these desperado women in their thirties and forties, no husband, not even a boyfriend, coming in 'cause they figure it's their last chance to have a baby, and they're just going to pick some random sperm from some stranger. I mean, it's pathetic. So they're going to have a baby on their own? And I think, Are you having this baby because you can't get a man? 'Cause you're lonely? Well, what about the baby? Doesn't that kid deserve a real family, with a mom and a dad? And brothers and sisters? Not be stuck with some old maid who's probably all bitter and who's going to make this kid crazy someday? When I see that, I get a little worried, you know?"

Annie sat motionless, never averting her gaze from Jill, but, inside, her heart was racing and her shoulder muscles were tightening. She began taking deep breaths through her nose, trying to calm down. She wondered if she'd have to excuse herself to go to the restroom and splash water on her face. But she could see that Jill was waiting for a response to her last "you know?" and she didn't want to raise any suspicions.

"Of course," Annie said, taking a sip of her water. "Of course you must worry a bit when you see all that."

No longer conflicted about what she was doing, Annie went in for the kill. "You must know that you're better than those women, Jill. What kind of values do you think they have? How were they raised? You've got the right values because you were raised by wonderful, caring, down-to-earth parents. You would never find yourself in that sort of situation. Besides, these women are probably in this mess because they concentrated too much on their jobs. I'm sure you won't give up your dreams of a husband and a family—a *real* family—for a silly job."

"Oh, you are so right, Annie. Thank you!"

Annie's affection for innocent little Jill had turned into all-out repulsion. Who did this girl think she was? Did she really think she was better than all those women who came to the sperm bank looking for one of the greatest gifts life had to offer? And did she honestly think that just because she was twenty-two and cute she would avoid the fate of all those intelligent, accomplished women whose only crime was an unwillingness to let their aging bodies dictate the course of their lives? Not only did Annie want Jill to hand over confidential information, she wanted this girl to throw away her chances of a meaningful career so she could meet some asshole who she would marry and have children with, only to one day become unhappy and disillusioned and realize that she'd given up her life for nothing.

"Jill, I cannot tell you how helpful this has been! You've given me so much insight. I can't imagine what this article would have been like without you!"

"Oh, it's my pleasure."

"Really. I'm thrilled we met. You're so wise for your young age. But surely you've been told that many times before."

"Yes, I have," said Jill, smiling. "I do think I've got lots to say. Sometimes I think I should start a blog."

"Definitely, you should!" said Annie. "Listen, Jill. There's one more thing. Of course I'm going to need to get a donor's perspective in this article, and, well, I don't know how I can do that without some help."

"Oh sure, I can help with that," said Jill. "In fact, I have a friend who just donated for the first time. He could—"

"Actually, I've been doing a little research in your database, and I came across one donor in particular who seems perfect for this story. Let's see," she said, flipping through her notebook. "I think I've got . . . Here it is. His number is 59873. I think he—"

"Wait a minute!" Jill shouted, her eyes widening. "Did you say 59873? Is that the one who wants to be a politician?"

"Yes, I think so. I think he did say that, yes," said Annie.

"You're not going to believe this, but last week I must have gotten, like, ten calls from people asking about 59873. That's how come I remember that number!"

"That's amazing!"

"Too funny! Oh, but I can imagine why all these women love Marcus."

"Marcus?"

"Yeah, that's his name. Marcus Reynolds. Nice sound. But he might want to go with Marc when he runs for office."

"Sure. Good idea."

"He's gorgeous. And so charming. I would have gone for him. These women are nuts because they can't get ahold of his sperm anymore."

"Really?"

"Yeah, he just got too busy to come in. Maybe he got a good job so he doesn't need the money anymore. They should take down his profile, but they leave it up there for the women who already have his sperm," said Jill. "Sure, I could find out his info for you."

"Actually, wait one minute," said Annie, pulling out her iPhone. "Hold on. Hmmm . . . Here we go. Marcus Reynolds, Kansas City, Missouri."

"That's right. He lives on the Missouri side. I remember 'cause he always complained about having to drive, like, half an hour to get here."

"Great," said Annie, scrolling down a list of "M Reynolds." She smiled when she saw there was only one Marcus. "Here we go. I found him."

"Well, if you can't reach him, give me a call."

"Will do, Jill," said Annie. "And thanks again for all your help."

The fact that Jill had no idea that she was doing anything wrong by disclosing Marcus's identity made it even easier for Annie. Kids today, she thought. No boundaries. No rules.

Back at the office, Annie spent the afternoon refining her plan of action on how she would meet Marcus. Every time her mind wandered toward the question of how she would procure a vial of his sperm, she stopped herself. One step at a time, she repeated, one step at a time.

A Google Maps search revealed that Marcus lived in a small bungalow, so as long as he didn't have a roommate, Annie could find out what he looked like and follow him with ease. Eager to begin the stalking phase, Annie decided she would take the next day off so she could get a full-day glimpse of Marcus Reynolds's comings and goings.

Marcus lived in Brookside, a neighborhood Annie always admired for its unique old houses and yards filled with huge maples, oaks, and elms. His street was lined with modest, well-kept homes where newlyweds, students, and young professionals lived.

She arrived at his house at six in the morning, just in case he left early for the gym or a morning run. She parked three houses away, using her binoculars for a better look. She kept her eyes peeled on the front door, not wanting to miss his inevitable exit. At seven, she longed to open her *New York Times,* but she couldn't risk diverting her attention. At eight she considered sneaking a peek at her email, but decided against it. At nine she wondered if maybe he had left the house at five-thirty.

Finally, at ten o'clock, a tall man with brown hair, dressed in a blue oxford shirt and khaki pants, walked out of the house. His back was turned to Annie as he locked the front door and walked to his car, parked in the driveway. She got only a brief view of his profile when he opened the door and slid into a dark green Honda Accord that looked about twenty years old. She quickly started her car and followed him down the street, traveling a good fifty feet away.

Annie smiled when she saw the back of the car covered with bumper stickers of Democratic presidential candidates from the last four election cycles. She liked Marcus's choices—his neighborhood, his home, his car, his political leanings. The more she learned, the more certain she was about what she was doing.

In less than five minutes they arrived at the University of Missouri–Kansas City campus. Marcus pulled into a parking lot and Annie waited on the street. She watched as he got out of the car and walked toward a large stone building, then disappeared into a quad. Annie decided that all she could do was wait by his car until he left, so she found a space on the street and parked where she could clearly see the green Honda.

Then Annie waited. Always keeping the car in the corner of her eye, she read the paper, played around on her phone, answered emails, ate the sandwich she'd brought with her, and drank a Diet Coke. At one point she had to pee, so she got out of the car and sprinted to a nearby Porta Potti that had been set up for a construction crew working on the road. When she felt herself drifting off to sleep, she turned on the radio. When the sound of pop music started to grate on her, she switched to NPR and listened to three afternoon news/talk programs. Then, an hour into *All Things Considered,* as she was listening to an in-depth report about mad cow disease, Marcus finally appeared.

Annie followed him to a nearby commercial district and watched him go into a coffee shop. She knew that this was her big chance. She knew she wouldn't be able to take off another day and spend it sitting in her car—watching and waiting. She had him cornered in a public place, a café where it was common for strangers to converse. She needed to go in and make a move.

After waiting in her car for ten minutes to make sure he wasn't just getting a take-out coffee, Annie walked in the door and headed straight for the counter. She got in line and noticed Marcus sitting at a communal table with his laptop open. There were two tables of people, all on laptops, and it seemed like they were there because the tables were close to a wall of outlets. Marcus looked so comfortable, even leaning over to one of the other computer users to ask a question, leading Annie to conjecture that he came there often to work. She realized that she needed to come back, with her laptop, and somehow find a place next to Marcus.

Rather than leaving, driving half an hour in rush-hour traffic to go home and get her computer, and then returning to find Marcus gone, Annie decided to come back the next evening, hoping his time spent at the coffee shop was a daily ritual.

The next day, Annie left work at four and headed straight to the café. When she arrived, there was plenty of room at the computer table, so she grabbed a seat and placed her sweater on a chair next to her, hoping she could arrange for Marcus to sit there. But although Annie spent two hours waiting, Marcus never showed up.

Annie hoped that it was perhaps an every-other-day ritual, so she returned the next evening, once again saving an extra place. This time, at five-ten, Marcus walked through the door. While he stood at the counter ordering, she slipped her sweater off the chair next to her and deftly tossed it across the table onto an empty chair that would not have afforded her easy access to her prey. Two people at the other table looked at her quizzically, but she didn't care. She didn't care about what anybody thought of her at that point—she cared only about Marcus.

The only two places available at Annie's table were on either side of her, but there was also an open spot at the next table. When Marcus got his coffee and walked toward the tables, Annie focused on her computer, holding her breath, praying that he would choose the right spot.

He did.

Not only did he sit right next to her, but he actually spoke. "Can I reach over and use that outlet?" he asked.

Annie lifted her head and took the opportunity to look straight into his eyes. For a brief moment, she didn't answer, mesmerized by his warm, inviting face. His eyes were a beautiful green, his longish, wavy hair brown with subtle streaks of blond. His lips were pink and full, his olive complexion perfectly smooth. He was one of the most beautiful men Annie had ever seen in person—or even not in person, for that matter—and she was afraid she would break out in an inexplicable grin at any second. But instead she forced herself to answer: "Sure."

She was nervous but relieved—relieved that he'd already broken the invisible boundary between them. Now if she was to say something it would be okay and not come off like she was hitting on him.

For the next fifteen minutes, Annie sat composing the perfect opening line. First she wrote down the requirements this sentence would have to fulfill. It would have to be casual. It would have to make sense within the context of the café, the neighborhood, the time of evening. It would have to be nonthreatening and not make her seem needy or on the make. Most of all, it would have to play to Marcus's interests, something Annie knew a lot about.

"I'm sorry," she said, eyes still on her computer, as if she was addressing anyone in the coffee shop who cared to listen. "Is there a Thai place somewhere around here? I can't seem to find it on this restaurant map."

Marcus immediately leaned toward her screen. "There." He pointed at an intersection. "It should be right there."

"Thanks," said Annie, looking up at him for a second and then back down. For some reason, every time she looked into those big green eyes she had to turn away, as if she were staring right into the sun. But then she steeled herself, glanced up again, and said, "Is it any good?"

"Yeah, it's the best in town."

"Great. I've got a friend coming in from New York and I can't take him to a bad Thai restaurant. I've got to prove I don't really live in the boonies." Annie was happy with this line. The New York mention made her sound cosmopolitan, and the reference to a male friend made her sound unavailable.

"Well, I don't know if it can compete with New York restaurants, but it's good for Kansas City."

Any other time, Annie would have let the conversation stop at that, fearing that she'd be overstaying her welcome. But this time, that was not an option. She had to push forward. This could be her last chance.

"Believe me, there are plenty of bad New York restaurants," she said knowingly.

"Hmmm. I don't know about that. Every restaurant I've ever been to in New York has been pretty amazing."

"So, you know New York?"

"Yes, I do!" Marcus said playfully.

"I'm sorry," said Annie, fearing she sounded too surprised.

"Don't worry about it."

"I should disclose that I'm a New Yorker."

Marcus's face lit up, and Annie could tell she had struck gold.

"Which part?" asked Marcus.

"I grew up on the Upper West Side."

"That's awesome," he said. "I spent a summer living on Amsterdam, right by Barney Greengrass."

"The Sturgeon King!" shouted Annie.

"I loved the sable," said Marcus.

"Oh, my God! The sable! Was that not incredible?"

"I'd go there every Sunday for brunch."

"Me too! With my family. But that was . . . years ago." For a moment, the thrill of finding someone at a random coffee shop in Kansas City who shared her love for an obscure Jewish delicacy that originated on the Lower East Side made Annie forget about her single-minded mission and just enjoy the happy coincidence.

"Actually, I kind of used the place as a litmus test for girl-friends," said Marcus. "If I brought her there and she didn't eat the smoked fish—ordered only the potato latkes or something—that would be it."

"Ouch. You're tough."

"Got to separate the wheat from the chaff."

"Or the fish from the latkes, as it were."

"As it always has been," said Marcus.

"You probably shouldn't try that with Kansas City girls," said Annie. "Else you'll be a lonely man."

"I know. I've got a whole other criteria now that I'm back here."

"Oh, yeah? What is it?"

"Well, let's say if they'd rather go to the Olive Garden than to Bryant's barbecue, we've got a problem."

Annie smiled. "Funny you should say that. I was just at the Olive Garden."

"You're kidding."

"Long story."

"I got time," said Marcus, holding up his watch.

"Do you?" asked Annie. "You seem like a guy who's got places to go."

"Yeah, I guess I do."

"Like?"

"I'm working on my MBA over at UMKC."

"Nice."

"And you?"

Annie hesitated. She hadn't really planned out what she would say about herself, whether she would make up an elaborate lie to better her chances at getting what she wanted or simply tell the truth. She decided she would have to go with the truth. "I work for Sprint."

"Huh. I never would have guessed. You don't come off like the corporate type."

"I guess that's a good thing. But, hey, you'll probably be begging me for a job someday."

"Maybe, but I'm more the entrepreneurial type," said Marcus.

"Okay, so I'll be begging you for a job."

"I think I'd have to give you one," he said with a smile. "You live in the neighborhood?"

"No, I live out by the office. But I try to get down here as much as I can."

"I don't think I've ever seen you here before," said Marcus.

"I just discovered this place." That was close, thought Annie to herself. Keep on your toes—don't get too comfortable.

"My name is Marcus, by the way," he said, and he held out his hand.

"I'm Annie," she said, giving his hand a firm shake. "Nice to meet you."

"Yeah," said Marcus, more to himself than to Annie. "Very nice."

Chapter Fifteen

Whenever Katie came over to Annie's house and walked through the cavernous entryway, saw the gigantic living room, and sat in her gourmet kitchen, she felt a little funny. How odd it was that this single, childless woman would have such a huge house, that a woman who'd never picked up a golf club in her life lived on a golf course, and that her uncultivated backyard was big enough for a jungle gym, a trampoline, and a swimming pool. She often imagined herself living there with Frank and Maggie, how they would have a playroom down in the basement, their own bathrooms, and even a special computer room. Katie had always been happy with her small house, had never wanted any more, but somehow seeing her friend with all this space made her feel jealous.

Of course, there was the added problem that Katie had just lost her job and was worried that she might not be able to pay her mortgage next month. She told herself to stop blaming her well-to-do friends for her own misfortune.

"So how's it going?" asked Annie, as she took a pile of fluffy towels out of the industrial-sized dryer located right off the kitchen. Katie admired its shiny navy-blue surface and thought how nice it would be if she didn't have to trudge down her basement stairs every time she did a load.

"Okay," answered Katie. She wasn't quite ready to tell anyone about being laid off. "Where's Claudia?"

"She called and said she wasn't coming," said Annie. "Said she wasn't feeling well. I could tell she was bullshitting, so I told her to get her ass over here."

"Is she?"

"I guess so. She's been acting really weird lately. She hasn't shown up for work for days. I'm afraid my boss might tell me to find a new PR firm."

"Maybe you should tell her," said Katie.

"I have. Doesn't seem to get through. Something's wrong." Annie took a bottle of white wine and a platter of fruit and cheese out of the refrigerator and brought it over to Katie, who was sitting on a couch in front of the kitchen's big stone fireplace. "Have you heard anything from Maxine?"

"Not a peep. I called her once but never heard back. I guess she's busy." Katie was actually hurt by Maxine's silence. The two had never gone this long without talking, and Katie was surprised that Maxine didn't want to share her experiences in L.A. with her.

Katie looked down at the coffee table, where last Sunday's *New York Times* was spread out. She noticed an article about online dating on the cover of the magazine. "Have you read that yet?"

"Oh, yeah. It's incredible!" said Annie. "It's all about women finding sugar daddies online. You should totally take it and read it."

"Okay," said Katie, picking it up and sticking it in her purse.

"I mean, if you're going to the trouble of dating some knuckle-head, he might as well be rich, right?"

Katie and Annie both turned toward the front door when they heard Claudia walk in.

"Hey, Claudia!" said Annie.

"Hey," Claudia said weakly. She shuffled over to the couch and plopped herself down next to Katie. Her face was pale, her eyes were puffy, and she was wearing an old gray sweat outfit that looked to be from her college days.

"Claudia, what's up?" asked Katie.

"Nothing," said Claudia.

"It's not nothing," said Annie. "Something's up. Why haven't you been at work? Have you been sick?"

"No, I'm not sick," said Claudia.

"Well, then, what is it? We want to help you."

"There's nothing you can do," said Claudia.

Katie and Annie sat and looked at her with concern, waiting for her to talk. Finally, Claudia burst into tears.

"I don't know, you guys," she sobbed, as both Annie and Katie held her shaking shoulders.

"What is it?" Annie asked.

Claudia let out a few more sobs, blew her nose in a napkin, and tried her best to compose herself. "Okay. So. I had an affair."

Annie and Katie looked at each other, eyes wide in amaze-ment.

"It was with a guy at work. I know it's wrong. I don't want to talk about that. I was . . . I . . . I think I was really in love with him. I know that sounds stupid, and you're probably thinking I'm crazy and of course I wasn't in love, I only wanted to do it to get away from Steve, but, honestly, I think I was in love and, you know, I don't care if anyone believes me or not because it just doesn't matter anymore."

"Of course it matters," said Katie. "If you're in love you need to be together."

"No, because he doesn't want to be with me. He said I'm a cheater and he doesn't want to be with a cheater."

Annie gave Katie a confused look. "Well . . . um, so is he."

"Yeah, but he wasn't married, and he didn't know what he was getting into, and blah, blah, blah. Bottom line, he doesn't want to be with me anymore."

"Okay," said Katie. "So now what? What about Steve?"

"I haven't told Steve, but what I did do was accidentally post the fact that I had an affair on Facebook—"

"Huh?" said Annie.

"I was writing someone and didn't realize I was posting to the general public and it just so happened that Marjorie Gooding saw it and told me I should take it down and she's really good friends with Steve or maybe even his lover for all I know—"

"Huh?" said Annie.

"I'm sure she's told him but he hasn't said anything so I just don't know."

"Oh, my God," said Katie.

"Yeah, oh, my God," said Claudia.

"Do you want to end it with Steve?" asked Annie.

"I don't know," said Claudia. "But I know that I don't want my marriage to be over because I don't know how to use Facebook!"

"Who's this Marjorie chick and why do you think she's Steve's lover?" asked Katie.

"She's his little Facebook friend, and I think they started meeting in real life too."

"Facebook is evil," said Annie.

"I've been saying that since day one and nobody listens to me," said Claudia. "People aren't supposed to have all that information about you. You're not supposed to be in constant contact with five hundred of your closest friends. We shouldn't be able to look up our high school sweetheart and reconnect and try to relive the past. It's not natural. Facebook makes people do weird things."

"Or maybe it hastens the inevitable," said Katie quietly, gently massaging Claudia's back.

This brought Claudia to tears once again.

"I'm sorry, Claudia," said Katie. "I didn't mean to—"

"No, it's okay," said Claudia. "You're probably right. Listen, can we stop talking about this now? Please? Just give me a glass of that wine and let's talk about something else."

Annie poured some wine for Claudia, and the three sat in silence.

"Okay, so I have something," said Annie, and the other two perked up excitedly.

"Oh, good, tell!" said Katie.

"Well, remember Rick? The mystery donor?"

"Oh, yeah!" said Claudia. She was glad she came. It felt good to get everything out, and now it felt good to leave it behind and hear about somebody else's life.

"I found out his name."

"Really?" said Katie. "How?"

"The receptionist at the sperm bank. Anyway, long story short, I met him at a coffee shop."

"Did you ask for his sperm?" said Claudia.

"No, haven't gotten around to that yet. But, you guys, he's incredible. Really. Just beautiful! And super charming and funny and nice. I like him a lot!"

"Like him like him?" asked Katie.

"No! I mean, I want him to be the father of my baby, that's all."

"Oh, right, that's all," said Claudia.

"We exchanged info, and I think he likes me too, you know, as a friend. We're going to check out this Russian deli that sells smoked fish this weekend."

"An obvious second date," said Katie.

"So how do you plan on going from salmon to sperm?" asked Claudia.

"I don't know. I figure if we can establish a friendship, maybe I can just come out and ask him for some."

"Stranger things have happened," said Katie. "I think."

"All right, enough about me," said Annie. "Your turn, Katie. What's up with the online dating thing?"

"It's okay," said Katie.

"Okay?" said Claudia. "You're going to have to do better than that."

But Katie wasn't sure she could do better than that. How could she tell them about Dave? About Henry? What would they think of her?

"Well, I've been dating this guy. Cute, fun, sweet. My age, this time." It was weird to think of Dave as her age. Yes, he was only two years younger, but he seemed to Katie to be of another generation.

"That's great!" said Annie.

"Then I started seeing his friend."

"Huh?" said Claudia.

"It's like, Dave, the guy, hangs out all the time at Mike's Pub. So I got to know all his friends. And one of his friends, Henry, starts hitting on me. And I'm all freaked out, and I tell Dave, and he tells me, 'Hey, go ahead and see him.' It's, like, that's what they do—share."

"Share?" asked Annie.

"The friends, all of them have dated each other, sometimes at the same time. So I figured, what the hell? It was starting to get kind of heavy with Dave, and I just didn't want to get all caught up in him, you know? I thought if I started seeing Henry too it would keep things light and casual. Do you think I'm a total slut?"

"Do I think you're a slut?" said Claudia. "Are you kidding me?"

"I don't think you're a slut either!" said Annie. "Look, guys do it all the time and nobody calls them sluts. What's wrong with it? You got their permission."

"Permission? They practically begged me to do it!"

"There you go!" said Claudia. "So it's good for everyone."

"It all sounds good, but I have to tell you, it feels kind of weird," said Katie. "I know guys do it and don't think twice. In fact, they probably love it. But, for me, it's kind of hard."

"That totally makes sense," said Annie. "But maybe it's good for you. Maybe you need to learn how to look at relationships differently. Not get too attached. Focus on getting what you need from a man."

"You sure do know what you need, Annie," said Claudia.

"Yeah, I know what I need," said Annie. "Now I just have to figure out how to get him to give it to me."

Chapter Sixteen

Annie's words kept replaying in Katie's head: "Focus on getting what you need." But Katie still wasn't sure what she needed. Months ago, she'd thought what she needed from a man was easy, fun sex. But now that she was getting it—from two different guys— she wasn't so sure. She actually thought all that sex was exactly what had gotten her into this mess.

Her boss told her she wasn't being fired because of anything she did, but Katie was convinced that all those hours of dating and drinking had led her to losing her job. And what about her kids? They felt neglected, and they were right. Katie had been busy and distracted and pushed them off on Rob as much as she could. No, Katie concluded, all this great sex was not what she needed.

Then what did she need?

The first thing she needed was a new job, so Katie threw her-self into a search. She blasted her résumé to every bank in town, answered ads for administrative assistants and receptionists, and joined every business networking site she could find. But after a couple of weeks of searching without a single response, she was worried.

Ever since the divorce, Katie had struggled to make ends meet. She'd never had the chance to build up any savings, either for re-tirement or for the kids' education. She lived from paycheck to paycheck, with Rob's meager child-support payment providing only a modicum of relief. She thought about going to her parents for help, but her dad was retired and they had already been help-ing out her brother and sister for years. The last thing she wanted to do was add to their burden.

Katie prided herself on her independence. She knew she would find a way.

Then she thought of the *Times* article she had taken from Annie, which was sitting on her nightstand. So she plopped down on her bed and began to read about SeekingArrangement.com, where young pretty women hooked up with rich older men.

"We stress relationships that are mutually beneficial," the website's founder said. "We ask people to really think about what they want in a relationship and what they have to offer. That kind of up-front honesty is a good basis for any relationship."

Yes! thought Katie. Wasn't that exactly what she'd been trying to do all these months—think about what she wanted from a rela-tionship?

Sure, the site had plenty of gold diggers and ditsy young things who only wanted a taste of the good life, but there were also a lot of intelligent young women trying to finish school or get through a rough patch, women who found older, wiser, wealthier men and established a meaningful—mutually beneficial—relationship with them.

Some of the men were married, but some of them weren't. Some of them provided monthly allowances of thousands of dollars, and some offered pocket change. Some wanted busty blond bimbos, while some wanted smart, attractive, independent women.

But was it wrong? wondered Katie. Was it just a flimsy disguise for prostitution?

The article quoted a history professor, who pointed out that, since the early 1900s, dating involved boys paying for "meals, entertainment, and transportation, and, in return, girls were to provide well-groomed company, rapt attention, and at least a certain amount of physical affection." According to her, SeekingArrangment.com was "a piece of contemporary society. It's simply more explicit and transparent about the bargains struck in the traditional model of dating."

Exactly! thought Katie. How tired she was of all the pretending, how no one wanted to admit the truth. Look at Ed. He was older and wealthier and took her out to fancy restaurants and gave her gifts. And what did she give? Her companionship, her affection, and her body. No, there was no quid pro quo, but how long would Ed have kept pulling out his credit card if Katie had been unwilling to put out?

This would be no different, except that she would be taking cash instead of jewelry—money that would help her keep her home and feed her children. Wasn't that better than a bunch of useless merchandise? Wouldn't the man feel all the more helpful and better about himself if he was making a real difference in someone's life?

Katie had been to so many of these dating sites that she wasn't even fazed when she visited the Seeking Arrangement home page and found a good-looking older man, graying at the temples, flanked by two scantily clad women busting out of their bikinis. Katie wondered if she could compete with that, but figured it was worth a try. Either there would be a nice older gentleman in search of a woman like herself or there wouldn't.

When she posted her pictures—the same ones she used for the other dating sites—she couldn't help but feel they weren't quite right for a site like this. Maybe she needed one that showed a bit more skin. So she put on a black tank top that offered a nice but minimal glimpse of her cleavage and went into the bathroom with her cell phone. When she posted the photo, it looked a little like low-budget porn, but, Katie thought, what the hell. Over the past months, she had already snuck into a boyfriend's house and watched as he screwed his old girlfriend. And she had already dated a man and his best friend simultaneously. How much further could she go?

As she was composing her new profile—one that accentuated all she had to offer and hinted at all she hoped to receive—Katie got a text from Dave, quickly followed by one from Henry. They both had been texting her incessantly over the past couple weeks, and she had put them off by telling them she was too busy dealing with her job search to even think about going out. But now she was ready to cut the cord completely. There was nothing Dave and Henry could give her at this point, and she was tired of giving of herself with nothing to show for it.

"Sorry," she texted to Dave. "Cant see you anymore. Too much going on. Need to focus on job and kids. Please understand."

She would have liked to send the exact same thing to Henry, but figured they might compare notes. So she wrote: "Hen, time to move on." She thought Henry would respond better to a more definitive break. "U r a fab guy. Take care." For this last text, she decided to adopt the annoying language she had shunned for so long. But never again, she thought.

The next day, Katie began to receive emails from arrangement seekers all over the country, even some from as far away as France and Dubai.

"Nice to see some new blood!" read one. "Mind sending me a bikini shot?"

Another had "Come to Daddy" in the subject line, and in the body it simply said: "Daddy's gonna make you come!"

One thirty-nine-year-old "Daddy" from Japan asked if Kansas City was near New York. Katie wondered how he'd managed to find SeekingArrangement.com but not MapQuest.

A seventy-eight-year-old Daddy seemed annoyed that thirty-four-year-old Katie would have the nerve to put herself forward as "Baby" material. "If you really think you're up for the role, maybe you should give us Daddies a better look at the goods," he wrote. Katie wondered how this so-called "captain of industry" found the time to write nasty emails to women he wasn't even interested in. Perhaps he was the self-appointed Seeking Arrangement police, on the lookout for "Babies" who were past their prime.

Then came one with the header "A Touch of Class." It read: "Why do women these days think they need to let it all hang out to be sexy? Don't they know there's nothing sexier than a little restraint? You seem like a classy lady. Bert."

Bert was fifty-seven years old, with a full head of dark gray hair and a brown complexion that looked fresh from the tanning bed. He listed his location as Wichita, Kansas City, Boston, and Brussels. His annual income was "more than $1 million" and his net worth was in the "$50 million to $100 million" range. He wrote that he was a "businessman" who was based in the Midwest but traveled frequently to the East Coast and Europe. His interests included opera, Renaissance art and architecture, tae kwon do, and cycling. He said that he was looking for a bright, attractive woman who could share his passions and introduce him to some of her own. His "budget" was "negotiable." Overall, his description was brief and vague, as if giving too many details about his charmed life would elicit too much attention from eager young women.

Katie was intrigued, but every time she moved to hit "reply," her eyes shifted to the number "57." He was fifty-seven, twenty-three years older than she was. Katie's father was sixty-two, only five years older than Bert.

Come on, Katie told herself, women do this all the time. She could tell that Bert was fit and in shape, probably in better shape than Ed was, and certainly had a lot more hair. She pictured Ed, with his balding head and significant paunch, and that's what pushed her over the edge.

"Hi, Bert. Thanks for the nice compliment. If you're looking for a woman who is not willing to parade around in skimpy lingerie for the entire online world to see, then I may just be the one for you. Katie."

Bert replied a few hours later with a "☺." He added: "I'll be in Kansas City on Friday. Can we meet?"

Katie agreed, but rather than meeting at a restaurant or bar, she suggested they meet at a park. For some reason, more than at any other time in her online-dating experience, Katie was nervous. She didn't want to feel constrained, locked into a booth and obliged to fumble with napkins and menus and cutlery. She thought a nice early-evening walk around a rose garden would calm her.

When Katie arrived at the large fountain at 5:05 p.m., Bert was already there. He was leaning against a black wrought-iron railing, talking on his cell phone. He was dressed in light-gray pants and a white shirt, his suit jacket slung over his shoulder.

Katie walked slowly down the stone steps that led to the fountain. She wore a cotton print dress covered in pink and yellow flowers with a loose-fitting white cardigan. When Bert looked up to see her, he flashed her a smile but kept talking on his phone.

Katie wondered whether she should take offense, whether he was being rude by not immediately hanging up, but she decided she was too relieved to be angry. She welcomed the extra few minutes to compose herself and assess the situation.

Bert was a handsome man, well groomed, trim, maybe a bit on the short side at about five foot nine, but still taller than Katie. He clearly took care of his appearance—his thick hair gelled back from his tanned face, his teeth shockingly white from numerous whitening treatments, his nails clean and filed down to a perfect length. While his suit made him look younger, it also made him look out of place in the outdoor setting, as if he couldn't wait to get back to his office or a lunch meeting or a jaunt on his private jet. Perhaps that was why he remained on his phone, trying to find a place of comfort and control. Katie wondered if she had made a mistake asking him to meet her out of his element.

"Hello, you must be Katie," Bert said, extending his hand. "Sorry about the phone. Some business I needed to take care of."

"No problem," said Katie, shaking his hand. She felt a little like she was on a job interview. Then she realized: She kind of was.

"Nice park," said Bert, looking around. "I've never been here."

"Yeah, it's so beautiful this time of year, with the roses starting to bloom and everything. Just thought it would be a nice change of pace."

"That's what I like about you, Katie. I can tell—you're different."

"I hope that's a good thing."

"Most women I meet, they want to go to an expensive restaurant. If I'm lucky they'll suggest the symphony. No one's ever said a park."

"Want to take a stroll?" she asked, pointing to a pathway lined with roses and big stone arches. Feeling her nerves starting to surface, Katie thought she could walk them off.

A moment of silence set in, and Katie felt obligated to fill it. "I used to come here a lot with my mom. She's very into gardening."

"So you grew up in Kansas City."

"Yup. Never left."

"Do much traveling?" Bert asked.

"Not really."

"But you'd like to?"

"Sure. Who wouldn't?"

"You never know. Some people are homebodies," he said. "What else would you like to do, Katie?"

Bert had a way of making everything he said sound charged with multilayered meanings. What did he want her to say? Was he looking for something sexual? Should she say she loved opera? That she was dying to see the Sistine Chapel? "Right now I'm open to anything. I guess you could say I'm searching."

"Ah, yes, I remember those days," said Bert. "Now I know exactly what I want and exactly how to get it."

"Lucky you." Oops, thought Katie. Her sarcasm was starting to seep through.

"Yes, I am lucky. Very lucky. But I also worked hard to get here."

Phew, Katie thought. Bert seemed to have taken her "lucky you" comment literally. Maybe he was one of those people who couldn't register irony.

"I'll tell you something, Katie. If you're going to be with me, you'll have to have a better idea about what you want. Because I don't want this to be a one-sided thing. I want both of our needs to be met. Do you know what I mean?"

"Yes, I think so," said Katie, not really knowing what he meant at all. On one hand, she felt like he was berating her for being a little lost. On the other, Bert seemed intent on meeting her needs.

"Before I went on Seeking Arrangement, I'd date women and it would always end badly. You know why? Because each of us had expectations. Whether we knew it or not, we had them. But they were never verbalized, never set out. And so one or the other or both would always feel cheated, like we weren't really getting what we wanted."

"That makes sense," said Katie.

"It's just the way it is. Right?" he asked, without actually wanting an answer. "But then I thought, there must be a way to avoid all that confusion and disappointment."

"And I guess you've found it?"

"I have," he said. "You must be wondering why I do this. A guy like me—I should be able to get women, no problem. I know I'm older, but, still, older men, especially men with . . . assets, don't usually have a hard time attracting younger women."

"No, they don't."

"But I prefer it this way. I prefer to be up front about our arrangement. What I expect and what you expect."

"I see your point."

Bert stopped and looked at Katie, smiling. "Would you mind if we adjourned to my car? I have some things I'd like to discuss with you—in private. I have a driver with me. You'll be perfectly safe."

Safe? wondered Katie. She hadn't once thought about her safety being imperiled with Bert. But now that he mentioned it, should she be getting into a car with him? Did his driver serve as a safety mechanism or an accomplice?

For the past months, ever since she posted her first photo on Match.com, Katie had felt like she was on a treadmill that she couldn't get off. Sometimes it went fast and sometimes it slowed down, but no matter the speed, she constantly felt impelled to move forward, unable to veer off course, unwilling to hit the big red "stop" button. Here she was again, at a moment in which she had to decide whether to continue on or bring everything to a halt.

"Okay," she said, and followed Bert out of the rose garden and toward the street, where a black limousine was waiting.

With just one seat in the back, it wasn't a stretch limo, but it was elegant and comfortable, with black leather and tinted windows. Bert introduced Katie to his driver, Lawrence, then promptly closed the automatic window that separated the back of the car from the front.

"We'll have complete privacy this way," he said.

"Okay," said Katie.

"Look, Katie, I feel right about this. I'd like to give it a try."

"Okay."

"Here's what I'm proposing. I've got a house in Wichita, but I've also got a loft here in KC."

At the mention of his house in Wichita, Katie immediately wondered if Bert had a family there—a wife, kids, dogs, cats. Why would anyone like Bert live in Wichita if he didn't have a family? Any other time, Katie would have made a sassy remark about this pretend family, something that suggested her suspicions while remaining playful. But she felt oddly intimidated by Bert, unable to serve up her usual sarcastic comments. She wanted this relationship to work out, she *needed* it to work out, and she didn't want to say anything that might threaten it.

"I'm here roughly four times a month. I've also got places in Boston and Brussels."

Here again, Katie wondered. What was waiting for Bert in Boston, in Brussels? A family? Or maybe a nice young woman like herself?

"I would like you to be available to see me four times a month. Most likely it would be two weekends and two weeknights, but that could vary."

Katie thought about her kids. She hadn't mentioned them in her profile because, interestingly enough, the profile never asked "number of children." Don't ask, don't tell, is what she figured.

"Does that sound feasible to you?" Bert asked.

Four times a month. That was it. It was a mere fraction of the time she spent with her previous boyfriends. Sure, it might require her to ask Rob for last-minute changes to their schedule or maybe even using a babysitter, but in the end she'd have much more time to spend with Maggie and Frank. "Yes, I think that's very feasible."

"When I'm in Kansas City, I like to go out. I like to listen to music, see plays, the museum. I like to eat out, but I've also got a beautiful kitchen in my loft. I like to cook."

"That's great," said Katie. "I like to be cooked for."

"Can you tolerate sitting through an entire opera?" he asked.

"I can more than tolerate it."

"Do you enjoy museums?"

"I minored in art history," said Katie. Actually, she'd taken only two art history courses, but she was never very clear about what it meant to "minor" in something.

"Excellent," said Bert. "Now the fun part." He took out a notepad and a pen from his briefcase. "Here's what I'm thinking for a monthly allowance." He scribbled a number on the pad of paper and handed it to Katie.

It read $4,000.

"Now, if you divide that into four, you get . . ." He took the pad back and wrote out "$1,000" four times. "Each time we meet counts for this much." He pointed to the "$1,000" written on the pad. "If you can't make it to one of our meetings, you simply lose that amount." Then he drew a line through the number. "But if for some reason I cancel our date, you still get that amount. Sound fair?"

"Yes, very fair," said Katie.

"Good," said Bert. "Like I said before, Katie, this needs to feel right for both of us."

He smiled and placed his hand gently on Katie's knee. Then,

suddenly, just as Katie was adjusting to the warmth of his hand, he withdrew it. "Oh, and one more very important thing. Never, and I mean never, do I want you to feel obligated to have sex with me. When I talk about dates, I mean just that—dates. It's a date like any date. While I'm comfortable asking you to be with me on any given day, to go out, to have fun, to enjoy each other's company, I am not comfortable requiring you to have sex. Is that understood?"

"Yes," said Katie.

"Good," said Bert. "Of course, it's my hope that you and I will be able to . . . connect in that way. I would hope that we would have feelings for each other—desires. This is what I would hope for. If that doesn't happen—on either end—well, it's something we would deal with, most likely by ending our agreement. Does that make sense?"

"Yes, it does," said Katie.

"Good," said Bert. Then he stopped talking and looked at Katie, smiling.

Bert has a nice smile, Katie said to herself. He's a good-looking man. Did she mind when he put his hand on her knee? she wondered. No, she didn't mind at all. In fact, she wouldn't mind if he did that again. Instead of doing that, though, he leaned in close to her. At first, Katie got a stronger whiff of his cologne, an agreeable, musky scent that she'd noticed when they first entered the car. But as he drew his face closer to hers, breathing out of his mouth, she noticed a sourness to his breath. Her instinct was to pull away, but she forced herself to remain still. You need to try this, she said to herself.

At first his dry lips felt good against her own, but then he opened his mouth and thrust his tongue into hers. It felt cold, like an unpleasant dip in the ocean on a cloudy day. She held her breath, trying to avoid the smell of his, but he kept kissing her, moving his tongue in a circular motion, pulling her in closer. She had to breathe, and when she did she could feel her whole body shudder. The longer they kissed, the more his mouth engulfed hers, the more she found herself thinking about the wetness, the saliva, the moist and mushy insides of his cavernous mouth.

Katie had not kissed that many men in her life, but the ones she had, she had wanted to kiss. She didn't remember ever dissecting a kiss in this way, so conscious of the mechanics of it, the exchange of bodily fluids. This kiss was different. This kiss she wanted to stop.

And finally, after months and months on that treadmill, jogging when it said to jog and sprinting when it said to sprint, Katie pushed the "stop" button.

As she walked away from the car—as quickly as she could without seeming to run—Katie couldn't remember what she'd said before pushing the door open and tripping out into the street. And because she had closed her eyes when she pulled away, she could only imagine the look on Bert's face when their passionate embrace ended so suddenly. But none of that mattered, because it was already forgotten. All of it.

When she got home that evening, she immediately went to her computer and began deleting—all the emails and all the photos and all the profiles used during those months of online dating.

She went to bed at nine o'clock and woke up eleven hours later with a powerful urge to see her children. She called Rob and asked if it would be okay if she picked them up early.

On the way to Rob's apartment, Katie thought about what she was going to do about money. Her mortgage was due in a few days and her bank account was below $1,000. She decided she would have to borrow on her credit cards or maybe she could get a decent loan from her friends at the bank. It will be okay, she told herself. She remembered when she and Rob first got married, how they carried debt for years before paying it off enough to afford a house. She could do it again, she thought. She could do it on her own.

"Hey, guys!" she practically shouted when Frank and Maggie piled into the car. "How's it going?"

"Fine," they said together in monotone.

"Only fine?" asked Katie. "Only fine? You've got to be great!"

They giggled. Katie thought they were probably happy to see their mother finally in a good mood.

"So what do you guys want to do today?"

"I'm hungry," said Maggie.

"Yeah," said Frank. "We didn't even have time for breakfast."

"Let's go out for breakfast!" said Maggie.

Katie hesitated. How could she justify going out for breakfast when she'd just resolved to use her credit card to pay her mortgage?

What the hell, thought Katie. What's twenty more dollars? It was time to celebrate.

"All right, let's go out. Where do you guys want to go?"

"Sharp's!" they said in unison.

"Sharp's? That place is always so crowded!"

"Sharp's!" they said again.

"Okay. Sharp's it is."

They waited thirty minutes before being seated at a booth big enough for eight.

"Awesome," said Frank, sprawling out on the seat, then rolling onto the floor. Maggie quickly followed, the two laughing hysterically under the table.

"Come on, you guys," said Katie, not very sternly. "Come up here and let's figure out what we want."

They climbed up onto the seat and immediately opened their packets of crayons and began coloring. Katie decided to relax and enjoy what was probably their last meal out for a very long time.

When the waitress came around with a steaming pot of coffee, Katie looked up from her menu and nodded with a smile. Then she noticed the growing crowd at the door of the restaurant, and there at the front, wearing a long-sleeved white shirt, black nylon pants, and a baseball hat, was a familiar face that she couldn't quite place.

As Katie stared at the man, trying to figure out who he was, he looked over and caught her eye. He, too, stared, giving her a look that said, "Do I know you?" Then, after a few seconds, his face changed with recognition and a huge smile overtook his face. He mouthed the word, "Katie?"

At that very second, Katie also figured out who he was. Nate. This was Nate, the first man she met on Match.com. Now here he was, standing in her and her kids' favorite breakfast spot, with what looked to be two kids of his own.

Katie found herself smiling too, not sure why but vaguely remembering that she had felt a fondness for Nate. But then she was overcome with embarrassment. She remembered that she had stopped emailing him suddenly, despite the fact that they had really hit it off, for no better reason than the fact that he made a lame joke about fondling melons at the grocery store.

She wanted to look down, hang her head low, but she couldn't tear herself away from Nate's wide friendly face peeking out from under the maroon baseball hat of a team she'd never heard of. In an instant, against her will, every moment of the past months flashed before her eyes—every sleazy, sordid, shameful moment— and she couldn't help but think it all could have been avoided if she had only chosen Nate, if she had only had the good sense to recognize that a harmless vulgar joke from a good man is far preferable to the insipid flattery of a scoundrel.

She looked over at her kids, coloring away, and thought about all that she had hidden from them these past months, all the secrets and lies and half-truths. She no longer wanted to keep anything from them. She would no longer let anyone or anything into her life that she wasn't prepared to share with them. She looked again at Nate, then at the two boys standing next to him, one probably Frank's age and one probably a little older. An overwhelming feeling of regret washed over her, a feeling that this was the direction she should have taken. But then she wondered, need it be a regret? Nate was smiling at her all this time. He didn't look angry or annoyed. Maybe he didn't hold Katie's rude behavior against her after all.

She lifted up her hand and waved. He waved back. Then she motioned for him to come over to her table. Nate bent down and told his sons something, then walked over to Katie's table.

"Nice to see you, Nate," said Katie, extending her hand. "Frank, Maggie, this is a friend of mine, Nate."

"Nice to meet you, Frank and Maggie," said Nate. "My kids are right over there. Walter and Nick."

"You know, this booth is pretty big," said Katie. "If you guys don't feel like waiting, you could sit with us."

"That sounds great," said Nate, and he turned and motioned to his kids to come over.

Once they all settled in and the crayons were evenly distributed, Katie said to Nate in a quiet voice, "Hey, I'm sorry about—"

"Stop," said Nate. "No need."

"It's just that—"

"I know how it goes," said Nate. "It's happened to me plenty of times. People change their minds. You don't have to apologize for that."

"Thanks," said Katie. "I think, well . . . I probably made a mistake."

"Maybe you did, maybe you didn't," said Nate.

"Maybe we could find out?" said Katie.

"Maybe," said Nate.

Chapter Seventeen

As Maxine walked with Ted and Bill along the steep, winding road that led to Jennifer Aniston's home, she experienced the uncomfortable realization that she had never been so excited about anything in her entire life. Not her marriage, not the birth of her children, not her first art exhibit—nothing in her life seemed to match this moment.

She felt like she was climbing a mountain, eager to reach the summit so she could ask the wise old man sitting cross-legged at the top what it's all about. Only she wasn't seeking the wisdom of a learned ascetic but rather a Hollywood starlet with no known credentials in any area besides acting.

Maxine could not be bothered to contemplate what all this said about her as a person, so she blocked it out of her mind and fo-

cused on the situation at hand. Here she was, steps from the house.
Who would answer the front door? Would it be Jen? Another ce-
lebrity friend? John Mayer? And what would she do once inside?
How would she get close enough to Jen to meet her, to talk to her?

When the three of them reached the steps that led up to the
house, Maxine suddenly heard an odd buzzing coming from her
purse, followed by a piercing chime. Startled, she looked at Ted
and Bill.

"Maxine?" said Ted.

"What was that?" asked Maxine.

"Um, could be a text?" said Bill with a slightly annoyed, Valley
Girl lilt.

"Oh!" said Maxine. While she had already sent texts to Jake,
Maxine had yet to receive one herself, so she hadn't ever heard
that particular vibrating ring tone before. She fumbled through
her purse and pulled out her phone—a small, out-of-date flip
phone. Still flustered, she couldn't figure out the right button to
press to read the text.

"Here, give it to me," said Bill, grabbing it out of Maxine's
hand. "Oh, my God, this phone is like straight out of 2005. Did
they give it to you for free when you signed up?"

"Yes," said Maxine sheepishly. She'd never before experienced
the unique embarrassment of having made a truly poor consumer
decision. "I'm sorry, I'm new to texting."

"It's okay, Maxine," said Ted, trying to make up for Bill's rude-
ness. "Some people's talents go far beyond being able to thumb a
tiny keyboard," he said, rolling his eyes at Bill.

"Whatever," said Bill, handing the phone back to Maxine.
"Who's Matthew?"

"My son!" Maxine shouted with sudden alarm, grabbing the
phone anxiously.

The text read: "Abby goin 2 call u but I dint do it! BTW, siked ur
texing!!!"

"What did he say?" asked Ted, genuinely concerned.

"He says my daughter is going to call me and he didn't do it. Do what? What didn't he do?"

"Why don't you ask him?" said Bill as he looked up at the house, which was rapidly filling with guests.

"But he said Abby is going to call," said Maxine. "Can I text and get a call at the same time?"

"Why don't you just call Abby?" suggested Ted, with a hint of growing impatience in his voice. He, too, was gazing longingly up at the house.

"Right, yes. Call Abby," said Maxine. "Should I call our home number?"

"Does Abby have a cell?" asked Bill exasperatedly.

"No. Right. Okay, home number is . . . Gosh, I haven't called the house in . . ." Maxine looked at Ted and Bill, who were staring at each other, their eyes wide, eyebrows raised. "You know what, why don't you two go ahead and I'll meet you up there."

"Awesome!" said Bill.

"Are you sure?" asked Ted.

"Yeah, I'll be fine."

"All right," said Ted, relieved. "So just give your name and tell the person at the door you're with us. Bill Miller. That's the name they have, right?" Ted asked Bill.

"Yeah," said Bill distractedly as he turned toward the house.

"Got it, thanks," said Maxine as she punched in the number.

"See you inside," said Ted hesitantly.

"Abby?" said Maxine.

"No, it's Suzanne. Mommy?"

"Hi, Suzanne." Maxine looked at her watch. "What are you doing up at this hour?"

"Abby and Matthew were fighting and they woke me up."

"You need to go back to bed, sweetie."

"I did, but then the phone rang."

"I'm sorry. Where's Abby?"

"In the bathroom. How are you, Mommy? Where are you? What are you doing?"

"Suzanne, sweetie? I need to talk to Abby first."

"Okay, but she locked herself in the bathroom after Matt pushed her."

"What?"

"Hang on, here she is."

"Mom?" came a muffled voice on the other end.

"Abby?"

"I wath going to caw you."

"Why are you talking like that, honey?"

"Becauth I have a nathkin on my ip."

"Well, take the napkin off your lip and talk to me," said Maxine. "What happened?"

"My lip is bleeding. Matt pushed me."

"Are you all right, Abby? Is it still bleeding?"

"I don't know. Hold on, let me check. No, I think it stopped."

"Why did Matthew push you?"

"I let him borrow my iPod because he couldn't find his, and then when he gave it back to me all of my music was wiped out! And then he pushed me!"

"Huh?"

"Okay, so first I pushed him, but then he pushed me and I bumped against his dresser and my lip started gushing blood!"

"Gushing!?" Maxine yelled, causing two guests who were walking up to the house to turn around and look at her.

"Maybe not gushing, but bleeding."

"Abby, where's your father?"

"He's at some meeting or something."

"Why didn't you call him?"

"I tried, but he's not picking up."

"Oh, God," mumbled Maxine under her breath. A meeting or

something? At this time of night? What the hell was he thinking? "Listen, Abby. Are you all right now? Did the bleeding stop?"

"I gueth," Abby said glumly, having replaced the napkin on her lip.

"Abby. Tell me you're okay."

"I'm okay."

"Listen. I have to go somewhere now. It's very important. If you need me, just call me. If for some reason your lip starts bleeding again. Okay? And tell Matthew to keep his hands to himself. All right?"

"Okay, Mom. Sorry."

"It's okay, honey."

"Mom?"

"Yes?"

"Are you having fun?"

"Yes," said Maxine, watching the people pass her by.

"What are you doing?"

"I'm sorry, honey. I can't talk now. I really gotta go."

"Suzanne wants to talk to you."

"Tell her I'll call back later, sweetheart," said Maxine. "You guys need to get to bed anyway. Good night, sweetie."

"Good night, Mom."

Maxine stuffed her phone back into her purse and hurried up the steps to the house. At the front door stood a young woman holding a walkie-talkie type of device and wearing headphones.

"Hi. I'm Maxine Walters."

The woman began scrolling through her clipboarded list.

"Oh, no. Um, it's not there. I'm with Ted. I mean, Bill. Bill . . ." Maxine was blank. "Ted's boyfriend? Bill . . . Miller! Yes! Bill Miller! That's it." Maxine smiled contentedly, looking over the woman's shoulder into the house. The rooms were sparsely furnished, with candles everywhere, giving off a soft orange glow.

"There's no Bill Miller," said the woman.

"What?" said Maxine.

"No Bill Miller," the woman repeated in a listless monotone, which signaled that she felt so far superior to Maxine that she wasn't even going to waste her energy being haughty. "Would you like me to look up another name?"

"Maybe it's under Ted? Ted . . . oh, what's Ted's last name? Did he ever tell me? I don't think so."

"Well, it doesn't matter, because I don't have any Teds either."

"This is crazy!" said Maxine. "They just walked in a few minutes ago. Two guys. Cute, young, gay."

"Uh-huh," said the woman with insincere patience.

"What do you mean, 'uh-huh'? What does that mean?" Maxine said heatedly.

"It means 'uh-huh,'" said the woman, finally allowing herself to show her disdain for Maxine.

"You don't need to talk to me like that," said Maxine. "I'm an invited guest to this party. I'm on the list!"

"No, you're not on the list."

"Well, my friend is."

"Actually, he's not on the list either."

"Well, he's in the party right now, and if you would let me go get him, he would tell you that I'm invited."

The woman gave Maxine a "yeah, right" look. "Why don't you call him?" she said.

"Right!" Maxine's face lit up with delight. "I can call him. Thank you!" she said with a smile. As Maxine scrolled through her contacts, looking for Ted's number, she noticed the woman staring at her phone with a confused look. "It's a loaner," said Maxine with annoyance. "My real one is in the shop." In the shop? Were phones like cars?

Maxine dialed, but the call went right to voice mail. It didn't even ring.

"He must have it turned off," she said to the woman, searching her face for a glimmer of sympathy.

"Sorry," said the woman, reverting back to her monotone.

"Listen," said Maxine. "You've got to understand. I'm not a crasher. I'm an artist. I've got a show at the Susan Shackelford Gallery. For real!"

"Look, Maxine—Maxine, is it? That's fine, but do you understand where you are?"

"Yes."

"Right. And do you think I can let anyone through these doors unless I'm one hundred percent positive that they are on the list?"

"Okay."

"Uh-huh. Because if I make a mistake and you go in there and do something crazy, which I can't say is out of the realm of possibility, then it's my job. Get it?"

The woman's guard seemed to be dropping ever so slightly. Maxine saw her chance.

"Of course, I understand. It's your job! But, I promise, I'm a normal person who wouldn't do anything to embarrass you. I mean, I'm from the Midwest!"

"I'm sorry, but I'm going to have to ask you to leave now," said the woman, as she smiled at a couple who had just arrived and were standing behind Maxine.

"Are you serious?" asked Maxine in genuine disbelief. "You're really not going to let me in?" Her voice was getting louder, her tone more angrily sarcastic. "Me? I'm a harmless forty-two-year-old mom! And you—some idiotic twenty-something starfucker—are going to turn me away?" Maxine paused to catch her breath and noticed the woman talking into her headpiece. "What? You're calling for help?"

Within a second the woman was joined by a tall man dressed in a suit with a similar headphone.

"May I assist you, ma'am?" he asked, clearly having no intention of helping Maxine in any way.

"Yes," said Maxine. "You see, I came here with—"

"Ma'am," the man said, cutting her off. "You don't need to do this. You need to leave. You need to leave right now."

Maxine stared at him in disbelief. "Really? You're going to make me turn around and walk down those steps and . . . and I don't even have a car! I don't even have a ride!" She looked at the woman, who had resumed greeting other guests. "Your job? What are you going to do when I end up getting murdered! Isn't that worse than losing your stupid goddamn job!?"

"Ma'am," said the man. "If you don't leave right now, I'm going to have to call security."

"Really?"

"Yes, really. And I don't think you want me to call security."

Maxine looked at the man defeatedly. "Right. Don't call security. But could you please call me a cab?"

As she rode back to her hotel, Maxine called home.

"Abby?"

"Hi, Mom."

"You okay?"

"Yeah. Why are you calling?"

"I'm sorry, Abby," said Maxine, feeling her throat tightening.

"Why? You didn't do anything."

"I'm sorry," she said, the tears welling up in her eyes.

"Mom? Are you crying?"

"No! No, I'm fine. I just feel bad for you. Your lip."

"Oh, it's fine. Matt apologized."

"That's great." said Maxine. "I'm so glad."

"Okay, Mom. I think I need to go to bed now."

"Yes, you do! It's late!"

"Good night."

"I love you, Abby."

"Love you too, Mom."

B y the time she reached the hotel, Maxine had decided that it was time to go home. At that moment, all she wanted was to see her children.

Then her phone rang.

"Maxine?"

"Ted?"

"Maxine! I'm so sorry! I feel so bad! When we walked in Bill gave his client's name. His name wasn't even on the list! And I didn't notice, because there were all these people and I was so anxious to get in . . . oh, my God, I'm such an asshole!"

"It's okay, Ted."

"Where are you?"

"I'm back at the hotel. I took a cab."

"Well, get right back into that cab and come over here! I talked to the people at the door and they're expecting you."

"No, Ted," said Maxine.

"No? But what about Jen? I swear, she's standing right over there!"

"No, I'm sorry, Ted. I'm done." Maxine was surprised at how easy the decision not to go back was. Not only that, she didn't feel an ounce of regret about not getting into the party.

"Maxine, this is once in a lifetime. You're going to regret this for as long as you live!"

"No, Ted. I'm pretty sure I won't," said Maxine. "Hey, I'm going to head back home tomorrow. Can you let Susan know?"

"Sure. Is everything okay? Are your kids all right?"

"Yes, they're fine. It's just time."

While Maxine could feel the love for her children stronger than ever before and could barely contain her desire to see them as soon as possible, she felt nothing but hostility toward Jake and complete dread at the thought of seeing him. No longer did she have a seed of doubt about his affair. Why else would he leave the kids alone at that time of night? Why didn't he pick up when they called?

She knew she should call to let Jake know that she was coming home early, but she worried about what she might say to him if she did. She was afraid she might end it over the phone.

But she knew it wouldn't be that easy. For the first time she allowed herself to imagine what getting a divorce from Jake would be like. Having the talks, telling the kids, maybe seeing a counselor, then the lawyers, the negotiating. It was all so exhausting, but Maxine knew in her heart it had to be done.

Usually, Maxine would spend an entire plane ride reading *People*, *Us*, or *In Touch*. But when she passed by the newsstands at LAX, she couldn't bring herself to even look at the magazine covers. It was like a miracle: Maxine had been broken of her celebrity habit.

When she arrived home that evening at half past seven, she noticed a strange car in the driveway. She walked in the back door, which opened onto the kitchen, and found her family—Jake, Matthew, Abby, Suzanne—sitting at the table, eating dinner with Deirdre.

"Mommy!" shouted Suzanne when she saw her mother. She and Abby leapt up from their chairs and ran to the door to give Maxine a hug.

"Hey, Mom!" said Matthew, too cool to get up and embrace his mother.

"Maxine," said Jake, getting up as if she were royalty, looking awkwardly at Deirdre, then avoiding her altogether.

"Welcome home, Maxine," said Deirdre, standing up alongside Jake, trying her best not to look the least bit perturbed.

"I thought you weren't getting back until Monday," said Jake.

"I know. I just thought I'd come back early and surprise you!" said Maxine, giving Abby and Suzanne another hug. As she squeezed them she could feel the tears coming. *Am I going to start crying?* she wondered. Maxine had felt so sure before arriving home, but now—seeing her kids, seeing Jake, and especially seeing Deirdre, sitting there with her family as if she owned the place—Maxine realized that this would be harder than she'd imagined.

"Deirdre came by to drop off some X rays, and the kids insisted she stay for dinner," said Jake.

"It's so nice to see you, Deirdre," said Maxine, ignoring Jake.

"Did you have a good time in L.A.?" Deirdre asked.

"Yes, it was great."

"Did you see any stars?" asked Abby.

"No," said Maxine. "No stars."

"How did the show go?" asked Jake. "I kept waiting for some word."

"Great. Sorry. I know I should have called, but I thought it would be more fun to surprise you and tell you all about it in person."

"Oh, yes, tell us about it," said Deirdre.

"Not now," said Maxine. "I'm beat."

"Come, sit down," said Jake. "I'll get you a plate."

Maxine knew what she *should* do. She should sit down with them and eat and show them she was fine, that she wasn't hurt or jealous or sad. She could handle anything. That's what she ought to do, but she simply couldn't. She could already feel her stomach turning, her palms sweating, the tears building up. She had to get away.

"You know what, why don't you all finish your meal and I'll go take a shower and unpack," said Maxine.

"Come on, Mom!" said Abby. "Stay with us. We missed you!"

"Thanks, sweetie," said Maxine. "I just need a few minutes and then we can talk. Okay?"

"Okay," said Abby.

After her shower, Maxine wrapped herself in towels and lay down on the bed to rest. Within minutes, she fell asleep. At ten o'clock, Jake walked into the room, and Maxine awoke with a start.

"Where are the kids?" said Maxine, disoriented, wondering if maybe she was back at the Chateau Marmont.

"Abby and Suzanne are in bed and Matthew is on his computer," said Jake calmly.

"Where's Deirdre?"

"She left."

Maxine stood up. "I should go say good night to the girls."

"They're asleep, Maxine. It's fine, you'll see them in the morning. Just relax."

Maxine sat back down on the bed, reluctantly.

"So tell me what's going on," said Jake.

"I think you're the one who needs to tell me what's going on."

"Maxine, there's nothing to tell," said Jake, in his most annoyingly patient doctor tone. "Like I said, Deirdre came by to drop off some X rays, and the kids wanted her to stay for dinner."

"So that's your story and you're sticking to it."

"It's not a story, it's the truth," said Jake, who was beginning to let his calm demeanor crack. "This is ridiculous!"

"Don't tell me I'm being ridiculous. I'm not the one having an affair," said Maxine.

"I am not having an affair!" Jake shouted.

"Look, Jake. It doesn't even matter. An affair is just a symptom of a bigger problem."

"Would you cut it out already?! I'm really getting sick of this. Why won't you believe me? What do I have to do to make you believe me?"

"I have to admit, it was hard seeing her sitting there with you and the kids," said Maxine. "Seeing my replacement. It's hard to feel so replaceable. And for a second I thought, Do I want to give this up? And, you know, I do. I do want to give it up. If you want to replace me with someone else, someone better and younger and more beautiful and more accomplished, that's fine. If you want to start over with Deirdre, I wish you all the best. Now that I know, I don't want this anymore. I want something different."

"You know what, Maxine? I think this whole Deirdre thing is a way for you to get out of our marriage. It's you who wants to end this, not me, and you're using Deirdre as an easy way out."

"Maybe I am. But if she's there, why not use her?"

"Because she's not there! We aren't having an affair. So don't ease your guilt in breaking us up by convincing yourself that I'm the bad guy."

As much as she tried not to, Maxine couldn't help but wonder if maybe Jake was telling the truth. "Okay, Jake. Let's just say, for the sake of argument, that Deirdre and you are not having an affair."

"Great."

"Then why—" Maxine stopped, and for the first time since she decided she wanted a divorce, she began to cry. "Then why don't you love me anymore?"

Jake, who had been sitting on the opposite end of the bed, got up and sat next to Maxine. He put his arms around her awkwardly and gently patted her head. "How can you say that? I do love you!"

"Look at yourself, Jake! You can barely touch me!"

"I am touching you."

"Yes, but you're so . . . uncomfortable. It's always like that! We don't hug, we don't kiss, we don't have sex. You can't stand me!" she said, starting to sob uncontrollably.

"Oh, God, Maxine. Please don't say that."

"But it's true!"

"It's not true," said Jake, now calm in the face of Maxine's hysterics.

"Then why don't you want me anymore? Why have you pulled away . . . so completely? It's not only the sex. It's everything!"

Jake sat quietly as Maxine cried, waiting patiently for her to let it all out. After a few minutes, he got up and brought her a box of tissues. Then he sat quietly and waited for her to clean herself up.

"You're right, Maxine."

"About what? That you hate me?"

"No. That I've . . . pulled away from you."

"Why?"

"I don't know."

"Are you not attracted to me anymore?"

"No, it's not . . . it's not that I'm not attracted to you, it's like . . . I'm not attracted to anyone."

"Are you gay?"

"No! But I . . . it's like . . . nothing's happening anymore . . . down there."

"You can't get it up?" asked Maxine. "Ever?"

"No. I mean yes. I mean—"

"Jake! You're a doctor, for God's sake! You probably just need some Viagra!"

"I think there's more to it than that, Maxine. It's not only physical, it's psychological. For so long, I haven't had it in me, and I felt bad about it. Guilty. I've had this feeling that I've been letting you down, not being a good husband to you, and so I guess I decided to withdraw."

"What about Deirdre?"

"Deirdre is a friend."

"But she's also a woman, and very beautiful."

"I think I felt safe with her, that I could have a close friendship with her because she didn't want anything from me, didn't need anything from me."

"Am I needy?"

"Of course not. But you're my wife and you deserve certain things—things that I couldn't give you."

"So what are we supposed to do now?" said Maxine.

"Well, it kind of sounds like you want to leave me."

"I think I felt that way because I thought you didn't love me anymore."

"I do love you."

"I love you too, Jake. But I also need . . . affection. Warmth, touching, sex. If I can't have that, then . . ."

"How about if I go and see someone?" asked Jake.

"Who? A psychiatrist? A urologist?"

"Both."

"I think that would be great."

"So you won't leave me?"

"No," said Maxine. "But I wish you had told me this sooner. I wish you'd been honest with me."

"I'm sorry, Maxine. I'm . . . you know, I'm just a typical guy. We have trouble talking. Right?"

"Yes, unfortunately you're right. But you're going to have to start talking."

"I will." Jake reached over and put his arms around Maxine once again, this time relaxing into it, allowing his body to press against hers.

"Jake?" said Maxine, slowly pulling away.

"Yeah?"

"One more thing. Can you please stop texting Deirdre?"

"Why?"

"Because it bugs the shit out of me."

Chapter Eighteen

The feeling of being depressed was not something Claudia was familiar with. Annoyed she knew well. Pissed, angry, aggravated. She knew bummed, glum, and sad. But she had never been so knocked out by an emotion as to be incapacitated.

Now she understood depression—at least the kind that left you so bereft of meaning and hope that you couldn't imagine doing anything else but sleeping.

Thankfully, Claudia could sleep. Her exhaustion was so acute that it was easy to convince herself and those around her that she was suffering from some debilitating illness like mononucleosis or chronic fatigue syndrome or Epstein–Barr. But there was one person who didn't seem to buy it—her daughter Janie.

"What's the matter with you, Mom?" asked Janie on day eight.

"I'm not sure, Janie," said Claudia, lying on her bed beneath a mountain of covers.

"So why don't you go to the doctor?"

"I will, but I'm too tired."

"Why don't you have any other symptoms? Like coughing or a fever or aches . . ."

"I'm pretty achy," said Claudia.

"Mom?"

"Yes?"

"You never get sick."

"I know."

"I've never seen you like this before," said Janie. "And it's kinda freaking me out."

Claudia looked at her daughter, who was on the verge of tears. "Janie, I'm sorry."

"You don't have to be sorry, Mom," she said, fighting back her own tears. "If you're sick and all. Right?"

"I know, but I'm sorry that I'm in bed and not . . . you know. There for you."

"I just want you to be better, okay?"

"Okay."

"I can't stand seeing you like this."

"Okay, honey, I'll try to get better."

That evening, while Steve was cooking dinner and the girls were doing their homework, Claudia took a shower. Then she dried her hair, put on real clothes—not pajamas or sweatpants—and emerged from the bedroom.

"What's for dinner?" she asked Steve, who looked up at her with alarm.

"Chicken cacciatore," he said rather fearfully, as if he expected her to find fault with his choice.

"That sounds good. Is it Rachael Ray's recipe?"

"Yeah, it is, actually. She made it today."

"Well, if it's okay with you, I think I'll join you."

"Sure, of course."

The next morning, as Claudia got ready for work, she smiled to herself. She had wondered for days whether she would have to go on one of those medications they advertised on TV—Abilify, Cymbalta, Zoloft. Now here she was, cured, from nothing more than her daughter's pain and frustration.

Okay, maybe not cured, thought Claudia, but at least she was out of bed. And she knew she had to go to work, even though she might very well run into Fred, because her family was counting on her.

Throughout her long week at home in bed, Claudia had managed to avoid talking to Steve. He slept in the guest room and pretty much left her alone in her room throughout the day. Claudia had no idea whether he knew about her affair or not. But now that she was back at work, seeing people face-to-face, talking to them and watching them as they talked to her, she found herself wondering with each and every interaction: Do they know?

During her affair with Fred, Claudia was so caught up in it that she never even considered what her coworkers were thinking. She convinced herself it was perfectly normal to go to lunch every day with a colleague. Plenty of people did it: John and Craig, Susie and Diana and Barbara, Wendy and Martin and Vanessa. But she had to admit, she couldn't think of any examples of a man and a woman going out together alone.

Now she had to wonder: What was everyone thinking?

Claudia found herself trying to decipher people's facial expressions, detect a tone of disapproval when they spoke, read between the lines of their email messages.

Then one day Susie and Diana passed by her cubicle on their way to lunch and Susie asked, "Hey, Claudia, want to come to lunch with us?"

"She goes to lunch with Fred," Diana quickly interjected. "Where is Fred, Claudia?"

Claudia didn't have to work too hard to find the contempt in Diana's remark.

She played a similar game with Steve at home, searching his every look and word for a clue as to what he knew. She couldn't imagine that Marjorie hadn't said something to him, but if she had, where was the anger, where was the indignation, where was the hurt?

Then Claudia started to wonder who else Marjorie had told and who else in her Facebook circle might have seen her posting.

"Heather? This is Claudia."

"Claudia! How are you?"

"All right. Listen, Heather. You know Marjorie Gooding? I need to find her."

"No problem. I can get you her number in just a . . ."

"Actually, I want to find her, like, bump into her. Not call her. You know what I mean?"

"What's up, Claudia?"

"I can't really get into it. I'm sorry. I . . ."

"That's okay. Hey, I've got an idea. Are you on Twitter?"

"Are you kidding?"

"Well, I am, sorry to say, and I'm one of Marjorie's followers."

"Seriously?"

"Whatever. So, anyway, she's always tweeting about where she is and what she's doing."

"I thought she was all into Facebook."

"She is, but she uses Twitter for more mundane stuff, like 'I'm getting my nails done at Rose Nails.'"

"Got it."

"So I can give you a call when I know exactly where she is."

"You're awesome, Heather. Thanks."

A few hours later, Heather called Claudia to report that Marjorie had just gone to the Starbucks at 119th and Metcalf to have a Mocha Frappuccino and work on her laptop. Claudia immediately left work, hopped in her car, and raced to confront Marjorie.

As she opened the glass door to the Starbucks, Claudia realized she had no idea what she would say, but she had faith that the right words would come to her. She scanned the store and spotted Marjorie sitting alone at a long table toward the back.

"Hi, Marjorie," she said, taking a seat across from her, trying to appear nonchalant.

"Claudia," said Marjorie, pasting on a smile to hide her nervousness. "How are you?"

"I wanted to talk with you." Claudia figured it was pointless to pretend this was a chance encounter.

Marjorie eyed Claudia suspiciously. "How did you know I was here?"

"Everyone knows you're here," said Claudia.

"Do you follow me on Twitter?" asked Marjorie, trying to hold back her smile as she imagined her public to be far greater than she had thought.

"I want to talk about that posting."

"Forget about it," said Marjorie, in a way that made it clear she would never forget about it.

"I wish I could," said Claudia. "I want to know if you told Steve about it."

"Why are you asking me? Why don't you ask him?"

"Because I . . . Can't you help me out here, Marjorie?"

"You know, maybe if you talked to your husband more, you wouldn't be in this situation."

"I am going to talk to Steve, but I thought that since you guys have been so tight lately—"

"What are you saying, Claudia? Are you implying that—"

"I'm not implying anything. I just know that Steve's been confiding in you."

"Right. And that's all. I would never have an affair," said Marjorie, her voice dripping with disdain.

"So does Don know about how close you and Steve have been getting?"

"My husband knows everything I do."

"Really? He knows about Steve and whoever else you've been compulsively emailing and IM'ing and whatever else you do?"

"I'm not compulsively doing anything."

"Because there's more to having an affair than sex. Right? There's the emotional connection. There's the sharing of feelings and personal information. Do you really think Don would be okay with that?"

"I've done nothing wrong, Claudia. And just because you have gives you no right to start accusing me."

"All I want from you is to know if you told Steve." But Claudia wondered if that *was* all she wanted.

"That would be violating his trust."

"A simple nod would do the trick."

"Don't forget, Claudia, I'm the one who pointed out your stupid mistake, remember? I'm the one who saved you a lot of embarrassment."

"Right. And after that, how many people did you go and tell?"

"No one!"

"Really? You can't get a cup of coffee without letting five hundred people know about it and you're telling me that you didn't tell one person that the wife of a friend of yours accidentally admitted to having an affair on Facebook?"

"You know what's so crazy about this, Claudia? It's that you're sitting here chastising me when you're the one who screwed around behind your husband's back."

"Right. So you know I'm probably not in the best state right now, and here I am, asking for one little bit of information, and all you have for me is a whole lot of disapproval."

"Sorry, Claudia, if I'm not full of forgiveness."

Is that what Claudia wanted? Forgiveness from Marjorie Gooding? Forgiveness from the person who had unintentionally been her confessor?

Suddenly Marjorie's cell phone began to vibrate. She picked it up to take a look. Then she started pressing buttons, as if she had forgotten that Claudia was sitting right there in front of her.

"What are you doing?" asked Claudia.

"Nothing," Marjorie said distractedly.

"What are you doing?!" Claudia demanded.

"I'm updating my Facebook status, if you must know!"

"My God!" Claudia shouted, causing everyone nearby to turn and look. "Do you ever stop? What are you writing? Are you writing about me? Are you writing about this conversation?"

"None of your business," said Marjorie, continuing to punch away.

"It is my business!" yelled Claudia, her voice getting louder and her face turning red.

"No, it's not!" said Marjorie, her voice also getting louder.

"Stop it!"

"No!"

Claudia reached across the table and snatched the phone out of Marjorie's hand.

For a split second, the two of them stared at each other in shock. Then Claudia, realizing what she had done, grabbed her purse and ran with the phone into the bathroom.

Claudia quickly locked herself in, and while Marjorie pounded on the door, Claudia read the message Marjorie was writing: "Wondering how a person can be so rude, especially when they're the one who just admitted to breaking one of the 10 commandme—"

Claudia pressed the "delete" button until all that was left was "wondering how a person can be so" and then added: "judgmental and unforgiving, especially when you're most weak and vulnerable. Maybe it's time we all got off these stupid machines and smiled at the next person we meet, no matter what kind of sin they just committed." Claudia hit "share" and, when she was sure the message went through, dumped the phone in the toilet.

When Claudia opened the door, Marjorie, who was still pounding away, practically fell on top of her. "Where's my phone?" she screamed.

Claudia pointed to the toilet. "Don't worry. I have a friend at Sprint. I'm sure she'll give you a good deal on a new one."

As Claudia drove home, surprised that she'd managed to get out without sustaining any physical harm, she realized that she would now have to accept—even embrace—her new persona. Surely Marjorie would tell as many people as she could what had happened, and there would be no way for Claudia to deny it. Not only would she be known as the adulterer, she would be known as the lunatic adulterer.

But she couldn't worry now about what the world thought of her. First and foremost, she needed to deal with Steve, the one person she'd been avoiding and neglecting for far too long.

It was three o'clock in the afternoon, and instead of going back to work, Claudia decided to go home and talk to Steve before the girls got home from soccer practice.

She found him in the kitchen, trying to lift a whole chicken out of a steaming stockpot. On the counter sat two pans of freshly baked sugar cookies. Ever since Claudia's weeklong sojourn in bed, Steve had stepped up to the plate and started cooking regularly. Not only that, but he seemed to be graduating from the no-fuss recipes of Sandra Lee and Rachael Ray to the more challenging concoctions of Martha Stewart and Bobby Flay.

"Whatcha making?" she asked.

"Just some chicken stock for a white bean and escarole soup."

"Yum," said Claudia. "And cookies?"

"Those are for a caramel sandwich cookie I saw Martha do yesterday. Do we have any powdered sugar?"

"I think so," she said as she went to the pantry to look. "Here you go."

"Thanks," said Steve. "Why are you home so early?"

"I wanted to talk to you," said Claudia.

"Uh-oh," said Steve, as he began to remove bones from the chicken.

Claudia smiled, appreciative of Steve's ability to lighten things up. "First, I want to say I'm sorry."

"For what?" asked Steve, his hands still deep in chicken skin and flesh.

"Where do I begin?" said Claudia, mostly to herself. "For being a bitch? For being unsympathetic? For spending an entire week in bed?"

"Look, Claudia. I need to apologize too. I mean, look at me. This is what I should have been doing all along, ever since I lost my job. I should have been cooking, taking care of the house, taking care of you—"

"Steve. Please don't apologize to me right now."

"Why not? I know what kind of a husband I've been and I just—"

"Steve! Stop. Please. Nothing you've done compares to what I've done."

"Claudia—"

"I had an affair."

Steve looked up and wiped the chicken fat off his hands with a dish towel. "I know."

"Marjorie told you?"

"Yeah."

"When?"

"A week or two ago."

"Why didn't you say anything?"

"I figured I should wait till you were ready to tell me."

"Wow," said Claudia.

"Marjorie told me what you wrote. I could see that you regretted it."

"You must have been angry."

"I was hurt."

"I'm so sorry, Steve."

"But it's not like I wasn't hurt already. I've been hurting for a long time."

"I know," said Claudia.

"We both have. It hasn't been good."

"No, it hasn't."

"So I know why you did it. For the same reason that I was getting so close to Marjorie."

"Did you and Marjorie—"

"No. We never even met in person."

"Really?"

"It was all on Facebook, a little on the phone."

At that moment, Claudia finally saw the value of Facebook: the ability to connect with people while keeping a safe distance. Yes, she had heard about old high school sweethearts reuniting there and leaving their husbands and wives in a quest to reignite a past flame and give a spark to their dim lives. But more often than not, people were using Facebook as a way to work through their fantasies without causing any harm. They could "friend" the captain of the football team or the head cheerleader they had a crush on and carry on a simulated relationship full of pictures and postings that led everyone to believe they were much happier and more successful than they actually were. People had affairs to boost their egos or to get the attention that they weren't getting from their spouse. Isn't that why she got together with Fred? So maybe it was better to get that ego boost or that extra attention from five hundred fantasy friends than one real live human being.

"I never even considered having an affair, Claudia. And, honestly, I wish you hadn't done it."

"I do too!" said Claudia pleadingly.

"But I understand. You were weak. And you probably wanted out but didn't know it."

"I don't know that—"

"I do. You took the cowardly way out," Steve said matter-of-factly.

"I know I did." It felt good to hear Steve talk like this to her, to call her weak and cowardly. Not since the day they first met at Kinko's had Steve been so willing to call out Claudia's deficiencies. She wondered if things would have been different if Steve had dealt with her like this more often.

"But that's what people do," said Steve. "They have affairs because they don't have the guts to say to their partner that they want out."

"I don't know if that's what I wanted. I still don't."

"I think it is," said Steve. "And, to be honest, I think I felt—feel—the same way. I was a coward too, only I just sat around playing on Facebook, waiting for you to do something."

"So you want out?" asked Claudia, a lump developing in her throat.

"I don't see any other way," said Steve. "I feel like too much has happened between us. We've gone too far. And neither of us has had the motivation to do anything about it."

"But maybe we do now."

"Why? Because you had an affair? That's the end, not the beginning. At least it is for me."

"Some people work things out after an affair."

"I know, but I can't. I just don't think it works."

"How can you be so sure?"

"Because I'll never be able to forget about it. I know myself."

"Oh, God," said Claudia, beginning to cry. "I feel like I'm damaged goods. That no one is ever going to want me again!"

Steve walked over to Claudia and put his arms around her. "You're not damaged goods, Claudia. You made a mistake. People make mistakes."

"I broke a commandment. That's what Marjorie said."

"Marjorie?" said Steve, pulling away.

"Oh, I ran into her. Long story," said Claudia. "I hate her, by the way. Please don't marry Marjorie. I don't want her to be Sandy and Janie's stepmom."

"I'm not going to marry Marjorie. I'm not going to marry anyone," said Steve.

"How do you know?"

"I need a break from marriage right now."

"Me too," said Claudia.

"And I'm in no hurry to find another wife."

"Me neither," said Claudia, smiling. "You're right. I shouldn't worry if another man ever wants to look at me again. Who needs men anyway?"

"That's right. We're all a bunch of good-for-nothings."

"Right."

"Speaking of that, I just got a call from a job prospect. They're having me back for a third interview."

"That's great!"

"Yeah, it's looking good. I think they want to talk money at this point."

"Wow. That's amazing news."

"Thanks. Listen, Claudia. I want to do this differently."

"What?"

"The divorce. I want to do it right. I'm not angry with you. I don't hate you. And I hope you don't hate me."

"I don't. Of course I don't."

"I wish people could learn how to break up amicably," said Steve. "Without all that venom and ill will."

"We can," said Claudia.

"I know we can."

Chapter Nineteen

Normally, when Annie was going to a place she'd never been before, she'd punch the address into her GPS and allow herself to be
guided effortlessly to her destination, guaranteeing that no time
would be wasted. But when she set out to find the purveyor of
smoked fish where she was to meet Marcus, she decided to forgo
that convenience. It had been so long since she'd explored the city
for something new or got lost in a strange part of town.

When she arrived at Stanislav's and saw Marcus's old green
Honda Accord parked out front, she could feel her stomach churn
in an oddly pleasant sort of way. She'd been anticipating this
meeting for days, in a way she hadn't anticipated seeing another
human being in a very, very long time.

Marcus was nowhere in sight, so Annie took a moment to peruse the deli case. It was nothing like the one at Barney Greengrass or Zabar's, where huge slabs of fish sat glistening in their own fat, adorned with strategically placed olives, sliced tomatoes, and sprigs of parsley. Here there was a rather puny stretch of salmon and a platter of whole whitefish surrounded by large bowls of unidentifiable salads swimming in mayonnaise.

Annie looked up at the man behind the counter. "No sable?"

The man smiled. "Ah, sable. You like sable?"

"Yes, I like sable. Doesn't everybody?" said Annie.

"Very difficult to get," said the man, shaking his head. "Also, not so many people want."

"Crazy," said Annie, shaking her head too.

"I tell you what," the man said conspiratorially. "You give me your name and I see what I can do for you. Okay?"

"Okay." Annie smiled.

"So what can I get for you today?"

"I should wait for my friend."

"Oh! You with that nice boy?"

"I think so."

"He went to the restroom. Nice boy. Very nice."

"Yes, he is."

Annie figured that Marcus inspired this reaction in everybody he came into contact with, and he probably didn't even have to open his mouth to get it. She wondered what it would be like to move through the world in that way, leaving hordes of admirers in your wake. Annie knew she would never know that feeling, but she was excited by the possibility that her child might.

"Hey!" said Marcus, giving Annie a hug as if she were an old friend.

"Hey, there," said Annie, awkwardly hugging him back. "Bad news. No sable."

"I know," said Marcus with exaggerated dejection. "But I wasn't real hopeful they'd have it. We're not in New York, after all."

"I guess I just wanted to believe."

"That's what I love about you. You're so optimistic."

Hearing the words "I," "love," and "you" fall from Marcus's lips so close together made Annie feel light-headed.

"What are you gonna get?" asked Marcus.

"I think I'll get one of those whole whitefish and put it on a bagel with cream cheese. Want to share?"

"Sure."

Annie stood on her tiptoes, lifted her head up to Marcus's ear, and whispered, "The whitefish salad looks a little soupy."

"I know," Marcus whispered back.

When they got their food and sat down at one of the small tables lined up in front of the window, Annie took charge of beheading and deboning the fish.

"I'm impressed," said Marcus. "Ever thought of becoming a surgeon?"

"Never. Blood freaks me out. Besides, I felt like I could really give back as a marketing director."

"It's a shame more people don't go into marketing," said Marcus, shaking his head.

"All right, all right. So I'm a complete sellout. But you're getting a business degree, for God's sake. What are you going to do with that? You can't fix cleft palates in India with an MBA."

"Actually, I want to get into microfinance."

"Microfinance?"

"You know, where they give small loans to people in developing countries so they can start businesses or increase their farming productivity and try to break the cycle of poverty."

"Oh."

"Yeah, I know, sounds crazy . . ."

"But it just might work," said Annie with a smile.

"Yes, it just might."

"I can't figure you out, Marcus. On one hand, you strike me as incredibly ambitious. On the other, you've got this idealistic streak."

"Are they mutually exclusive?"

"I guess not. Or maybe I've never seen them coexist like this before." All wrapped up in such a gorgeous package, thought Annie.

"Enough about me," said Marcus. "Let's talk about you."

"What do you want to know?"

"I still can't figure out how you ended up here."

"I can't either. I was on the same track as all my friends at Horace Mann."

"Horace Mann? Really?"

"Then Yale, Wharton—"

"Wow. Annie."

"Whatever. I mean, I had all the credentials. But for some reason, I was intrigued by the idea of doing something completely different from all my friends."

"That's cool."

"Right. But the problem is that my friends were doing the most amazing things. They were becoming artists and government officials and foreign correspondents and CEOs of innovative start-ups. So choosing to do the opposite of my classmates was actually a pretty stupid idea."

"I don't think so," said Marcus.

"Oh, yeah?"

"Yeah! I mean, the bottom line is you didn't want to be a sheep and follow everyone else. You wanted to pave your own way, even if that meant taking a more traditional route. But it wasn't traditional for you. Coming to Kansas City and working for a big corporation—for you that was kind of exotic. Right?"

"I couldn't have said it better myself."

"We all need to find our own way," said Marcus. "And the worst thing you can do is start comparing yourself to others."

"How did you get to be so wise, young man?"

"I'm not so young."

"Younger than me."

Annie was fine with telling Marcus how old she was but was glad when he didn't ask.

"I'm actually pretty cool with living here," said Annie. "I've found some great friends. And it's a very livable city."

"A great place to raise kids," said Marcus.

At that, Annie almost choked on her bagel. "Yeah. So I hear." She hesitated for a second, wondering whether she should remain on the topic of kids. But she decided not to, worried that if things got too heavy too fast, Marcus might get scared away.

"My favorite place to hang out is the Nelson," she said.

"What a great museum!"

"I know! It's kind of incredible that it's here. And they've got some amazing stuff," said Annie. "Sometimes I'll plop myself down in front of my favorite painting and sit there and stare."

"What's your favorite painting?" asked Marcus.

"The Caravaggio. *John the Baptist.*"

"Too weird. That's my favorite painting too."

Annie smiled to herself but kept a straight face. "I'm not surprised at all."

"Me neither. Caravaggio and sable. Makes sense to me."

Annie thought how easy it would have been to simply use the information that Marcus had included in his sperm-bank profile to forge common ground. Yet here she was, hitting on obscure things they both loved, and without even trying.

"It's weird, Annie. I feel so comfortable with you."

"Me too. But you seem like the kind of guy who's comfortable with everyone."

"It's not that. I'm just very good at making other people feel comfortable."

"I see."

"Most women I meet . . ."

Women he meets? thought Annie. Did Marcus really look at her as a woman rather than as a person who happened to be female?

"I always feel like they want something from me," he said.

Oh, God, thought Annie. He likes me because I don't want anything from him. Perfect. "What do you mean?" she asked, hoping that perhaps DNA did not fall onto the list of annoying things women wanted from him.

"Well, I don't want to sound conceited . . ."

"It's okay, Marcus. I know you're not conceited."

"But I always feel like women want to get together with me . . . right away. When they hardly know me."

"That's because you're so handsome," said Annie, trying to sound disinterested in his appearance.

"And then when they get to know me, I feel like they just want more."

"Like what?"

"More . . . more intense."

"Marriage?"

"Yeah, sometimes."

"Well, that's common among women your age. They want to get married. What can I tell you?"

"You don't?"

"No."

"Never?"

"Never."

"That's kind of weird," said Marcus.

"I guess," said Annie. "I came close a few years ago, and when that didn't work out I think I sort of lost interest."

"I see. But you probably shouldn't rule it out completely."

"You're right. I probably shouldn't. There you go again, being all wise."

"I really like you, Annie," said Marcus, with a shyness that he seemed unaccustomed to.

"I like you too!" said Annie spunkily, trying to gloss over the awkwardness and ensure that they were talking only as friends.

"So the new Charlie Kaufman movie is finally playing here," said Marcus.

"I love Charlie Kaufman!"

"Of course you do," said Marcus, smiling. "Why don't we go see it tomorrow night?"

"It's a date," said Annie, immediately regretting her word choice.

From the beginning, Annie knew what she wanted from Marcus—his sperm. And as outlandish as that might sound in any normal situation, Annie convinced herself that, because Marcus had given freely of his sperm to countless women in the greater metropolitan area, he wouldn't mind giving some to her, especially if he liked her and respected her as a person. However, Annie was well aware that if Marcus felt more about her—if he was interested in her romantically—giving his sperm would suddenly become more complicated. So there was the difficult balance for Annie: making Marcus like her, but not too much.

At first, Annie felt confident that she was so out of Marcus's league that there would be no danger of him falling for her. How could he possibly fall for a woman ten years older than him, not nearly as good-looking, who had settled for a quiet life in the Midwest working for a telecommunications company? But the more they saw each other, the more Marcus seemed to be doing just that. As much as she tried, Annie couldn't ignore all the "I really like you's, all the "We have so much in common's, all the "I've never met anyone like you before's. Getting the attention of a guy like Marcus was flattering, but all it served to do was threaten Annie's best-laid plans.

While her feelings about Marcus's interest were mixed, Annie couldn't help mentioning it to her mom when she called one Sunday morning.

"There's a boy," she said cryptically. "And he likes me a lot."

"Oh, Annie!" her mother practically shouted with joy.

Annie wondered why she was getting into all this with her mother, but a part of her needed her to know she wasn't a complete loser after all when it came to men. Besides, in the end her mother had been supportive of her decision to have a child on her own—she was with Annie one hundred percent. Maybe she'd surprise her this time as well.

"Remember the sperm donor I told you about? The smart, cute one?"

"Yes."

"Well, this is him."

"I don't understand."

"It's a long story, Mom, but, basically, I tracked him down because I couldn't get his sperm from the bank and so I thought I'd try to just ask him for some."

"You know, Annie, there are other ways of getting a man's sperm besides asking for it."

"Mother!"

"Oh, calm down. I only mean if you're together and you like each other, well, why not have a baby the old-fashioned way?"

"Because it wouldn't work that way."

"Why not?"

"Because men never do what you want them to do."

"Boy, that Ben really screwed you up, didn't he?"

"Yeah, I guess he did. But it's not just him. They're all like that. You think they want what you want, or they will someday, and they don't."

"It's not always like that."

"I know, but the odds aren't in my favor. Sure, wouldn't it be great if Marcus—"

"Marcus?"

"The guy. Wouldn't it be great if he fell in love with me and was a wonderful husband and he wanted to have a child with me right away? But, Mom, that isn't going to happen! If we got together, who knows how long it would last? Besides, he's young and ambitious and he's not going to want to settle down and start having kids anytime soon."

"You're right."

"What?" Annie said in disbelief.

"You're right," repeated her mother. "Men are not dependable. And, sure, he'd probably stick around long enough for a few good lays—"

"Mom!"

"And then he'd be long gone."

"You really think that?"

"You convinced me, Annie," said her mother. "You keep telling me how awful men are these days."

"Not awful, but not . . . dependable."

"Okay, not dependable. You've decided to take matters into your own hands and have a baby. So do it. Screw this guy. I mean, not literally."

"But that's the problem. If he likes me—you know, likes me likes me—he won't want to give me his sperm."

"Then maybe you should screw him—literally."

"Oh, I don't think I could do that."

"Why not? You think women don't do that all the time? He'll never know. Jeez, he's been doling it out to the sperm bank like it's going out of style. What's one more little Marcus roaming around Kansas City?"

"You've got a point there."

"I know I do. Just think about it, Annie. Don't rule anything out. You've got him right where you want him."

It was a strange feeling for Annie—to finally be the one with the upper hand. Of course, the tragedy was that she didn't want a relationship with Marcus. She had arrived at a point where she truly didn't need a man, where all she wanted was a child, and now she was being given the chance to be with the man of her—of every woman's—dreams.

She forced herself to reconsider. Why not give in to Marcus and see where it could lead? she thought. But she knew that each day she put off getting pregnant diminished the odds of ever being able to have a child. Still, could she really let a guy like Marcus slip away?

Over the next few weeks, Annie and Marcus saw each other almost every other day, going to movies, art exhibits, dinners and lunches out, or sometimes just meeting at their favorite coffee shop, where they sat side by side working on their computers. Annie was biding her time, waiting for the right opportunity to bring up the sperm question. But then Marcus told her he'd like to cook dinner for her at his house, and Annie realized she needed to act fast.

As she drove down Marcus's street, a canopy of trees above her, each house with its own unique charm—whether it was painted in an unusual shade of green or red or it had a funky sculpture in the yard—Annie couldn't help thinking of her own neighborhood, with its scarcity of trees, mammoth houses all painted beige or taupe, and manicured lawns that looked more like golf courses than anything that had been touched by human hands. She imagined herself living in this neighborhood—maybe even living in Marcus's house—and how different her life would be.

Standing outside his front door, waiting to be let in, Annie braced herself for the bachelor pad she was likely to encounter. She figured there would be an old used black leather couch, a massive media center housed in a fake-wood cabinet, a four-chaired colonial dining set, and a dirty shag rug. But when she walked in, she found a cozy home decorated to a T.

There was a big, fluffy off-white couch with brightly colored throw pillows of yellow and teal, a distressed-wood coffee table, and an old-fashioned wingback chair. The dining room had a long harvest table with antique mismatched chairs around it. The kitchen was small but neat, with shiny black appliances and a center island covered in a maroon tile.

"Nice," said Annie as she surveyed the small space. "Did an ex-girlfriend help you decorate?"

"No!" answered Marcus with mock indignation. "But my mom did help a little."

"That's okay," said Annie. "Maybe she could come over and decorate my place."

"I'm sure she'd love it!"

"So, what's for dinner?" asked Annie, trying to move the subject off meeting Marcus's mother.

"Pad Thai," said Marcus, giving Annie a knowing look.

"What?"

"Don't you remember? When we met, you were checking out a Thai restaurant to take your friend to."

"Oh, yeah."

"How'd it go, anyway? Did he like it?"

Annie couldn't bring herself to lie and have to describe her meal course by course, so she said, "He didn't end up coming."

"You eat shrimp, right?" asked Marcus as he headed for the kitchen.

"Sure!" said Annie, following close behind.

"I thought maybe you . . . kept kosher or something."

"I'm not Jewish, Marcus."

"Well, I wasn't sure."

"Why does everybody think I'm Jewish?"

"I don't know. Maybe because you're from New York and you like smoked fish?"

"Makes sense. You know, that actually got me into trouble a long time ago."

"Oh, yeah? What happened?"

"Let's just say that if I were Jewish, I'd probably be Annie Weiner right now."

"Then it's a good thing you're not."

"Yeah, good thing. Ben Weiner was a weenie."

"Most men are, right?" said Marcus playfully.

"Totally! And weenies don't know how to make Pad Thai!"

"So I guess I'm not a weenie?"

"No way!"

After dinner, Marcus and Annie brought their wineglasses over to the couch and plopped down amid the pillows and overstuffed cushions.

"This is comfy," said Annie, feeling stuffed, happy, and light-headed.

"I know. A little girly, but I don't care."

"I don't think anyone would mistake you for being gay," said Annie, more flirtatiously than she had meant.

"Why not?" asked Marcus, feigning offense. "I could be gay."

"Okay, okay, you could definitely be gay," placated Annie. "Are you gay?"

Marcus smiled at Annie, not saying a word. Then he reached over, cradled her chin in his hand, and kissed her.

Many thoughts ran through Annie's head as Marcus gently pressed his warm lips against hers, such as, How could I let so much time go by without kissing a man? and Why does this spectacularly gorgeous man want to kiss me? and Am I doing this right?

"You're not gay," she said when he pulled away.

"I could be bi," he said with a smile. Then he leaned in for another kiss, this time letting his tongue enter her mouth.

At first, Annie sat passively, letting Marcus take the lead. But as the kissing got more intense, she allowed herself to respond, to push closer to him, to touch his arms and his chest.

Taking this as a signal that Annie wanted more, Marcus caressed the outer part of her breast through her blouse with one hand, the other moving down her back.

Annie could see where this was going but couldn't bring herself to stop it. She kept kissing him as he ran his hands along her body, as he began to unbutton her shirt. She kept thinking, I shouldn't do this, I shouldn't do this. All the planning and all the work would all go to waste if she slept with Marcus now.

But then again, she hadn't felt this good in years, hadn't met a man with whom she felt so in tune on every level—intellectually, sexually, emotionally. As much as Annie tried to deny it, she and Marcus seemed perfect for each other. So how could she let this go? And what about what her mom said? Why not just do it, do it without protection and get his sperm that way? But, no, she could never do something so deceitful. She could never bring a baby into the world like that.

It was all going too fast. She needed time. "I think we should slow down," she said, placing her hand over the few buttons that were still intact.

"Okay," said Marcus. "Sure."

"I'm sorry," said Annie, buttoning herself up.

"No, you're right. We should slow down."

"I should go," said Annie, knowing she was being too abrupt

but also knowing that, if she stayed, she might not be able to say no again.

As she drove home, Annie began to enumerate all the many flaws in her plan. Did she really think she could befriend Marcus and ask him for a jar of sperm? Did she really think he would knowingly become the father of her child and never have anything to do with his own offspring? The sperm bank was different, anonymous. There was a reason for that anonymity, and Annie was stupid not to see it. And now that Marcus felt something for her, whether they consummated those feelings or not, her plan was shot. Unless Annie and Marcus got married and lived happily ever after, she would not be able to have his baby.

When she arrived home, Annie sat down at her desk and stared at her computer. She tried to project into the future, to see what would happen between Marcus and her. What she saw was the same story she'd seen over and over and experienced herself. She would imagine a future with Marcus, creating a family with him, and she would count on that future and plan for it and need it to feel fulfilled. But Marcus would have something else in mind, and one day out of nowhere she would discover that, and all her hopes and dreams and desires would be dashed.

Annie thought about Ben Weiner, how she'd promised herself never to get in a position like that again. Here alone, in her home, away from Marcus, she had the strength to do it—the strength to say no.

Annie booted up her computer and went to the Olathe Cryobank website. She pulled up her saved searches and found Donor No. 43009—Bob. Without reading over his profile, without giving it another thought, she scrolled down to the big red "purchase" button. And then she clicked.

Chapter Twenty

Match.com

K-K-K-KATIE

NO LONGER LOOKING . . . YIPPEEEE!

RELATIONSHIPS: Happily Divorced/Happily Dating

HAVE KIDS: Yes

WANT KIDS: I guess I'll keep the ones I have

MY JOB: Part-time bank teller

MY EDUCATION: Currently attending nursing school. I decided to become a nurse because I wanted to help people—

no, really! Also because I heard nursing is recession-proof

FAVORITE HOT SPOTS: Anywhere but Mike's Pub

TURN-ONS: Flirting, public displays of affection, skinny-dipping, thunderstorms

TURNOFFS: Flirting, public displays of affection, skinny-dipping, thunderstorms (with the wrong person)

IN MY OWN WORDS: I know I'm not supposed to be on Match .com, since I already found someone, but I just wanted to tell all of you who are still looking that there is hope.

I've been divorced almost three years and am now in a committed relationship with a man who I love but never want to marry.

I met my man on Match. (Sort of.) So it really works! (Sort of.) Just beware. You may meet the love of your life, or you may meet someone pretending to be the love of your life but who really only wants to screw with your mind and make you question the goodness and decency of humanity. So my advice is this: If it looks too good to be true, it probably is.

USMagazine.com

ARTIST TO THE STARS SAYS VIAGRA SAVED HER MARRIAGE

Celebrity artist Maxine Walters, whose paintings hang in houses belonging to Khloe Kardashian, Justin Timberlake, and Jennifer Aniston, says the prescription medication Viagra saved her marriage to renowned physician Jake Walters.

"We were totally headed to divorce court," quips the ultratalented Ms. Walters. "It's amazing what a little blue pill can do for a relationship. It's never been better!"

Click here to see photos of other stars· dealing with erectile dysfunction!

According to Walters, lack of movement in the penile area had an overall negative effect on her relationship with her husband. "He felt bad, I felt bad—it was a tough time for both of us," she explains. At first, Walters was sure her husband was no longer interested in her. Turns out, he was interested—but just couldn't get it up!

"I was so embarrassed," admitted Dr. Walters. "So I withdrew completely. Now I know there are millions of men just like me out there. That's why I'm speaking out, so maybe I can convince others to come forward and get the help they need."

Can you match the celebrity with the mortifying detail about their personal life?

Walters insists divorce is no longer in the cards. "I was kind of getting psyched about the whole divorce thing and being single again," she confides. "All my friends are doing it. But I figure, I might as well stay in it for the kids—and the big hard dick!"

Facebook.com

Claudia Spinelli just gave her two weeks' notice and starts her new job as development director at Goodwill on Monday.

Wondering if working in corporate PR is like smoking—how long does it take for all that nasty black soot to get out of your system???

3 people like this.

KATIE RAWLINGS: Hurray, Claudia! I'm so proud of you!

MAXINE WALTERS: You've been doing PR for what . . . 13 years? So in another 13 years you'll be pure as the driven snow.

MARJORIE GOODING: Pure as the driven snow, my ass! Claudia, you are going straight to hell, no matter how much phony nonprofit work you do!

ANNIE SAX: Watch it, Marj, or else I'll take back that fancy new phone I got you and tell my friends at Sprint to cut off your account.

JANIE SPINELLI: Yay, Mom! But does this mean I can't go to soccer camp in Wisconsin this summer?

STEVE SPINELLI: Don't worry, sweetheart, I've got you covered. Great work, Claudia! And, Marjorie, why don't you lay off Claudia already? I don't know why she hasn't defriended you by now.

CLAUDIA SPINELLI: I'm keeping her on—sort of like a punishment.

MARJORIE GOODING: Don't use me to absolve your sins! I'm outta here . . .

OlatheCryobank.com

TESTIMONIAL

I can't begin to thank Olathe Cryobank enough! Here I am, cradling this little bundle of joy in my arms, and I owe it all to OC. Your database is amazing—and all that information! Well, maybe TOO much information, especially for someone as anal as me. And, of course, your staff was so attentive and understanding. I'd like to give special thanks to Jill in reception, who not only helped me get this gorgeous child but also helped me get a gorgeous boyfriend to go with him! Thanks, Jill! Can't wait to give little Bob a brother or sister, but I think next time we won't be needing the Cryobank's services . . .

Acknowledgments

Thanks to Ellen Levine, as smart and kind an agent as any writer could hope for.

To my editor, Kelli Fillingim, whose enthusiasm brought this book to print and whose wise editing enriched it.

To Susan Byrnes, Julie Fingersh, Paul Greenberg, Loren Miller, and Greg Sax for their insightful critiques and lifelong friendship.

To Bryan Steiner, who not only helped inspire this story but made life fun during the writing of it.

To my family, who have provided me with endless amounts of love and hilarity. Most of all, thanks to my parents, Patti and Al Shapiro, who dedicated their lives to my siblings and me and always made us feel it was their privilege to do it.

About the Author

MOLLY SHAPIRO is the author of
Eternal City, winner of the Willa Cather
Fiction Prize. She earned a bachelor's
degree in semiotics from Brown and
a master's degree in creative writing
from Columbia. She has lived and
worked in New York, San Francisco,
Seattle, Boston, and Rome. She
currently lives in Kansas City,
Missouri, with her two children,
Harry and Fanny.